Somebody at the Door

Somebody at the Door

Raymond Postgate

With an Introduction
by Martin Edwards

Poisoned Pen Press

Originally published in 1943 by Michael Joseph
Copyright © 2017 Estate of Raymond Postgate
Introduction copyright © 2017 Martin Edwards
Published by Poisoned Pen Press in association with the
British Library

First Edition 2017
First US Trade Paperback Edition

10 9 8 7 6 5 4 3 2 1

Library of Congress Catalog Card Number: 2017945973

ISBN: 9781464209123   Trade Paperback
      9781464209130   Ebook

Poisoned Pen Press
4014 N. Goldwater Boulevard, #201
Scottsdale, Arizona 85251
www.poisonedpenpress.com
info@poisonedpenpress.com

Printed in the United States of America

Introduction

Somebody at the Door was Raymond Postgate's second crime novel, a successor to the outstanding *Verdict of Twelve*. He wrote the book during the dark days of the Second World War, and the mood of the story reflects the sombre atmosphere of the times. On a bleak Friday evening in January 1942, Henry Grayling is on his way home from work. He catches the train from Euston, and manages to find a seat in a busy carriage. His travelling companions, a mixed bunch, include five men known to him: a work colleague, a German refugee, a vicar who is a fellow town councillor, a corporal from his Home Guard platoon, and a young man with a club foot.

By the end of that night, Grayling is dead, and the staff wages, which he was carrying home with him for safe-keeping over the weekend, have gone missing. The cause of death is at first mysterious, and although it soon becomes clear that Grayling was murdered, it is far from clear how the crime was committed, let alone by whom. Inspector Holly, a diligent representative of the forces of law and order, embarks on a challenging investigation. Soon he discovers that Grayling was—just like those villainous blackmailers, shady financiers, and miserly old relatives who provided so many motives for murder in more conventional Golden Age detective stories—an unpleasant individual who supplied several people with reasons to hate him. Is it possible that the culprit may have been one of Grayling's fellow passengers?

The bulk of the novel is devoted to sections detailing the past lives of the prime suspects. A varied pattern of possible motives for murder emerges from the murky backstories, and, with ingenuity worthy of Agatha Christie, Postgate shows how the unusual *modus operandi* might conceivably have been adopted by several of the candidates for the role of murderer. Clever, too, is the way in which Postgate tailors the crime to the backdrop; it is not giving too much away to say that the culprit's plan depends on circumstances unique to war-time.

Somebody at the Door provides plentiful evidence of the literary gifts of Raymond William Postgate (1896–1971), but he was not first and foremost a novelist. A journalist by profession, he had a strong interest in history, biography, and above all politics. After working for the *Daily Herald* and various other publications, including *The Communist* and the *Encyclopaedia Britannica*, he became editor of *Tribune* in 1940. By that time, he had established himself as a prolific author of non-fiction, his early titles including *The Bolshevik Theory* (1920), *Revolutionary Biographies* (1922), and *A Workers' History of the Great Strike* (1927). *No Epitaph* (1932), not a genre work, was his first novel, but eight years then passed before he published *Verdict of Twelve*.

In his first venture into crime fiction, he focused on the ways in which the life histories of members of a jury at a murder trial may affect their attitude to justice. *Somebody at the Door* varies that pattern, by utilizing biographical sketches to show how a diverse group of individuals might all have cause to kill the same person. As American critic Jeanne F. Bedell said in *Twentieth Century Crime and Mystery*

Writers (1980): "Although deterministic, Postgate's view of character does not negate individuality: rather it enhances it. His novels are filled with fully realized, recognizable human beings who come alive as do few characters in detective fiction."

Postgate's preoccupations and beliefs are reflected in the story, and give it a richness of texture that is appealing even if one does not share his views. He was an atheist and a one-time Communist, as one might guess from his disdainful portrait of the Vicar of Croxburn, who happens to be a conservatively inclined local councillor, and who "felt himself like a man sitting by the wayside, dressed in sacred raiment, each piece of which had a noble and ancient history; and the people ignored him and went to the pictures". He also provides a satiric description of a publishing firm (whose senior partner, Sir Herbert Brown-Cotton, made clear to a young employee that "the great British reading public was deeply moral") which is both entertaining and relevant to the plot.

Postgate delights in describing the involvement of the murder victim—a reactionary and a bully—in local government corruption, concluding: "Grayling did not note down that he was witnessing a fundamental change in economics and the structure of society. He was not inclined for reflexion upon the structure and implications of the late stage of finance-capitalism. All he saw was a system of graft beginning to wither away before he had had a real opportunity to exploit it." At times, for instance when complaining about the British government's conduct in the lead-up to war, Postgate falls into the same trap as Sir Herbert, and over-does the sermonizing; this failing is a reminder that he was, as a crime novelist, a talented if occasionally wayward amateur rather than a seasoned professional.

Postgate had, nonetheless, an abiding interest in crime, real and fictional. He edited a book of notable English trials, reviewed detective fiction, and put together an anthology, *Detective Stories of Today* (1940), which featured stories by such authors as Margery Allingham, E. C. Bentley, Anthony Berkeley, and Dorothy L. Sayers. The other contributors included the husband-and-wife duo G. D. H. and Margaret Cole, whose political views were closely allied to Postgate's. Margaret happened to be Postgate's sister, and Postgate collaborated with Douglas Cole on *The Common People 1746–1938* (1938).

After publishing *Somebody at the Door*, Postgate did not return to crime fiction for a decade. *The Ledger is Kept* (1953) was much admired by Bedell, but perhaps inevitably, he again failed to surpass the excellence of *Verdict of Twelve*, and this may in part explain why he produced no more mystery novels. By that time, he was in any event editing *The Good Food Guide*, having founded the Good Food Club in 1950, the achievement for which he remains best remembered. When his last published book, *Portuguese Wine*, appeared in 1969, his work in the crime genre had almost been forgotten. Yet *Somebody at the Door* illustrates the gifts of a versatile and accomplished author, as well as offering an intriguing picture of life during a dark and disturbing period of British history.

Martin Edwards
www.martinedwardsbooks.com

How often I have smiled to see, in a story which pretended to show me the life of Paris or of London, five or six persons, always the same, meet by chance in the most varying places. "From their box the Mortevilles suddenly saw the Duponts sitting in the stalls"; next, "on entering the enclosure the first pretty woman Jacques Dupont met was Alice Morteville"; next, "from the surging crowd of demonstrators Pierre Morteville saw rising the energetic head of Jacques Dupont." The author may work as hard as he chooses after that in describing to us the immense surging crowd, the brilliant attendance in the enclosure, and paint in the background as much as he can; the poor man does not realize that his Duponts and Mortevilles, as soon as they "meet" and because they meet with such deplorable ease, annihilate all immensity around themselves, prevent me believing that Paris or London are anything enormous, where one may be lost, and make these cities suddenly little places like Landerneau…

The reader will not see this vast work arrange itself, according to traditional artifice, around a miraculously chosen central figure. He cannot count on a rectilinear action, whose movement will carry you along without troubling your laziness, nor even on a too-simple harmony between multiple actions, which in its turn becomes a convention. He will guess that very often the thread of the story will seem to break, and the interest be suspended or scattered—that at the moment when he begins to be familiar with a character, to enter into his cares and his little world, and to watch the future through the same window as he does, he will be suddenly requested to transport himself far away from there, and take up quite different disputes.

(Extracts from the Preface to *Men of Good Will* by Jules Romains, restating the principles of Unanimism.)

Chapter I

1

January, 1942, was a hard month in London. Friday, January 16th, was one of its bleakest days. Snow had fallen on the Wednesday and Thursday, rain during Thursday night. Enough snow had been left by the rain to form piles of slush in gutters and side roads. Early in the morning it had frozen; the slush had become hard rutted cakes, and a thin film of ice had formed on the roads and sidewalks. Some, but not much, of this had been melted by the dull red sun which shone for a little while through the mist in the middle of the day. By 4.30 the sun was obscured by clouds; soon sleet began to fall, and a strong, bitterly cold wind sprang up. By six o'clock, when the darkness was pitch-black, the thermometer touched the lowest point yet that winter.

On this dreary day probably the dreariest place was a railway terminus. Those who were hurrying to catch the 6.12 at Euston may have thought so, if they had any thoughts to spare from their aching ears and fingers. One of them, Councillor Henry James Grayling, a thin man looking about 50, cursed the station and the railway company aloud. Entering from the side, not through the grotesque, vast, black Euston arch, he had slipped on the frozen cobbles nearly in front of a lorry coming out in the darkness. He had fallen on his side and only been saved from injury by young Evetts, an assistant in the chemist's department of his own firm—a man whom he did not like or trust. He had not known Evetts was near to him; he did not like the officious way in which the young man pulled him to his feet and ran his hands all over his clothes. "I'm all right. Thank you. Disgracefully dangerous place. Confound the company," he said, ungraciously and reluctantly.

To evade his rescuer, as much as for any other reason, he crossed slantwise towards the refreshment room, picking his way in the faint blue light which was all that black-out rules allowed. He pushed through the swing doors, and then through the light-trap—a curtain—into the tearoom. It was brilliantly bright, close and hot after the dark and cold platforms.

Grayling stood for a moment, dazzled by the light and blinded by the film of steam that formed on his glasses. Waiting for it to clear, he decided that he might for once break a habit and really take a cup of coffee or tea before the train left. It would not be an indulgence, he reasoned; he was extremely cold, he had definite catarrh, and the price was low. But when the room cleared into his sight, he hesitated. The place was crowded, and it would take some time to get served. The cakes on the counter looked stale and unattractive. The tea would be served with tinned milk, if any milk were served at all; it would be scalding hot, and he had but five minutes to spare. His grey eyes, reddened at the corners, rested on a group of sailors who had been drinking beer and were shouting. One had a whisky in his hand. Grayling was a teetotaller, and envy or principle made him scowl; then, almost at once, he saw another thing which made up his mind for him. Near the door, in the crowd through which he had just pushed his way, was standing the square dark figure of a German refugee doctor—so-called—whom he knew and viewed with personal dislike and political suspicion. He turned sharply and walked through the door, pushing fairly rudely against the doctor on his way. In his belief the German jostled him deliberately in return—a fresh offence.

The month before, a large number of trains had been taken off because of fuel shortage. His favourite 5.57 no longer ran. There was a crowd thrusting on to the platform where the 6.12 would come in; Grayling took his place in the queue and pushed past the barrier with the others.

The platform was already filling up; he had to thread his way to reach the far end, where he always waited for the train. To be at the end saved him perhaps a minute on arrival at Croxburn; besides, the carriages near the end tended to be less full. Inside the station the wind did not blow so continuously and hard as outside; it eddied and whirled. But it was cold enough for him to press his attaché case close to him and to fold his hands across his chest; with his case held in front of his breast he looked oddly like a man with his gasmask at the "alert." When he reached his chosen place he stared out into the greater darkness from which the train would come. It was just possible to make out the edge of the station roof, a great dark arc against the darker sky. In the picture which it framed, the only visible things were the signal lights, red and green. They were of an unimaginable brilliance—unimaginable, that is, to those who only knew the pre-war station, whose brilliant lighting reduced the signals to unimportant glitters. Now they shone out from the thick, almost furry blackness with strong, unwinking cones of light. There seemed to be hundreds of them. Even Grayling, little accustomed to reflect on what he saw around him, wondered at the strength of the green lights. It wasn't safe, he reflected. A plain signal to German aircraft.

The train was now five minutes overdue. The platform was getting crowded. Among the people standing near, Grayling recognized, or thought he did, men with whom he travelled up every day. He was quite certain of one—the young man Evetts had reappeared. He began to edge away from him, still further up the platform, hugging his case. There was about £120 in that case, in pound notes and silver; he was not taking any risks.

Just then a flickering yellow light appeared among the reds and greens. The crowd moved, and a sound like a communal grunt of hope appeared; perhaps that was the light on the front of the engine of the delayed train? It jigged tantalizingly, but did not seem to come nearer. At last, but so slowly, it grew brighter, then it swerved to one side, and then, quite suddenly, there appeared behind it the black bulk of an engine, and rattling and panting the train pulled in, dead and dark with all its blinds drawn. As it came in Grayling saw that the company had made some effort to allow for the increased traffic. Extra carriages had been added; and, in common with other cautious passengers he ran forward to where the platform sloped down in a long ramp, in order to get into these additional and probably less crowded carriages. Once again, to his annoyance, he was jostled in the rush, and lost his favourable position by clinging anxiously to his case. When he did enter a carriage he found indignantly that all the corner seats had been taken, one, of course, by the wretched man Evetts. There was no sense in going to find another carriage, and in any case he was being pushed from behind by other travellers. He sat next to Evetts, coughing pointedly from the fumes of the large and foul pipe which the young man was smoking. The hint, if it was one, was not taken. Next to him there sat down with a thump a rather heavy man in clerical dress; he recognized in the dim light of the two lamps that were allowed the Vicar of Croxburn, his colleague on the Town Council. He nodded to him curtly: the Vicar was like himself a Conservative—or Ratepayers' Association member as they called themselves—but the two were all the same generally in disagreement. He recognized two other persons in the carriage. In the corner opposite was a large-nosed dark little man, just outside the pool of the lamplight; he was fairly sure that that was Ransom, a corporal in the Home Guard platoon in which he was a second lieutenant, and a damned bad corporal at that. A little further along on the same side was a handsome, fair young man with a club foot; he glanced at Grayling, blushed scarlet with embarrassment and looked away. Grayling's face became harder and angrier; but just at this moment a heavy bulk pushed in between them, and there sat down, dead opposite to him, the refugee doctor. Grayling drew himself back, hideously and openly affronted. But there was nothing that he could do to expel the German. He pulled himself stiffly back and took out his handkerchief, deliberately holding it in front of his nose, as if to protect himself from a disgusting smell. The German took no notice; or, if he did, did not show it.

In the far corner there was a fat middle-aged woman whom Grayling did not recognize; with her there was a small girl of about thirteen, in school uniform and with a running nose. Opposite them were two young working men in overalls whom he didn't know either. Something appeared to have amused them excessively; they kept bursting into fits of loud laughter and exchanging half sentences, incomprehensible to the outsider, about an event that had apparently occurred at work. Their most frequent word was "bloody," but they suppressed more coloured adjectives in deference to the company. The Vicar blew his nose with some violence, and Evetts withdrew his pipe to sneeze. Infected by their example, Grayling also blew his nose, and for a moment the carriage was echoing with sneezes, nose-blows and coughs. At that moment the train started with a violent jerk, the passengers were thrown forward and Evetts' bag, which he had put in the rack, fell on to Grayling's head. Evetts leant forward, apologized, and pulled it back again; Grayling replied inaudibly.

Thereafter the train ran its usual course, stopping at each station as suburban trains do. After the fourth station, one of the exuberant workmen turned his attention to reading the inscriptions inside the carriage. It was an old carriage, brought back into service for the war period; and its notices had had more than their fair share of schoolboy emendations. The jests were neither very good nor very new, but the reader professed to find them overwhelming. To decipher them, he had to peer very closely, right past Grayling's shoulder in one case, and to move right down the carriage, which he did without embarrassment. "Please res*t*rain your ticket," and "Do not lea*p* out of the window" were established jokes; but he appeared never before to have seen the simple injunction: "Before alighting, wait until the rain stops." On the door itself the advice "To lower window, pull strap towards you" had defeated the inscription writer: he had got as far as "To love widow," but had then given up in despair. The explorer's colleague began to offer suggestions but was hastily hushed. The cream, however, was a notice above Grayling's head, newly put up because of the war. By the simple but grandiose process of turning an "i" into an "o" it had been made to read: "During the blackout, blonds must be pulled down and kept down." The Vicar was moved to protest at the delighted elaboration of this thesis that followed, and the reader fell into an abashed silence.

Nothing else noteworthy occurred. The passengers were silent, seeming to dislike each other's company. Most had colds; all were cold. The young man who had blushed so darkly at the sight of Grayling, glanced at him once or twice with a very queer expression, but said nothing.

After three-quarters of an hour, the train pulled into the suburb of Croxburn. Most of the passengers got out, leaving the woman and her child, and the two workmen to go on to a later station. Grayling avoided speaking to anyone of his companions, got first through the turnstile, and was almost immediately hidden in the moonless night.

2

The Vicar made his way cautiously home; he had no electric torch and the ground was slippery underfoot. He prodded carefully with his umbrella when he thought that he had reached the kerb, or when he perceived what might be a lump of half-frozen slush. Though there was no fog, his eyes were sore, and the wind seemed to chafe his face unreasonably. He wrapped his scarf round his cheeks, but they had become so tender he pulled it away again. It was half an hour's walk to the Vicarage, and he was never more glad to arrive than he was that evening.

As he switched on the light, having carefully closed the door first, his housekeeper, who had come out to meet him, gave a faint squeal: "Oh, sir, you've got that barber's rash again. Look at your face!" The Vicar stared at himself in the long hall mirror, as much as his smarting eyes would allow. It was true; the left side of his face was covered by a pink rash, and it was certainly itching very unpleasantly. Some months before he had been troubled by a skin disease caught from a barber's shop; he tutted irritably at this sign of its return.

He went upstairs rather heavily, and routed out from a medicine cupboard the remains of a zinc ointment prescribed for him at the time. In the bathroom, he rubbed some of it on lightly, and at the same time bathed his eyes with boracic lotion. These amateur operations eased his discomfort to some extent, and he was able to eat his dinner. But his eyes and skin still remained troublesome, and half-past ten he was wondering whether it was not worth while, even on so foul a night, to go down the road to call on Dr. Hopkins. At that moment the telephone bell rang. He lumbered across the room and answered it.

"Croxburn 0015."

A cold, level feminine voice replied: "Is that the Vicar speaking?"

"Yes."

"This is Mrs. Grayling. I wonder if you could spare the time to come and see my husband."

"I think so—I mean I—" The Vicar was puzzled at the request, and showed it.

"I think he is dying" went on the voice, which seemed to have some difficulty in selecting its words, but showed no other emotion at all. "That is to say, he is certainly very ill. The doctor is with him now. But as he is one of your churchwardens, I thought perhaps you should be there." It might have been a committee meeting to which Mrs. Grayling was inviting the Vicar.

"Oh, dear me, dear me. I *am* sorry. Has he—er—asked for me?"

"He cannot speak."

"Oh." The Vicar was distinctly jolted. "I will come at once."

Croxburn is one of the many huge "dormitory" suburbs round London, mostly built up in the between-wars period. There is a small nucleus of the old village, consisting of undistinguished Victorian houses, but the body of the borough consists of two-storey houses, sold to middle-class occupants by building societies, on the instalment plan. Like every other, it has its Park Drive, Elm Avenue, Laburnum Grove and such roads, all alike and with identical houses, but made to curl and wind in a manner intended to recall an old English village. It makes it very easy for the stranger to lose his way, and even for the native it enforces long detours.

It took the Vicar half an hour to reach the Grayling house, and he had ample time to reflect on the character of the man to whose side he had been called.

His emotion was chiefly that of surprise. It was true that Grayling was a churchwarden at St. Mary's, but he very much doubted whether he had any religious feeling. He was quite sure Mrs. Grayling had none at all. She was a very good-looking, self-possessed woman some twenty years or so younger than her husband; and the last time that the Vicar had taken tea at their house—a long while ago—she had told him she was not a Christian, and had spent most of her time trying to vex him with the more childish atheist puzzlers, such as "Who was Cain's wife?" Grayling himself was one of the well-established clique which had had the Town Council in its pocket ever since there had been a Town Council. He had attached himself to the parish church of St. Mary the Virgin for no better reason, the Vicar thought, than that it was a form of municipal activity, and he intended to keep his hand on every local affair that he could. The Vicar had attempted, not being High Church, to drop "the Virgin" from the church's name; Grayling had succeeded in preventing him, and the Vicar did not think he was uncharitable in saying (and he had done so more than once) that conviction played no part in the Councillor's interference. Grayling attended service as rarely as was compatible with his churchwardenship; since the Home Guard had taken to parading every Sunday he had not attended at all, though Evensong never clashed with his military duties. The Vicar wondered if he could bring himself to believe that danger had brought out unsuspected spiritual earnestness in the Councillor. Forgetting for the minute that Mrs. Grayling had said her husband could not speak, the Vicar allowed himself to play with the idea that he might be being summoned to hear a confession. The near approach of death had a chastening effect on even the most hardy. He had long suspected Councillor Grayling and certain other members of the Council of corruption. The Gas Committee, of which Grayling was chairman, published very attenuated accounts, and the Vicar had been given three very circumstantial stories of graft—two dealing with the allocation of contracts and one with secret rebates. He had been investigating these, as he believed, privately. (But here he was wrong; his activities were well known to those concerned. The Vicar believed himself to be a patient man with plenty of worldly cunning; as are most people who hold that belief he was short-tempered and naïve.) He wondered if, before meeting his Maker, Grayling had decided to tell the truth and disclose the facts to the one man on the Council who could be trusted not to hesitate in clearing out evil. He pondered over this, remembered Grayling's character and decided it was unfortunately a very improbable hypothesis.

Mrs. Grayling answered the door when he arrived. She was between thirty and forty, with a rather lean face— pointed nose, pointed chin and thinnish lips. She had wide dark brown eyes and a head of dark brown hair. Her face was devoid of any marked signs of distress; it had an impersonal expression like that of a hospital nurse. "I am afraid I have brought you out for no reason, Vicar," she said. "I telephoned your house, but I was too late. He cannot speak or see now. There is nothing you can do for him. Dr. Hopkins is upstairs with him now. I expect he will be down soon and we will ask him. But he warned me against expecting any good news."

"What is wrong with your husband?"

Mrs. Grayling spread out her hands in a gesture of ignorance.

"The doctor doesn't say. I think he doesn't know. It is something to do with his lungs, I gather. But it is very sudden, for lung trouble, surely."

"Yes. Yes, indeed. And he looked perfectly well this evening," said the Vicar unhappily.

"Oh," said Mrs. Grayling indifferently, "did you travel with him? What am I thinking of, keeping you standing here? Please come into the drawing-room and sit down."

She led the way and they waited in the drawing-room in silence. After about half an hour Dr. Hopkins, a greying man with a half-bald head, came in. "He is very ill," he said without preamble, "and—oh, are you here, Vicar?—and I am afraid that you must prepare yourself for the worst, Mrs. Grayling." He stopped short, looking at her uncomfortably. He felt he should have said more, but what could he say? The Vicar stepped in: "Perhaps I could see Mr. Grayling a minute?" he said. "I do not think Mrs. Grayling—" "Why certainly," fussed the doctor, "I think it would be better for Mrs. Grayling not to come up, unless she insists; but certainly you can come. I must go up now; I cannot leave the nurse alone there any longer."

Mrs. Grayling made no move; and did not speak.

Just as they were going she said in a rather low voice: "What exactly is wrong, doctor?" "Lesions in the lungs, chiefly," answered the doctor, "but there are other complicating symptoms. And it is not clear what has caused them. This sudden onset is most peculiar."

Twenty minutes later the two men returned to the drawing-room. The Vicar advanced with outstretched hands. "He passed away while I was with him," he said gently.

He held Mrs. Grayling's hands between his. "My dear," he said, "is there anything I can do?" He checked himself from offering to pray with her.

She looked up at him gratefully. "You are very kind," she said. "I mean that. You are *really* very kind. But I don't think so. I think you had better leave me to myself. And him."

Dr. Hopkins spoke. "I am sorry to trouble you at this time, but there will have to be a post-mortem. I am going to ring up the police surgeon now. We will cause as little inconvenience as we can, I promise you."

3

"I assure you, Inspector, I am only too glad to answer your questions. There is no need for these apologies. I am really distracted, and I only wish you could take complete control of this house and everything in it." Mrs. Grayling's voice did at last show some emotion, if it was only that of exasperation. "To answer the telephone calls from Barrow and Furness's branches alone is really too much for me. Please sit down. I will tell you anything I can. I suppose you will ask me my name, though you know it quite well, of course. Renata Grayling. My age—well, I really think that is not wholly your business—"

Inspector Holly broke in gently. "I shouldn't think of asking you questions like that, ma'am. I want to spare you trouble, not make it. I am so sorry that you have been worried by your husband's firm telephoning. I will see if I can stop it. I cannot understand why they should do such a thing."

"Oh, don't blame them. What else can they do? They want to pay their people. They keep asking what Henry has done with the money. I can't tell them."

"With the money?"

"Didn't you know? Henry always brought home with him, every Friday, the money to pay the staff in five branches of Barrow and Furness. Quite a lot of money, he used to say. He had them made out into packets and on Saturday morning three of the shops sent round for theirs while he took the packets for High Street and Austen Road himself. Austen Road has telephoned me twice already, and the manager of Neville Road was here at 8.30 this morning. But Henry didn't bring the money."

Inspector Holly said nothing about any reflections that that last sentence caused. "I will certainly see that you aren't worried any more," he said.

"Meanwhile could you—would you mind telling me just what happened last night, as far as you know it?"

"Yes. It was about 7.30 or a quarter to 8—I can't be sure exactly, but it must have been after half-past seven, because I remember thinking Henry was late and might have missed his train—he was very regular in his ways, and it was unusual for him not to be in strictly to time. I remember saying to myself that perhaps the bad weather had delayed the train and then that if he had missed the train I ought to go and take the dinner out of the oven or it would spoil. Alice's evening out is Friday, you see, and I was alone in the house and had prepared our dinner. I was just idly wondering like that, thinking of nothing in particular, when I thought I heard a sort of soft thump against the door. I wasn't sure, and I went out into the hall to listen; and then I seemed to hear a sort of scrabbling against the door."

A slight, almost imperceptible grimace as of horror went across her face.

"Well, I turned out the light, and opened the door; and Henry practically fell on me. He must have been leaning against the door, unable to stand up. He must have been on his knees, I think, for when he fell down his body was only half across the threshold. I didn't realize what had happened; I couldn't understand it at all. I couldn't see much anyway; you know how dark it is in the black-out, especially a night like last night; and I had just come out of a lighted room.

I did look round, but I couldn't see more than a few feet. It was all blackness. There wasn't anyone using a torch or anything, not even a bicycle lamp. I could see that the snow on the garden path had been sort of smeared and brushed about. I suppose Henry had dragged himself on all fours up the path. Well"—Mrs. Grayling began to speak more hurriedly now—"I dragged Henry into the hall by his arms as best I could, and as soon as I had shut the hall door I turned on the light, and then I could see he was in a terrible condition. There was blood down his chin and on to his tie, and he had been sick. He couldn't stand or speak, and he kept clutching at his throat. His face looked as if he was in most hideous pain, and was all blotchy. And while I looked at him he coughed up a fresh lot of blood and spittle, but he couldn't say anything but make a faint sort of moaning noise, though I'm sure he was trying to tell me something. I went straight to the telephone and got Dr. Hopkins, and told him my husband was taken horribly ill, and he must come at once; and must see that a nurse came too. Well, he did so; and while I was waiting for him I managed to get Henry to bed and out of his clothes. And the rest I think you know."

Mrs. Grayling drew in her breath and let it out with a sound which was neither quite a gasp nor a sigh.

The Inspector said: "Yes. Thank you very much. Thank you very much indeed. I have talked to Dr. Hopkins, and I do know the rest. You've told me everything very clearly. There's only one other thing I would like to ask you—did your husband have a case or a bag with him?"

"No. He hadn't got anything in his hands. And he hadn't his hat on. He usually carries an attaché case and he set out with it that morning. Have you found it?"

"I think we have. We found a case fifty yards or so down the road. It was open and had some Barrow and Furness notepaper in it. Nothing else. No money. I'll ask you to look at it later, if I may, to identify it. And Mr. Grayling's hat, which was not far away. A black felt, with H.J.G. on the band. But there's no hurry about that.

"It's very kind of you to have helped us so much. I want to express again, er, our deep sympathy in your bereavement and our thanks again. I will not intrude on you any more. I will go and deal with these telephone calls."

And thus, clumsily, the Inspector took his leave.

4

Inspector Holly walked slowly back to the police station after he had left Mrs. Grayling. He was a tall, thin man with iron-grey hair; he was walking just now with a slight stoop and with his lips pursed up as for a soundless whistle. He looked perplexed, as, in fact, he was. He was not a native of Croxburn; he was a Devonshire man who only recently had been transferred. He wished he knew more about the people concerned. For example, Mrs. Grayling had said he knew her name was "Renata"; but he had not known even that. He knew Grayling's own position—that is, he knew that he was a very influential councillor, though not a very well-liked one. The Vicar he knew too: he rather liked him; he regarded him as a busybody, but an honest busybody. But he knew none of the gossip that an old inhabitant would know—not even enough to know where to look and what to ask.

He put aside his worry for the minute with the reflection that after all it was not certain that much inquiry would be needed. The death was an odd one, it was true; but there was after all no very clear reason to assume it was anything but natural. The disappearance of the money that Grayling seemed to have been carrying was obviously something requiring investigation. But it did not seem a serious problem. If Grayling had been suddenly taken ill, he might well have dropped the case from his hand; and afterwards staggered home without it. He was probably trying to tell Mrs. Grayling about it when she picked him up. Meanwhile some passer-by in the dark found the case and opened it—or maybe it had flown open as it fell—and when he saw the packets of money inside, pinched them. If so, he was probably a local man; no one else was likely to be wandering about suburban roads late on a January evening. There were no fingerprints on the case, but that was not surprising. Anyone who had gloves would be wearing them on a night like that. Nor did it matter; if it was a local sneak-thief who had collected over £120 in one windfall he would fairly quickly give himself away. He would be caught spending it.

The Inspector decided more cheerfully that he had reconstructed the course of events correctly; he straightened himself and began to walk briskly. All that remained was to confirm from the doctors that Grayling's death had been natural.

He found Dr. Hopkins with Police-Surgeon Campbell. He respected Dr. Hopkins as a hard-working, unpretentious G.P., quite competent to deal with any case likely to come his way; he neither respected nor liked Dr. Campbell. He could not follow easily what he said, for the doctor's broad Scots was never in the least moderated for his Devon ears; he believed that the doctor regarded him as an intruder and was intentionally rude; he suspected that he drank whisky too freely and was inaccurate in his work. But he was the police doctor, and there was nothing Holly could do about it—not, anyway, until he had been in Croxburn considerably longer.

"So ye've come, have ye?" said Campbell. (There is no possibility of attempting to reproduce his accent.) "Maybe ye will explain the case to the Inspector, Dr. Hopkins; I doubt I could make him understand."

Ignoring him Holly turned to the smaller man. Dr. Hopkins began fumblingly: "The case presents, um, several features of difficulty. I am not quite sure how to present— that is, to explain exactly…"

"Dinna haver, man," said his colleague. "Tell Mr. Holly we don't know how the man died; and then tell him why we don't know how he died. Be very simple for the Inspector."

"Well, it is not strictly true that we don't know how he died. He died of heart failure, if you are going to be exact, Campbell," said Dr. Hopkins. "But what induced the heart failure is, of course, as usual, the real question."

"And at that he may have died of choking," interpolated the other.

"Choking?" almost shouted Holly.

"Ye see, ye have to be careful with the Inspector," sneered Campbell. "Choking doesn't necessarily mean someone strangled him. Explain it, Hopkins, in words of one syllable."

Dr. Hopkins, blushing scarlet for Campbell's boorishness, went on: "The condition of the body, Inspector, is very strange. Grayling died of heart failure consequent on two, er, causes. That is to say, it might have been due to either one of them. They were: loss of blood, and suffocation. Both his lungs and throat were terribly affected. There was œdema of the lungs, and the symptoms of very severe laryngitis. The latter was the reason why he could not speak; there were even what are called pseudo-membranes in the throat. The tissues were very severely affected…"

"Blood must have been pouring into his lungs," grunted Campbell. "Sodden like sponges they were."

"What caused all this, Doctor?" asked the Inspector.

"We don't know. There was no previous history of bronchial trouble or throat trouble that we know of, and in any case it is doubtful if that would explain the attack. It must have been almost in the nature of a seizure. Most extraordinary. We did have," Dr. Hopkins coughed deprecatingly, "an idea which momentarily seemed to explain the affair; but it had to be abandoned." He stopped speaking; Holly wordlessly urged him to go on. "Well, we thought that possibly someone might have thrown vitriol at him."

"Vitriol!"

"Yes; you see we found marked traces of burning round the nose and mouth. The eyes were badly affected. I think, indeed, that towards the end he was partly if not totally blind. The skin of the face seemed in parts to be almost raw. But although some of his appearance was consistent with an attack by a vitriol-thrower, that was all that could be said. It doesn't explain the rest of the symptoms. And it was those after all that caused his death."

"The man didna die of a burnt face, ye ken," added Campbell. "The long and short of it is, we canna tell ye how he died, and ye must bring in Sir James from the Home Office."

"He won't be able to get here till Monday," objected Holly.

"Then ye must e'en wait till Monday."

Dr. Campbell clearly enjoyed leaving the Inspector on that sentence.

5

The Inspector had had a talk with the Superintendent, who had told him to do just what he had expected. Since no clear lead had come from the doctors, he was instructed to be on the safe side and inquire as fully as he could into the whole circumstances. If he had to have a hypothesis, let it be that Grayling had been attacked by vitriol at some time. But it would be better to have no hypothesis. He was just to reconstruct as closely as he possibly could Grayling's actions that day, especially on his homeward journey. His first calls should be on the Vicar, who had travelled down with him and the manager of Barrow and Furness who would know about his actions during the day. It would be as well to make those calls early ones. Memories faded only too quickly.

That was exactly what the Inspector had expected the Superintendent to say. It was the only correct thing to say, and if he had been in the Superintendent's place he would have said it. But it was no more agreeable for that. It meant, in effect, going to look for something and not knowing what that something was. In the Inspector's opinion, this talk about forming no hypothesis without sufficient facts was like the Judges' Rules—something theoretically sound but, in fact, quite impracticable. To have no hypothesis was to have no object: to have a hypothesis which one knew to be untrue was no better.

All the same, work had to be done, he telephoned both the Vicar and the manager of Barrow and Furness—the latter first, in order to catch him before he left the office. (It was now 11.30 on Saturday morning.)

The manager had a disagreeable voice, and he seemed in a disagreeable temper. He appeared to hold the police and Grayling equally responsible for the loss of the money which should have paid the staff in the North-Western branches. Holly elicited from him, or was presented with this information:

That the sum lost was exactly £124 10s. 3d.

That he, the manager, was about to go away for the week-end by the 12.15, and that he would not adjourn his departure, nor give the Inspector an interview, nor disclose his week-end address. He would answer what questions he could on the telephone, forthwith or on Monday afternoon. He might find time to see the Inspector in the week. That the staff at the North-Western branches would merely not be paid that week-end. Something would no doubt be done on Monday. Inconvenience to the staff? The inconvenience of a heavy loss to the firm was his sole concern.

That Mr. Grayling was one of four assistant cashiers, all of whom had been with the firm many years and possessed the firm's confidence. That he had arrived at the usual time, 9.30, and left at 5.30, and spent his day as usual at his desk. All the assistant cashiers sat at desks which were visible from his, the manager's desk, and nothing in any way unusual had occurred yesterday. He had no conversation with Mr. Grayling except a few words of greeting or farewell. On the question of the money, the manager said this:

"Originally, the wages of the staff were sent out by special messengers on Friday afternoon. With the outbreak of war this expense seemed unreasonable. Besides, the men whom we employed being strong and healthy, would naturally at once wish to answer their country's call. In any case, we dispensed with their services, and arranged for each assistant cashier to take home on Friday night with him the wage packets for the area with which he was concerned. In the morning he would deliver some, and some would be called for at his house.

"He made his own arrangements about that. The position was quite clear. The money was in the assistant cashier's charge until it was delivered to the various branch managers. In consequence, the loss of this particular sum is the concern of the late Mr. Grayling's estate. I have been endeavouring to make this point clear to his representatives, but have not succeeded."

Holly was used to callousness, but this was too much. "I had heard," he said, "that Mr. Grayling's widow was being pestered by telephone calls of some such kind, immediately after her bereavement. I am glad to say I have arranged with the telephone exchange that the nuisance shall cease."

The manager made a strangled noise.

"One more question," continued Holly. "To how many people was this arrangement known?"

"I—um—that is to say," replied the manager more subduedly, "it was not a secret in any way. I could not say how many knew of it. Anyone who chose, of our headquarters staff, that is."

"But your staff was paid on Saturday at midday, not on Friday."

"And why not?" said the manager, recovering himself. "Our business is run to suit the convenience of our customers, not of our employees."

"No doubt. I was not interested in that aspect of the matter. I was remarking that your outside staffs, also, would presumably know of the arrangement."

"Yes. I suppose so," agreed the manager reluctantly.

6

The Vicar. Not a troublesome man, like the manager, Inspector Holly had no difficulty with him. Only the smallest amount of guile was needed in approaching him.

The Inspector sat in his study, tastelessly furnished by a multiple store, and said:

"I've come to you for help, sir, because you know the parish so well. I'm relatively a newcomer, and I'll have to rely on you. I'm sure I can trust in your discretion if I speak to you a little more freely than I would to the ordinary man."

The Vicar's large, rather pink face beamed at him. It gave the illusion of literally shining. Nothing could be more flattering to its possessor than this approach. Though he was far from being High Church, and regarded Anglo-Catholicism with deep suspicion, the Vicar had a strong sense of history and an elevated estimate of the importance which he should possess in the life of the community. In Croxburn, he was the parish priest. His position should be no less—it should indeed be greater—than that of the Mayor, the M.P., the Medical Officer of Health, and other functionaries whom everyone knew. But what were the facts? Very few people even knew of him. He ministered in an ugly, dark, middle-sized church, rebuilt and spoilt in 1851; he lived in a false Tudor-timbered semi-detached house, differing only from its neighbours in that the freehold was held by the Ecclesiastical Commissioners instead of a building society. His congregation was small, and its members were chiefly ageing. His attempts to advertise himself, his church and his religion were unsuccessful, and on looking back at them he often found them humiliating. He would have been able to bear it if the citizens of Croxburn had attended the synagogue, the Wesleyan Methodist Chapel, the Pillar of Fire Gospel Hall, or even Our Lady of Sorrows with its detestable, shifty Irish "Father." That would have meant that heresy was rampant, and he could fight heresy, ramp how it might. But they did not: they passed them all by. The Vicar felt himself like a man sitting by the wayside, dressed in sacred raiment, each piece of which had a noble and ancient history, offering eternal truths; and the people ignored him and went to the pictures.

Now, for the first time, a man in charge of the civil power, having the right to bind and to loose, was calling on him for advice and help, deferring to him as one who knew the truth about the parish. (How wise Holly had been to use the word "parish," how nearly he had forgotten to do so!)

"My dear Inspector, I am so glad you have come to me. I will give you every help I can. And most certainly I shall treat as absolutely confidential anything you think you should tell me. Please tell me what I may do."

Campbell would talk anyway, reflected the Inspector; it was as well to make a virtue of necessity.

"I expect you have guessed already what it is about, sir," he said. "It is the death of Councillor Grayling. We are completely at a dead end. The strangest thing has happened. The doctors do not know how he died. We are having to call in specialists, and hope that they will tell us. I have never known such a thing; we simply do not know if the death was natural or not."

"But Dr. Hopkins was with him when he died."

"Why, yes, sir, strictly speaking we do know *how* he died: lung trouble, as I understand it. But what caused this sudden attack—that is what the doctors cannot say.

"Now, sir, we all hope it was a natural death. But, as policemen, we may not take chances. It might not be a natural death. I hope, sir, you will not let it be known I said this."

"Of course not."

"If it isn't a natural death, then we shall have to find the murderer, to put it bluntly. We shall in due course, there is no doubt, be told whether it was natural or not. But meanwhile we had better proceed on the assumption of the worst. Clues are evanescent: men's memories are short. But if it came to anyone's ears that I was investigating and that the police entertained a suspicion of murder—consider the scandal! And then if after all, we were to find out that our alarms were baseless. We might have done untold damage."

"Quite. Exactly so." The Vicar removed his eyeglasses and fixed on the Inspector a strained glare which was intended to suggest both concentrated attention and phenomenal acuteness. It gave him a slight squint.

"So I am going to ask you, sir, to tell me all you can about two subjects. The first is—Councillor Grayling himself. Give me an idea of the man, tell me what he did, what enemies he had, and anything in his life that was—well, in any way irregular or likely to lead to consequences. The second is more easy. I want as full an account as possible of his journey back home with you last night."

"The man himself..." The Vicar abandoned his stare and looked pensively up at the electric chandelier, whose glass had a pattern of Greek keys in orange on it. He must be honest, but charitable; fair but precise. "That is a very hard question. I will do my best. Henry Grayling was a church-warden, but I never felt he was a man of strong religious views. I regarded his wardenship as a tribute to the conventions. We never had any conversation on serious subjects, and that I think was not only because he was a silent man. His wife, as you may know, is an infidel."

"I did not," said Holly, surprised by the antiquated word.

"He himself was what used to be called a worldly man and, since you have asked me to speak freely, I suppose I should say that I have had laid before me some evidence about him that might have become your affair later in any case. There were three different cases which had been brought to me. You probably know that Grayling is, or was, Chair-man of the Gas Committee of the Council. Both the man-ager and the majority of the committee belong to a clique which, in the opinion of many citizens, runs our municipal affairs to its own private advantage. These three cases refer to the Light and Power Station."

"Don't you think," asked the Inspector, "that you ought to be more explicit? You said they were a police matter."

"I said they might *become* one. Frankly, I can't say more, because I haven't proof. I will go so far as this: two cases allege the giving of secret commissions to three Councillors, of whom Grayling was one, to secure contracts either for repairs or for the supply of necessary raw materials. If and when I get evidence amounting to proof, which I have not got now, I was going to expose the matter at a Council meeting. I shall do so still."

"Well," said Holly, "I won't press you, sir, at the moment. I may have to do so later. Is there anything more that you can tell me? About his private life, for example?"

The Vicar looked highly embarrassed. At last he said: "There is nothing else that I know." There was just a faint emphasis on the last word.

Holly said gently: "If you have any suspicion, I think you should tell me. We are speaking in confidence, after all; and I have learned to be discreet."

Cornered, the Vicar thought unhappily of the figure of Mrs. Buttlin, once the Grayling's cook, housekeeper, and still a regular attender at his church. *"A whore, and the wife of a churchwarden. You shouldn't be afraid of a scriptural word, a person shouldn't. A whore, that's what I said."* Indeed, that had been what she said, but not by any means all that she said. He made up his mind.

"A servant who left them brought me a detailed and unpleasant story charging Mrs. Grayling with adultery. She added that Mr. Grayling was refusing a divorce on religious grounds. I did not, and do not, believe that. And as for the main allegation, I told my informant—as soon as I could get a chance to speak—that I would not listen to gossip."

"You gained no idea of who might be the guilty man—if there was one?"

"No, indeed."

"But would you tell me who it was who spoke to you?"

The Vicar scratched his head and then ran his finger round his neck inside his dog-collar. "Well, I suppose. Yes. Mrs. Adelaide Buttlin; she lives at 34, Chamberlain Gardens, with her niece; but I believe she is away at the moment. I would rather you did not mention my name."

"I certainly will not. Now, about my other question. Would you give me an account of your journey home with Mr. Grayling?"

The Vicar's relief was obvious. "With pleasure, with pleasure. I can remember the carriage and its occupants well. In fact, if you wish, I could do more."

"H'm?"

"I could identify the carriage. I could point out in it precisely where each person sat. I think I could also recite everything that occurred on the journey, such as it was."

"Identify the carriage! May I ask you how you could manage to do that?"

The Inspector thought that after all there might be traces in the carriage. Traces of what? Heaven knew. Not of vitriol, anyway. Confound this case.

"By certain—er—marks that I noticed," the Vicar was saying rather archly.

"I think I will take advantage of your offer," said the Inspector. "If I may use your telephone? Tell me, first, what part of the train was your carriage in."

"By all means. We were in the very first coach."

"Thank you."

The Inspector took a little time in getting on to the Traffic Superintendent from the local station, and then back to the local station. Eventually he had unexpected good fortune. The coach in question was easily identified, it was standing in a shed at Croxburn and had not been used since the previous night. Saturday traffic being noticeably less than other days, trains were shorter, and it was not wanted.

"If you will be so very kind as to come with me," he said to the Vicar, "I'll put your promise to the test. The station-master says we can go over the coach now, if we choose. It is not being used to-day; it's in a siding."

A little while later, accompanied by the Inspector and an inquisitive stationmaster in a hard hat, the Vicar gleefully picked his way across the railway tracks. For the most part he was as excited as a schoolboy, but once he was badly frightened. His umbrella caught in the loose stones between the sleepers and nearly tripped him. At that moment a light engine, roaring and blowing like a dragon, rushed towards him and appeared to be about to crush him. "Steady, sir!" said the stationmaster, and pulled him up; the engine swerved on to a side line and ran fuming away about its own affairs.

At last they arrived at the coach. Standing alone, away from any platform, it seemed unexpectedly tall. The Vicar had to be hauled up into it. He inspected first one carriage, then a second, pursing his lips and wagging his head to and fro. At the third, he said triumphantly: "This is it."

"Are you certain?" said the Inspector.

"Yes. I am certain."

"Do you mind my asking why?"

Slightly less triumphantly the Vicar answered: "Because of the, um, modifications of the inscriptions."

"The what, sir?"

The Vicar pointed to notices which said:

Wait until the rain stops.

Please restrain your ticket.

"Ho!" said the stationmaster. "I wouldn't go much by that. You'll find them in most carriages of this type, I'm afraid. Passengers have been doing that for years. Especially school-children, on these local trains."

"I am aware of that," said the Vicar, a great austerity filling his countenance. "But I had reason to notice that these mutilations were carried to a greater extent than usual. There is, for example, that notice which was behind my head as I sat, and which seemed to amuse some of my fellow passengers."

The notice originally dealt with the pulling down of blinds. But it now said: DURING THE BLACKOUT, BLONDS MUST BE PULLED DOWN AND KEPT DOWN. The stationmaster, a man of noticeable vulgarity, who had risen from the ranks, let out a horse-laugh, "Ha, ha, ha! Hoo, hoo, hoo! Blonds must be pulled down. I should shay sho!"—an ancient Edwardian catchword which vexed the Vicar exceedingly. "It's a very unusual one, that," he continued, speaking to the clergyman as one collector to another. "It's a long time since I saw it."

Holly intervened.

"Could you tell us where you sat, sir, and, as far as possible, how the rest of the carriage was filled?"

"I can tell you with great exactitude," replied the Vicar, turning with pleasure from the gross-minded railwayman. "I sat here. Immediately to my left sat Councillor Grayling. To his left, in the corner, sat a young man smoking a rather foul pipe: I think he was known to the Councillor personally. When the train started it jerked a bag or parcel off the rack on to Grayling's head and this young man retrieved it. They exchanged a few words, and I think Grayling called him 'Everitt' or 'Evetts,' I am not sure which.

"On my other hand, on my right, sat two young men of the artisan class. They were rather boisterous. I did not know them, and as they did not leave the carriage at Croxburn I suppose they lived further up the line. Those were all the passengers on this side of the carriage."

The Inspector looked at the long seat and fixed its population in his mind. From one corner to the other it had been as follows:

Young man with pipe, Evetts or Everitt.
Grayling.
The Vicar.
A boisterous workman.

Another of the same.

Five on the one side, a full complement, especially as the Vicar was a Broad Churchman physically as well as theologically.

"Here was where you said Mr. Grayling sat?"

The Vicar nodded.

Holly inspected the place carefully. He could see no traces of burning, discoloration, or anything to indicate the presence of an acid. However, he was no expert, and after all he did not know what he was looking for.

"I'll ask you to let one of my men go over this thoroughly," he said to the stationmaster.

"When? Can't keep this coach out of commission indefinitely: it'll be needed Monday," said the stationmaster.

"To-day or to-morrow. And now the other side, sir."

"Yes," said the Vicar. "Now, in the corner opposite the young man with the pipe, there was a man whom I didn't see clearly. There were only two lamps in the carriage, as you see, and they were encased in those two black cones, because of the black-out rules. They made two sorts of circles of light, and this man, who was rather a small fellow, was mostly outside the light. I have an idea that I've seen him before, in Home Guard uniform, but I'm not sure.

"Directly opposite the Councillor was a man whom I know well by sight, a dark, square largish man with glasses. A refugee, I have been told. I have been told his name too, but didn't remember it.

"Next him was a fair young man, good-looking, but with an injured foot. He is an acquaintance of the Graylings, and his name is Hugh Rolandson. You will find him easily. Then there was a middle-aged lady with a schoolgirl of about thirteen with her. I didn't know them: they also went on past Croxburn. I can't remember anything distinctive about them except that the girl had a bad cold and sniffed continually.

A little disagreeable, still, we nearly all had colds, and were coughing or sneezing most of the time."

"Thank you."

Holly memorized this side of the carriage too.

Slight man, possibly Home Guard.

Large Refugee.

Hugh Rolandson.

Unknown woman and her daughter.

As they picked their way home, he asked the Vicar: "You were going to tell me about the journey, would you do so?"

"I think I've told you most. The train was late and the platform was crowded. I don't remember seeing Mr. Grayling there. But a rush was made to the far end of the train, and when I got into the carriage he was already sitting down next to the young man with the pipe. I am not sure if I spoke to him, or if I merely nodded. The German refugee sat down opposite, and Mr. Grayling did a curious thing, which I thought rather offensive. He drew out his handkerchief and held it before his nose, as if the poor man smelt. But I may be doing him an injustice: he certainly had a cold and blew his nose more than once. I couldn't tell you, otherwise, in what order the others sat down.

"When the train started, it did so with a violent jerk. First backwards, as if the engine had charged it, and then forward again. I cannot imagine how engine drivers manage to do such complicated things with their machines. Certainly, the two men opposite were flung almost into the arms of myself and Grayling, and then, when they were jerked back, the young man Everitt or Evetts' bag fell on his head. Everitt or Evetts apologized and rescued it. I got a good sight of him and could recognize him.

"Nothing that I can remember happened during the journey, except that one of the workmen, who had been talking rather loudly and sillily, read those notices aloud. He got up to read the one that I mentioned and leaned over between me and Mr. Grayling, without any apology. I rebuked him for a rather gross comment, and his behaviour was more seemly for the rest of the journey.

"Everyone got out at Croxburn except the two workmen, and the lady with the small girl. I think Mr. Grayling must have gone out of the station very quickly, for I could not see him when I looked round."

"Thank you very much, sir. That has been very clear. I won't trouble you any more for the minute." Inspector Holly saluted and turned on his way to the police station.

7

Later in the day he summarized his results to the Superintendent.

"Until we know the facts of his death we can't go very far. This is all I've got—

"On his way home from Croxburn Station he may have met somebody or may not. It was a pitch-black night; and the black-out was made for crime.

"If he met anyone in the streets of London, we shan't know it either. But we do know who was with him in the carriage, and could possibly have followed him home. We can't rule out of the question someone having lurked waiting for him at Croxburn Station; inquiries merely show that no one was *noticed* there. These are the people who were in the carriage, anyway."

Holly summarized the Vicar's description, and went on:

"Supposing there has been any funny business, had any of these people a grudge? Well, sir, it's early to say. £124 in notes, anyway, is as good a motive as a grudge. But for what it is, here's all I know.

"The Vicar clearly did not like Grayling. He tells me he had something on him and expected shortly to expose a first-rate scandal and drive him from public life and possibly get him quodded. Not a motive for murder. Might have been, the other way round. Nor do I think that the Vicar wants £124 very badly. If things become serious, though, we might have to inspect his banking account."

The Superintendent shook his head.

"I've found nothing about the two workmen or the woman and girl. But after all they didn't get off here. Nor do I know who was the alleged Home Guard. But there is an H.G. parade to-morrow, and Major Ramsay has agreed to make an announcement and ask the man who travelled down with Grayling to report to us.

"Evetts or Everitt I haven't traced yet. It shouldn't be difficult, if he was an acquaintance of Grayling's. He may have been a fellow-employee, in which case he would know about the money.

"About the fair young man, Rolandson, I do know something. The Grayling's maid, Alice Williams, indicated to me that if Mrs. Grayling had done any sleeping-out, Mr. Rolandson was the boy friend. There had been rows between the Graylings about him. I'll get more when Mrs. Buttlin comes back.

"The German, too, is a possible line. Refugees are a Home Office matter, and Inspector Atkins deals with them. But I remember him telling me about one, who sounds very like this man, whom Grayling was making a dead set at. I can't remember the name, but Atkins will when he comes in. Grayling had written both to us and to the Home Secretary charging the man with being a spy, possessing a bicycle and a radio, and passing himself off falsely as a refugee, using the name of someone the Nazis had, in fact, killed. We didn't pay much attention, because Grayling had recently become very violent about such things and talked rather wildly. But I seem to remember Atkins spoke as if an arrest wasn't unlikely.

"That's all I have. What shall I do next?"

The Superintendent spread out his hands like a Jewish stall-keeper. "What can I say? You know as well as I do. Follow up all these people, and pray that the doctors make their minds up soon. You know where most of them could be found. You could ring up the deceased's firm about the young man Evetts or whatever his name is."

Chapter II

*	Snuffly Girl	A Workman	*
*	A Mother	A Workman	*
*	Hugh Rolandson	The Vicar	*
*	A German	H. J. Grayling	×
*	A Home Guard	• C. J. F. Evetts	*

1

"What are you going to do about it?" snivelled Ann Darling. ("Ann Darling!" and to think he had once made lover-like play with the words.) It was the sixth time, at least, that she had said it; and for the sixth time Charlie Evetts answered sourly: "I don't know."

What on earth had induced him to sleep with her at all? he wondered. She had thick legs, she was dull and had little to say for herself, and she couldn't be called pretty. She had a youthful bloom and cheerfulness which enabled her to get by—not at the moment, though, with a reddened nose and weepy eyes. A miserable lump of wet clay. Not the least chance of pretending that the baby wouldn't be his, either, with a girl with a face like that. What made me do it? he thought, looking at her venomously. Rebound after Veronica, I suppose.

He cast his mind back to the evening responsible. He reflected, as George Moore did with more elegance in *Hail and Farewell*, that you could always remember anything but the ultimate act of pleasure. You could keep a pretty vivid picture of a golden head looking down while its owner peeled a long silk stocking off a white thigh. But after all, what you came for wasn't that. And you never could recall that what you did come for was like. You just remembered the extras. Precious little of the extras he had had with clumsy Ann. Fumbling in the dark on the beach behind a breakwater. The most expensive and the least worth while.

Now if it had been Veronica. Damn her for walking out on him. He'd have married her, he would really, if she'd wanted it. He'd never thought that of any other girl. With her you almost could remember. A series of erotic and highly valued pictures began to unroll in his mind, until Ann's snuffles recalled him. What a time to be thinking of that. He never thought about anything else, they used to say at school. Damn right too. But what else was there worth thinking about? Well, it had got him in the bloody pit now, all right.

"I tell you I don't know, Ann. I'm trying to think," he answered to a half-heard whine.

He made an effort to consider his circumstances. Charles James Fox Evetts, aged 24, second assistant in the Chemistry and Drugs at Messrs. Barrow and Furness, wholesale. Wages, £4 4s. 0d. Resources, £18 in the Post Office savings bank. Some bits of furniture in his room, but nothing of value. His landlady was perfectly indifferent to any "goings-on"; he could, as he had discovered, behave like a tomcat with his girls so long as he didn't make the same noises as a tomcat. Once he and Elmer Evans— He sharply pulled his wandering thoughts back. His landlady's complaisance would most certainly not extend to an illegitimate birth in her house.

"You could marry me," said an ignoble and choking voice. He looked at her exasperatedly.

"I didn't think you would," said Ann, even more meekly. He felt a spasm of pity; she was so abject, and it wasn't her fault more than his. Perhaps he could borrow off his father, living in Runcorn on a pension. Not very likely. Maybe the old man would be good for £10; well, he had £18 and could surely get £2 more somewhere. Thirty pounds.

"Look, Ann," he said, kindly as he could; "I'll try to borrow something off father. I don't know, but I may be able to raise as much as thirty quid. Then we could get a doctor who—"

She jumped off the hassock on which she was sitting, with a squeal. "I won't," she said. "You know what happened to Jessie. I won't. You can die with those operations. Dirty black doctors. I won't have them touch me. Ever."

She walked to the door, anger and fear contending in her face. "Make up your mind to it, Charlie," she said. "You work in that chemist's department. You can get me something to bring it on, and you've got to do it. If you don't, I'll…I'll go round to your General Manager and tell *him.* And I'll face father, and he'll get an order against you. So make up your mind to it. Get that stuff, and get it by Saturday."

She faced him for a minute with the trembling ferocity of a cornered rabbit; and then darted out of the door, slamming it behind her.

2

Next morning at work was not an easy morning. Harry Kelvin, who shared a desk with him, noticed and commented on his strained look. All the morning he was seeing with his mind's eye the inside of the great stockroom and the exact shelf and carton where there was the stock of ergoapiol. It would be possible to steal two of the small bottles without immediate detection. He had to go in at regular intervals and dish out stock. There were two of them always on it, in addition to the man who came with the requisition. Generally, Harry went in with him; they both worked at the same time. The man called out what he wanted off the requisition, and they fetched each item in turn. Then they both checked over the amounts with the man, signed his copy of the list, and he went off. It would be easy to slip two ergoapiol bottles into his pocket when fetching something nearby. Well, fairly easy.

But some day it was bound to be found out. Grayling, the disagreeable assistant cashier, frequently carried out extra checks on the stock out of sheer spite and the hope of catching someone out. So Charlie believed anyway; and if he didn't there would still be the routine check in a month's time. And there'd be a bloody awful row about it. No ergot preparations were allowed to go out without a doctor's order. It would be just as safe as trying to pinch one of the poisons. Pretty easy to pin on him, too; there were very few people who had access to the stockroom.

And when it was found out, he'd be fired. For him to be fired, that wasn't like a miner or a railwayman losing his job. Easy come and easy go, that sort of common job. Besides, they had their union behind them, and everyone knew—Charlie thought—how unions tyrannized. They pushed back that sort of tough into a job though he might be hopelessly unfit for it. It was only decently educated and superior types like himself who always got the dirty end of the stick. If a chemist's assistant got fired for knocking off an abortion medicine, *he* wouldn't get another job. Not ever, not with any firm. Washout; complete washout.

But what was he going to do?

He cursed under his breath; and cursing was almost no relief at all.

About twelve he got out of his seat without a word and walked straight into the stockroom. He had no very clear idea of what he would do; he stood for a moment staring towards the carton in the corner. As he did so, steps sounded behind him; he turned to see the grey and suspicious face of the assistant cashier.

"What are you doing here, Evetts?" Grayling said.

"Nothing in particular. Do you want anything, Grayling?" The reply was a double offence, both in its matter and in the omission of the word "Mr." before "Grayling." Grayling held that his juniors should treat him with respect. He drew his lips back in a mirthless grin, but all he said was: "I shall have to check over stock again soon."

"Any other time when you've got no work to do suits me," replied Charlie with polite insolence. But he went back to his desk subdued. Was that old sod going to dog his steps? Another snag he hadn't thought of. And this was Thursday. Ann would split on him on Saturday if he didn't get the stuff. She would too; obstinate little cow.

To-morrow was his last chance.

During the night, in which he didn't sleep much, he decided to take that last chance.

After all, he reasoned, there was a chance he might get away unnoticed. And if he didn't, well, there was a way out, a rather desperate way. He'd send in his resignation and walk into the Army.

He was reserved because of his occupation now, and there was nothing that he wished less, in late 1941, than to be messed about in the Army and probably sent out to Libya to be killed. He supposed Hitler had got to be stopped, but that was other people's affair. Not for Charlie. But still, if the worst came to the worst, he *could* do what other people had done. Then he'd become a volunteer who threw up a safe job to defend his country. He'd probably be able to get a job in a chemist's department after the war. Not Barrow and Furness, of course, but somewhere. The idea, of course, would be not to wait till he was found out, but to enlist as soon as things looked fishy. As long as he got out before a definite accusation was made, the firm might be as suspicious as hell, but it wouldn't dare say anything. Not against a returned hero after the war. But no amount of reasoning could make it a pleasant prospect. Even the thought of a uniform, whose absence had been recorded aloud by one or two young ladies, was little consolation. He tried to envisage himself on embarkation leave; it was only reasonable to suppose that even the most difficult would refuse nothing to a gallant fellow who might never return. Suppose he had seven days; could he spend each night victoriously with a different companion? He tried to thumb over his address book in his mind; but for once he found himself listless. Trouble was too near.

3

He began to make the build-up right away. Friday morning he said to Harry Kelvin: "You know, Harry, fellows like you and me ought to be in the Army. There's no excuse, really." Harry gasped at him, as if he had gone mad; Charlie abandoned the line hastily.

Friday afternoon he did the trick, while making up a consignment for Deptford branch. Clumsily and nervously—he was almost sure Harry noticed something. And he didn't, in his haste, get ergoapiol; he got another ergot preparation next to it.

But he had got two bottles, anyhow; and the consignment had been checked and taken away. No one, not even Harry, had said anything.

Next morning he passed the bottles to Ann, with a word of warning which she disregarded. She took the full contents of both bottles that night.

4

He heard nothing from Ann on Sunday; nor on Monday, nor on Tuesday, nor Wednesday morning. Wednesday midday he and Harry Kelvin were in the gents' lavatory, and Kelvin was smoothing down his hair with a brush he had just dipped in the handbasin. He had black shiny hair, very natty, and kept it carefully in order. He was watching Charlie carefully—that is, he was not looking at him direct but watching his image in the mirror. He said:

"You knew Ann Darling, didn't you?"

"Yes, I know her," said Charlie, on guard.

"Heard about her?"

"Heard what?"

"She's dead. She had a miss on Sunday, and told nobody. She bled so they couldn't save her. Elmer told me—"

The room swayed round Charlie and he had to grip the marble side of the basin. His face was yellow, and greasy with sweat. Harry stopped in the middle of a remark about you never could tell with the quiet ones, and stared. After a second or two he walked out of the lavatory, silent and thoughtful.

5

Harry Kelvin thought to some purpose. A quick young man with his way to make had to be right on the job, at the right minute, never miss a chance; and he was a quick young man with his way to make. He attached himself to the bigger man when they left the office. Charlie didn't want him—never had liked the slick little fellow with his fast moving eyes—but he couldn't do anything about it.

"I been in the stockroom," said Harry. His grammar was worse than Charlie's, because his education had been worse. But, as he always said, he knew enough to get around.

Charlie said nothing. Nothing to say, anyway.

"You done it, didn you?" continued Harry, still in the tone of one carrying on a quite idle conversation. "Knocked her up, and then pinched the stuff from store to bring on a miss. Well, I'll be damned. J'expect to get away with it?"

Charlie muttered an exhortation to mind his own affairs.

Harry did not wish to do so. "I suppose you might get away with it, arter all. There's not anyone but me knows you took that ergot. Not yet anyway. Did you know it'd do her in?"

This was too much. "How the hell did I know she'd take too much? I told her to be careful. It's not my fault," protested Charlie.

"Ah, that's what they all say. Fat lot of good it'll do you when they find out the stuff's gone, and what it's gone for too. They must find it out, too. At least, I suppose that *is* a way out." Harry feigned hesitation and thought.

"How?" Charlie turned a haggard look on him.

"You did do it then. I thought you did. Now you just told me. I thought you was up to something on Friday, but I couldn't quite see you." Harry seemed satisfied about something; and so he might well be. Every career has to have a beginning; a man may rise to be a Capone or a Himmler when he only begins by blackmailing a clerk. But he must start well; even his first efforts should show the master-hand. And it had been a master's stroke to get the subject to admit the necessary fact himself. Later on, maybe, Harry would learn to operate on a probability, but for a green hand it was far better to work on a certainty. Now it was a clear canter home. He went on, still in a careless tone:

"Well, the way I'd figure it is this. Suppose I didn' say anything, and you got out the copy of the Deptford order. Put a piece of carbon over it and alter the order of 23 bottles there to 25. You can do it easy if you're neat. There'll be no check on that for three months or six. Then when they do find the Deptford stock's not right, it'll look much more as if the faking had been done on the top sheet, the one they've got down there, and the two bottles been knocked off on the way there or down there. It's easier to fake a top sheet; so people think, anyway. And both you and I will remember there was 25; no fault of ours if we were fooled into passing out two more'n we should. That's the way I'd do it."

For the first time in his life, and the last time, Charlie looked at the shiny young man with respect and the beginning of liking. "Gor," he said, "you've got a brain, Harry. That's the way to do it. Will you? Will you?"

"I didn' say I would do it. I said that's the way I'd do it if I was in the muck you're in.

"Nothing to do with me and no reason I should stick my neck out. My duty's to go and tell the manager just what I know, and have him check the stock to-morrow. Or I could tell Grayling. It'd be a pleasure to him, I daresay." Harry looked at Charlie very closely; the reaction was all he could wish.

"Harry, you mustn't; Harry, you can't; it'd ruin me. It's only a little thing to do. And, Christ, I didn't mean the girl any harm; it was only to oblige her I got it. Harry, be a decent fellow."

Harry looked squarely at the foolish-handsome face in front of him—the manly pipe stuck back again in the white teeth, and the Nordic blue eyes imploring. Then he let him have it.

"Make it worth my while," he said, not casually at all now; and walked on. Charlie followed him.

"How much?" he said, after a few seconds.

"I can use a hundred pounds," said Harry.

The answer was what he expected. "A hundred pounds! You're crazy. I've never even seen that amount of money. I've got ten pounds in the bank, and that's all. I'll pass you five to keep quiet and back me up."

Now was the time to be firm. Charlie Evetts was rattled and would come across in due course. This clamour was nothing but a try to get out.

"You heard what I said. I can use a hundred pounds. Else I'm not interested, and things'll just take their course. I don't want to screw you down, of course. I realize you maybe can't arrange to pay it all right away. You got to get it together. You can pay me by instalments, see. Just you make a proposition and I'll be reasonable. But don't try and cut it down below a hundred, that's all."

"I tell you I haven't got so much money, or anything like it."

"I'll give you a week to think it over," answered Harry, "and that's my last word. A hundred, mind."

He turned abruptly and crossed the road. From over the other side he watched Charlie dejectedly walking on towards Euston. He found to his surprise that he enjoyed a greater pleasure than the simple prospect of gain which he had expected. Something about the humiliation of Charlie's stance pleased him. A bedraggled peacock. So often he had cut Harry out; he had not only talked about his conquests—Harry could do that—but he had actually made those conquests. He had always been the informed victor; he could look at almost any personable girl of their common acquaintance and say if she would or she wouldn't, or how far she'd go, with a marked precision of detail and almost unvarying accuracy; he would even at times pass on the information condescendingly to Harry himself ("not that it's likely to be of use to *you*, twerpie"). Now look at him. No patronizing now. The sight made Harry feel a fuller and rounder person. As he thought it over, he decided he too might be a success with the girls. Show them money, show them a good time, and you could do what you liked. They're the same as everyone else. When he got that hundred he could take his pick of Charlie-boy's skirts.

6

For six days Charlie Evetts thought. Connected thought, except on one subject, had been unusual for him since the days when he ceased worrying about exams at school. But that did not mean that he was a fool, as many of his acquaintances assumed. What are flatteringly called Don Juans are not fools. The siege of female virtue—even if the strongholds are less firmly defended than once—is an art, perhaps a science; certainly it cannot be successfully practised without skill and intelligence. Sexual attractiveness alone is not sufficient: the beautiful young man, at whose head girls throw themselves for years on end, exists mostly in young men's day-dreams. Certainly, if he is unintelligent, the male beauty's run is very short. He is very swiftly attached, after a brief and possibly bitter struggle, by the most determined and well-equipped young woman; and once he is married no man without plenty of intelligence can escape the firm bonds she lays on him. Conversely, a man may be very ugly, and yet have the most universal amatory success, as is shown by Jack Wilkes' portraits. To do this, he has, of course, to be as clever as Wilkes. Charlie was not as clever as Wilkes; he was also not as ugly. But he had spent five years in an earnest study and practice of the art on which the great democrat spent forty-two years. Like Wilkes, he had only to transfer to another sphere the cunning he had already learnt.

Some payment, he decided, would have to be made to Harry. But it need not be the whole hundred pounds. True, he ruled out any hope of appealing to Harry for a reduction. Harry's tone had been wholly convincing about the figure of £100. But the reduction might be secured indirectly. This way.

Blackmailers, Charlie argued, were in nearly as dangerous a position as their victims. Somehow he could use this fact. Once he had got some evidence, he and Harry would be at an equal disadvantage. It wouldn't be any good asking for a receipt for the money as paid over: Harry would be too fly for that. But what he could do was to tell Harry that he could get money slowly, and piece by piece, from his father. He would pay him first ten pounds and then five, and then perhaps five once again, or maybe twice. Also he would change his account from the Post Office to an ordinary bank. Then, at the proper moment, there would be a conversation which would run like this:

"*Charlie:* I've been thinking over our little financial arrangement, Harry. I've decided not to pay you anything more. Nothing at all.

"*Harry:* You're a fool, then. I'll go and tell Grayling to-day.

"*Charlie:* Oh, no, you won't; and you know you won't. Harry's going to be a good little boy, Harry is. Harry knows when he's sunk, and Harry's sunk now.

"*Harry:* Whatjer talking about?

"*Charlie:* The moment you go to Grayling—the moment you so much as drop a hint, I'm going to the police.

"*Harry:* Police! They can't do anything.

"*Charlie:* Oh, can't they? I shall tell them the exact story of what I did, and how you've been blackmailing me. I'll tell them I'm sick of being bled and decided to make a clean breast of it. And I'll show them the cancelled cheques I've got back from the bank. Pay Harry Kelvin ten pounds. Harry Kelvin five pounds. Harry Kelvin five pounds. And Harry's signature on the back. Try explaining that away. What'd I be paying you regularly sums like that for?

"You've been too smart. If you talk, I get fired—oh, I know that. But you get what they give blackmailers. That's five years penal servitude. Or seven if the judge is nasty to you."

The conversation varied, but that was its general theme.

The only point to be settled was: how many payments to Harry would be enough to commit him hopelessly? One wouldn't do: it could be explained away or even wholly denied. Two? Three? Charlie hesitated between three and four, and decided to leave that question for later decision.

Meanwhile he wrote a begging letter to his father, and on Thursday told Harry that he would try and scrape the money together.

"I can get ten pounds from father," he said, "and after that I'll maybe be able to get £5 regularly a fortnight. I can't promise. I'll do my best."

"You'd better had," said Harry. "I'm not joking, and I'm not standing for any funny business."

Charlie shrugged his shoulders.

That afternoon, Harry standing at the stockroom door, he faked the figures on the Deptford chit. When he had done it, he felt an immense relief. He even spared time to be sorry about Ann.

He drew ten pounds next day from the Post Office—the maximum that can be drawn at a day's notice—and with it opened an account at the Croxburn branch of the Midland Bank.

7

Three days later he handed Harry the cheque. *Pay Harry Kelvin*, it said, *ten pounds*.

"What's this?" said Harry.

"Ten Pounds. I told you that's all I could manage," answered Charlie.

Harry tore the cheque, very carefully, into small pieces.

"You think I'm a fool, don't you?" he said. "Ten pounds, I said. In one pound notes. And, by the way, not new ones. Don't try this on again, Charlie boy."

Harry sneered at him, and the abyss opened before his feet.

One hundred pounds.

Chapter III

1

Sir James Mackenzie, white-haired, dignified—in full morning dress and with gold-rimmed eyeglasses—had spent but a little time examining the remains of Councillor Grayling. Still, he seemed more than usually interested by his inspection.

"Well, that is quite remarkable," he told Inspector Holly and Dr. Campbell, as he came into the Inspector's office. He actually rubbed his hands. "Most unusual. But quite easy to diagnose," he added, disregarding Campbell's feelings, to Holly's pleasure. "Rather unexpected, I suppose. That must be why you missed it. But there's no doubt. No doubt whatever."

"Then what is it?" said Campbell, bellicosely.

"Why, the man was killed in a gas attack."

"What nonsense is this?" snorted Campbell. "Gas attack! There's been no gas attack yet in the whole of Britain. Rubbish, man. There was not a single plane over that night at all, anyway."

"You question my diagnosis?" asked Sir James with chilly politeness. "Then perhaps you will tell me some other way of explaining the œdema of the lungs, and the inflammation of the throat leading to the sloughing off of tissue sufficient to cause suffocation. I know no other cause adequate to account for the pseudo-membranes. In addition, there are clear markings on the face of the distinctive yperite burns. Perhaps you would like to examine the body again? I can see certain reasons for surprise, but none for doubt. Surprise, because the means of application of the gas do not seem very clear. But there is nothing that would cast doubt on the diagnosis, from the medical end. You yourself informed me that the man was nearly blind; anyway, there are unmistakable evidences of severe inflammation in the eyes.

"There are the symptoms that I mentioned in the throat and lungs, which your report had led me to expect. There are those highly typical burns and blisters. All of these are consonant with the results of yperite. Some of them are not consonant with anything else—in my opinion at least," went on Sir James, menacing Dr. Campbell with his eyeglass. "The pulmonary œdema, for example, or the condition of the trachea, which was covered with a thick purulent membrane. You may care to compare the symptoms with the classical case of Gunner B in the reports of the Chemical Warfare, Medical Research Committee, Number 17, Case 6, page eight," he continued relentlessly.

"The only variation is in the swiftness of death. That is unusual. But I should point out, to begin with, that we are not sure *when* the attack was made. Though that point is not, perhaps, very valid. Whatever be the date of the attack, the symptoms developed at far higher speed than in the classical cases. The *tempo* of dissolution, so to speak, was accelerated. This is explicable. It can be due to two things. Firstly, Mr. Grayling was an oldish man—older, I think, by some twenty years than the average soldier who was attacked by poison gas in the cases recorded, and certainly in much worse health. His resistance would be less. Secondly, we have to postulate a higher concentration of gas than was usual in the last war. How that was achieved is another matter, on which I express no opinion."

He paused, for dissent or applause, and received neither. He turned to Holly, and said, more urbanely: "In non-technical terms, Inspector, the man died of mustard gas poisoning. Gas, of course, is in some ways a misleading term. The stuff—dichlorethyl-sulphide it's called—is really a liquid, giving off lethal vapour. The symptoms are very well known. They have been carefully studied and are theoretically familiar to every A.R.P. worker. In addition, we older men, can remember cases from the last war. Of course, it's twenty years since there was an instance. But there is no doubt in my mind at all."

"Gas!" said the Inspector, groping. "Of course I wouldn't question your verdict, Sir James. But it does take one aback a bit. Gas. I'll consult the Civil Defence people, but I don't expect they will help us. There was no enemy plane signalled that night at all."

Dr. Campbell appeared to have nothing to say. He was bright red and looked very embarrassed. Sir James offered some aid:

"I can't tell you how it was administered. I can only tell you what it was, and that I've done. I can see it's very perplexing. Is it possible that one of our own planes had some sort of an accident? For example: let's suppose we are making practice flights, and that by some error a small poison gas bomb—a live one—was being carried on a training plane, and an inexpert or frightened pilot released it. It might have burst more or less in the dead man's face. That would be compatible with the injuries received."

"It's possible," said Holly. "Only just possible. I'll make enquiries at the Air Ministry. I don't think it's likely, though. It would be a most extraordinary piece of inefficiency.

Besides, we should have found traces of the bomb. The bomb case, for example."

"Tck," said Sir James. "Well, that's your problem, Inspector. A mustard gas bomb doesn't have to be dropped from a plane, I suppose. There may be other ways of killing a man with it. I confess I can't think of a plausible one at the minute, though."

2

Inspector Holly reported this verdict later to the Superintendent.

"I see," said the latter. "And that takes us nowhere. Have you got anything else?"

"Hardly anything, sir," replied Holly. "I've interviewed the young man who sat next to Grayling. Evetts, not Everitt, his name is; he works in the same firm and lives in Croxburn. There was no difficulty in finding him."

"Yes. And then what?"

"Well, he's a young man, I should say good-looking, but at present in rather poor physical condition. His eyes were bunged up, and he had a sore throat and a cough so continuous that between the two he could scarcely speak. He works fairly near to Grayling in the office: he's in the chemicals department and has something to do with sending out the stores—though he made quite a point of telling me that nothing was sent out except under double check. He has a dispenser's certificate—the thing that you need to have to handle poisons."

"That isn't necessarily 'hardly anything,' Holly; maybe you have got hold of something there. Compare the young man's condition with what Sir James has said. Find if it would fit in with mustard gas poisoning."

"I have done so, sir." There was the faintest shade of rebuke in the Inspector's tone. "The symptoms are in the

A.R.P. Manual, and they are more or less what Evetts has, as far as a layman can see. Supposing Grayling had been without his mask during a severe gas attack, as in the last war, and Evetts had been in the same attack and had got his mask on rather late—that would have produced, I would think, the phenomena that I observed. But of course that is absurd. I do remember noticing that the Vicar, too, seemed to have trouble with his eyes or throat and a skin-rash. But even if that, too, was due to mustard gas, it doesn't make the whole thing any less preposterous.

"I suppose it's possible that young Evetts could have been monkeying with mustard gas, for the purpose of giving it to Grayling, and through carelessness got a snort of it himself. I don't know how he would do it, though. I don't think the Vicar would have helped him."

"What sort of man is this Evetts? Why isn't he in the army?" asked the Superintendent.

"Reserved. As a chemist. I don't know but what the new call up will catch him, though. As for what he is—well, it's hard to say exactly. There's no trace whatever, that I can find yet, of any motive against Grayling. He insists he scarcely knew him, except as a rather grumpy old man who sometimes travelled in the same carriage with him. They aren't neighbours—he lives nearly two miles away. He claims he didn't even know there was a Mrs. Grayling, which was a line I was going to follow up. You see, all I can find against him is that he has a pretty hot reputation with the girls. A great dancer too. Before the Palais de Danse closed he used to be there two or three times a week. Frequently acted as M.C.; but I understand there had been complaints from some of the girls about his style of petting and he had not been asked to act as M.C. for some time. I'm trying to follow that up: I don't really know what I can expect from it, though. Unless he was going off the rails with Mrs. Grayling, it doesn't seem to fit in."

"Any signs of extravagance? Is he supposed to be in want of money? Girls aren't always cheap," said the Superintendent.

"No rumours yet. I saw him in his room at Halifax Grove: it was plainly furnished. There was a radiogram that looked a bit expensive, but he's getting four guineas a week and could probably afford it on the never-never. Nothing else. Most of his decorations consisted of a large number of female photographs on the mantelpiece, which he swept off when I came and threw in a drawer. He didn't say why; but it needn't necessarily be a grave matter. Girl friends sign their names quite often, and policemen are nosey. He couldn't take the pictures off the wall, though."

"Were they, er, hum?" enquired the Superintendent.

"Oh, no; not really," said the Inspector broadly. "Nothing that couldn't be sold in a shop; semi-nude girls: the sort of thing that in our day was done by Rudolf Kirchner. I don't know who does it now."

"A man called Varga, I think," the Superintendent informed him, and then looked embarrassed at his own knowledge.

"The thing which does worry me a little," said the Inspector finally, "is that I got the impression that the young man was scared stiff of me when I came. I mean that he had something to hide. It may not have been about Grayling—at least he answered everything about him quite readily and said he was very anxious to help. But he seemed very uncomfortable at any general remark—about the pictures, the girls' photos, and even when I asked him if he liked dancing. It's a little difficult to be sure, when a man's voice is almost inaudible, anyway. But I did get the impression that he had got something on his conscience. Something rather serious."

Chapter IV

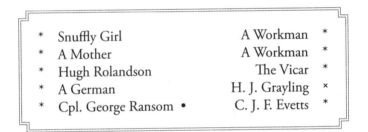

*	Snuffly Girl	A Workman	*
*	A Mother	A Workman	*
*	Hugh Rolandson	The Vicar	*
*	A German	H. J. Grayling	×
*	Cpl. George Ransom •	C. J. F. Evetts	*

1

Corporal George Ransom was a dark, short, tired-looking man of middle age. He had a rather large nose, and eyes small and close together. He was among the least noticeable of the members of "C" Platoon of the ——th Company, ——th Battalion, of a certain Zone of the Home Guard. He wore on his blouse the two ribbons of the 1914–18 war, called by the young and irreverent "Mutt and Jeff," and that was not distinctive either. Even the Mons ribbon was pretty common among his colleagues; of these two there seemed to be more men with than without. The ribbons did not, in Ransom's case, indicate any extensive service; indeed, he had sometimes wondered whether he ought to put them up at all. He had never actually seen a shot fired. He had been young in the last war; in addition he had been called up late, through no fault of his own. He had been sent to the front, nominally, in October, 1918. Counter-orders had stopped his unit when it was going up the line. Then it was switched towards Le Quesnoy, to take over from the New Zealanders. It arrived on the night of November 10th. In the morning, on parade, Ransom had heard the famous colloquy reported by Colonel Lushington in his Memoirs.

"Mr. Straker."

"Sir."

"You can fall out the men for breakfast. The war is over."

"Very good, sir."

One of the pigeons which the Colonel noticed as "circling around" messed on his shoulder; it was the nearest thing that he received to an enemy hit.

At the time, he had been unfeignedly delighted to get off so easily. Most of his fellows had felt the same; 1918 was a disillusioned year.

He did not, now, talk about the violent pacifist sentiments he had assented to then; it is not very certain that he even remembered them. Certainly, few volunteers could have been more warlike in the Home Guard than he. He seemed to find marked comfort, a relief from some private trouble, in attending to the minute physical details of the training. For some time he had been part of a Lewis machine-gun unit, and had even given instruction, to the extent that the initial shortage of ammunition allowed. He delighted in taking the gun into its sixty-two pieces, naming each, and reassembling it.

"The gun," he would say reverently, "is actuated by the force of the gases released by the explosion of the cartridge. These gases are trapped by a cup at the end of the gas piston, and you will perceive there are three rings behind this cup.

This ingenious device makes it sure that the maximum pressure will be exercised by the gases and none will escape uselessly." His satisfaction could not have been greater if he had invented the ingenious device himself.

He could scarcely bear to allow the recruits to handle the various parts: however well they might reassemble it, he would take the gun to pieces afterwards, oil it, and put it together himself. (The result was that the small stock of Lewis guns was generally rather over-oiled: one, indeed, tried on the range, produced a great cloud of stinking blue smoke and a hostile comment from the Regular instructor.)

"This is *my* weapon," Ransom used to tell his squad. "You can have your so and so and so—and—so" (he named two of the secret Reception arrangements for welcoming German tanks), "but when the balloon goes up this is the bastard I want to be behind. There's nothing at all like it. You can sweep a whole area: or you can pick off a single man. All you've got to do is to learn some simple commonsense rules of where to place yourself, and you can stop Jerry as long as you please. More or less, anyway. I don't deny it can't penetrate a tank. You've got to stop a tank with other means. But when they're stopped, what then? You've got to deal with the Nazis as they get out. And this is the boy to do it.

"You think of parachute troops," he would go on, patting the large barrel affectionately. "A rifle's all very well, but think how you could wipe 'em up with this. If you didn't kill them off, you could pin them down so's they were afraid to move."

It was no pleasure to him that his zeal had caused his transference. He knew the Lewis M.G. too well: the C.O. decided he must add another to his qualifications. He was taken away from the arcs and cones of fire he had earnestly mastered and made corporal-in-charge of anti-gas instruction. There was nothing in that sphere which he could *touch*: it was mainly theoretical work, and in addition he did not believe it would ever be wanted. Gas, he thought, would never be used. He did his best to absorb the necessary information, and to retail it; but his heart was elsewhere. Further, the folding and rolling of the gas cape was difficult, and he frequently mismanaged it. Even the respirator caused him trouble. On one occasion, he was in charge of men mustered for a gas test at the wardens' experimental station, and was nearly responsible for a major disaster.

The warden took him aside, and said:

"I'm giving your boys a specially strong concentration." (The nearest "boy" was a vastly fat man, with a bald, shiny head and a Boer war ribbon.) "You see, the way I figure it is this. We wardens may have to do our work when planes have dropped gas bombs. Okay. But you chaps may have to face a regular gas attack: you may have to *advance* into gas, actually. You'll have to fight in it, quite possibly. So you want a severer test. I've made a mixture of double strength." He then gave the constituents and strength of the gas he had prepared, and perceiving no comprehension in Ransom's face, said: "Take a look at that."

"That," was a small cardboard box, rather the shape and size of the puzzle boxes with glass lids, which used to be sold at Christmas, with two or three small silver pellets inside, which the purchaser had to shake and coax into a certain pattern. Instead of the glass, however, there was an arrangement of four small glass tubes let into the cardboard and numbered. One contained mustard gas—liquid, and rather impure, since it was dark brown. (Mustard gas is browner the more impure it is; absolutely pure mustard gas is, or would be, colourless.) The other tubes contained other gases, also in liquid form—one equally or more poisonous, the other two relatively harmless. They were named, but there is no need to name them here.

"I am using two parts of One and one of Three," continued the warden. At that point Ransom, fumbling with cold fingers, dropped the whole box face down. They were standing on the steps of the experimental station, some twenty feet away from the hut which was used as the treating-room. The box fell on the edge of a stone step.

"Hell," said the warden, and, covering his face with his handkerchief, hastily bent down and picked up the box, holding it by its edges. "You bloody damned fool," he said, and ran indoors with the box. "The blasted thing's leaking now."

He came out again after a minute, in no agreeable temper. "You'd better get your men in, before anything else happens," he said. "Form them in squads of five. Check the fitting of their respirators yourself. There ought to be someone else here," he continued dissatisfiedly. "Sending only a corporal in charge, I don't like it."

"Second Lieutenant Grayling should be here," said Ransom, unhappily. "I don't know what's happened to him."

"Well, we can't wait for him."

Ransom formed his men up in fives, and sent them through as instructed. But he was badly rattled, and did not check the adjustment of the respirators properly. Three men out of the first squad come running out of the testing-room, choking and with tears pouring from their eyes. At that moment, naturally, Second Lieutenant Grayling came up.

He glared at the Corporal and the distressed man; then he said: "As soon as you've finished with them, Corporal, I want to speak to you."

He was in a very disagreeable temper. He knew he had no business to be late, and in addition what had delayed him had been alarming to his dignity. His superior, the company commander, Captain Sawyer, about to retire, had sent for him; Grayling had hoped that it was to announce a step up. Sawyer was an old friend, who had been Mayor when the Home Guard was formed, in the old days when it was called the L.D.V. Both he and Grayling, as local politicians of eminence, had automatically taken a prominent part. But local politicians are not necessarily the best leaders of a popular army (or any army). Increasingly onerous duties, pressure of discontent from below, and latterly from above, had removed several of Sawyer's colleagues. Grayling himself had not had the promotion he expected. Now, what Sawyer had told Grayling was that his, Sawyer's, resignation was not really voluntary at all. Headquarters had (though he did not say this), at last understood that a sedentary, overweight tradesman, good-natured but not very intelligent or very honest, was not an efficient company commander, and had in effect told him to go. Sawyer's summons to Grayling was to communicate this, to complain of ingratitude, and to tell him that he believed all local worthies were to be treated in the same summary way. So far from Grayling receiving a second or third pip, he might consider himself lucky if he stayed at all. Certainly, the relatively easy time he had had was over: the new C.O., Williams, was no friend of his, and was determined to "pull things together sharply."

This was partly responsible for the tone in which Grayling spoke to Ransom. "What is the reason for these men's respirators not fitting?" he said. "Don't you know it is your duty to inspect the fitting yourself?"

"I did inspect them, sir," mumbled Ransom. "They appeared all right, the straps I mean."

"It is inexcusable stupidity," said Grayling. "The consequences might have been disastrous. You are unfit to have your stripes when you can be guilty of such gross neglect and incompetence."

The pomposity and unfairness nettled Ransom. "If you had been present in time, Mr. Grayling," he said, loudly, "and

I had had your assistance, I could have given each man a thorough examination. This is not my fault, whoever's it is."

Grayling shouted. "That's a piece of damned insolence, and I shall report you. You fail in your duty and then you're impudent. Let me tell you, the time's gone by when you can pull those tricks. This isn't a volunteer army any more, or won't be in a week or two, anyway. You're under military law, and you can't get away with it. You'll be sorry for your behaviour, and I'll make you sorry."

Ransom turned away, flushing. Grayling called him back. "Ransom!"

"Sir."

"Salute properly when you leave an officer."

There was a short hesitation, and then Ransom walked away, without saluting.

He did not hear any more of that particular incident, but he remained worried. The new C.O. was something of a martinet, and Grayling was malicious. The weeks were marching on fast and soon the date would come when he could not legally resign from the Home Guard. The coming of conscription for the Guard had been announced in the Press. The pleasant days, the comradeship, the understanding, the freedom and equality would be over, he thought. Incompetent, minor bullies, old fools and worse like Grayling would boss you around. Yet how could he go? The unit held him. He was a lonely man; he had little else to be loyal to. When he joined, in August, 1940, he had found happiness again: after years of shame he had known what it was to be needed and busy.

He had not changed wholly, nor had he changed suddenly. Men don't. But the day on which he had signed the declaration had begun an alteration. The act of enrolment had been a voluntary act, a decision of his own will, as it had been with a million other men. But such a decision had been unknown to him for some years: he had been consistently shiftless and hopeless, and what decisions he had made had either been to meet some immediate financial need or to avoid some trouble. This time he had deliberately, at some inconvenience, sought out the L.D.V. office, waited his turn to be enrolled, filled up a form for no other inducement but an appeal on the wireless to his hatred of Nazism, and waited anxiously to know that he had been passed—had been given permission, that is, to spend a great deal of time and trouble for no personal gain. A pukka sahib with a toothbrush moustache, an officer-wallah of the type he disliked, had read his form carefully. When he had approved it, the officer-wallah had stood up (following his usual routine), grasped Ransom by the hand, shaken it and grunted: "Welcome you into —th Company L.D.V."

George Ransom had been startled and moved by this action. He had not been able to analyse its effect on him, except in so far as it caused him to change his opinion of officers with small moustaches and abrupt manners. If he had done, he might have considered himself as a man who was climbing out of one condition of mind and life into another. His action in joining the Volunteers had been the announcement to himself that he had ceased to be a wreck, a drifting thing, but had become a vessel under control—a man and a citizen. The handshake of Mr. Alistair Edgwarebury-Caine (whom he never saw again) was an acknowledgement of that change by outside authority. In the next few months, Ransom not only attended to his Home Guard duties with exemplary keenness, but he also made a serious effort to put his personal financial affairs in tolerable condition.

They were in a sordid enough mess, which was far from being his own fault. He told the story, once, on a sudden burst of confidence, to a fellow Home Guard during a two-hour watch on a November night: even the manner in which he told it was significant. For the first time, there was no tinge of whining or self-pity in his account, even to himself; his story was one of things which had been hard to bear, but had been borne; the reaction expected was not commiseration but astonishment. He described his experiences not so badly as his limited education might have justified: indeed, he spoke with a clearness of accent and sensitiveness in description which did not fit with his generally shabby appearance. He had been educated in a mixed Church school in a village in a backward county, so indifferently run that if it had not been for the Rector's influence it could hardly have been allowed to continue, even thirty years ago. The instruction in arithmetic was wretchedly bad, and science or language teaching did not exist. Miss Grinngamble, the overworked teacher, was harried by her pupils and disliked them. In only one thing did she take an interest, and that was the English language. Not in spelling—Ransom was still unable to write down a sentence of any length correctly. But Miss Grinngamble made her charges read aloud, from plays and from novels, and, because she had no time to correct essays, made them stand up and speak. Each one of the children who showed any ability was required to deliver aloud the equivalent of an essay on a set subject, or a reproduction or variation of a story read or told the day before. Not only did Miss Grinngamble thus save the trouble of reading and correcting forty-three essays, she was also enabled to concentrate for once her attention on the children who showed intelligence. The rest, after blundering once or twice, were relegated to the position of audience; and they were an obedient and attentive audience. At all other times Miss Grinngamble was too tired or indifferent to repress disorder, idleness, or even impudence, but during English any attempt at mockery or disorder was put down grimly by the instant and pretty hard application of a ruler to knuckles or the tightly stretched seat of cotton knickers. A proportion, therefore, of the pupils of Brengton Village "National School" left with an exceptionally low equipment in arithmetic, general knowledge, and spelling, but an oddly full vocabulary and confidence in expressing themselves. George Ransom was one.

Yet he would probably not have talked as freely or well as he did if it had not been for the circumstances.

2

It was a November night, 1940, and the moon rose late; it was past the full. Ransom was on guard at company head-quarters; he was not then a corporal, but only a rank and file volunteer. The guard assembled at 7.45 p.m., which meant that Ransom had to leave his room at twenty-past seven in uniform; it was then deep darkness. As he waited for the bus, he noticed that an inspector came up and spoke to the conductor of the 48 which preceded his own bus. Half the lights were turned off, and the bus went on dimmed. "The first warning's come through," he thought, a little dully. "They'll be over again to-night."

The guard consisted of eight men; they took two-hour shifts of watch, in pairs, except for the cycle orderly and the N.C.O. in charge, who were, more or less, always available. The N.C.O. selected the pairs for the night. He partnered Ransom with a volunteer named Fremont, and allotted them the two spans 10 to 12 and 4 to 6—or, as he meticulously called them, twenty-two hours to twenty-four hours and oh-four hours to oh-six.

At five minutes past nine the wireless news (on full in the guardroom) suddenly dropped in volume; at twenty past nine the sirens went. Ransom felt his usual reaction of tired irritation at the noise. "It looks like the hump and it gives you the hump," he thought. The siren note started low, rose slowly to a higher volume of howling misery and then sank again; climbed again, wailed, and sank; and so on for the whole minute. The rise and fall made a picture in Ransom's mind, as of a series of humps of a string of Bactrian camels. He was no more, and no less, courageous than the next Londoner who enlisted in the Home Guard, A.R.P., or any of the Civil Defence services. He was not the indomitable, always gay Cockney of the kinder American correspondents. He did not enjoy the raids; he found them a strain. But equally they had no serious effect on his morale: the thought of surrender never even occurred to him. Communists and Fascists, in a tacit alliance in those days, were beginning a "campaign for a people's peace." The occasional evidences that Ransom came across—a sticker on a tube advertisement, an abandoned copy of the *Daily Worker*—affected him so little that he was not even angry. The effect of the strain on him was only to release certain inhibitions. It made him, in general, more incautious. If he was annoyed, he would use language that he once would have avoided. If he was in the mood for autobiography, he would disclose things that once he hid carefully.

Fremont, who was killed soon after in a raid, was a man likely to provoke confidence. Grey-haired, fifty-two, placid, the father of a grown-up family, he had already struck up a friendship with Ransom. Now the editor and part owner of the *Croxburn Weekly Argus and Guardian*, he had spent most of his life in daily journalism, from London to Shanghai. He was, in Ransom's verdict, "broadminded"; he had travelled pretty close to the edge of the legally permissible more than once; he was very kind and obliging; he had retired to his present occupation from Fleet Street with the same sort of deliberation as a prize-fighter once would leave the ring while still unconquered and take over a little "Physical Academy for Young Gentlemen" in a small provincial town.

The two men took up their position as ten struck in the church clock one block away. Headquarters were the premises of the Croxburn County School (pupils partly evacuated, partly transferred to another school), only partially occupied by the Home Guard. It was surrounded on two sides by an asphalt playground. The two sentries stood as usual between the main doorway and the entrance gate. Fremont had bayonet and rifle; Ransom rifle only. From time to time one or the other would walk round the side of the building and cast his eye over the length of the playground. Mostly they stood still and watched; or talked in low voices.

There was not much yet to be seen, or heard. The moon had not yet indicated her coming. The sky was clear black, with a wild scattering of stars. From time to time, a sudden low flash of faintly green light would appear on the eastern horizon: the sentries debated, as they did every night, whether these were very distant gun flashes from the estuary or less distant flashes from electric trains passing points. Once, a sudden illumination occurred: from all around (as it seemed) pillars of light arose, ending sometimes in blurs, when the beam caught a wisp of cloud, but mostly towering away without end into the high sky. The searchlight beams moved and crossed, stiffly as if they were performing a ceremonious dance; and then abruptly, on some unseen order, vanished instantaneously, leaving an even deeper darkness.

It was like village life, Ransom thought; not only had the red glow of London wholly vanished, along with the local bright lights of cinemas and street lamps, but the noise had gone too. The continuous hum and bumble, the great unindividual grumble which had been the unending voice of pre-war London was silenced. It was possible, now, to hear separate noises; and sometimes to hear nothing at all. A late bus, starting, running, and stopping, could be identified from many streets away. Every five minutes the toilets across the playground automatically flushed themselves, and that was a major noise. Far away, on some steam railway, an engine shrieked its complaint against an opposing signal; the noise came through as distant and clear as if nothing but hills and trees intervened. No sound of bombers or of guns was yet to be heard.

Fremont was telling a trivial anecdote of a device by which he had jumped himself into a chief reporter's job in 1919. Then he asked Ransom, carelessly and with no special interest:

"What did you do when you got out of the army, last time?"

Ransom hesitated for a moment, listened to the lavatories swishing water down and ending in a satisfied gurgle, and then began to speak.

3

It's a long story (began Ransom), and I'm not sure it will interest you. However, I'll tell you a bit of it.

You being born a Londoner won't easily understand the atmosphere I was brought up in, and I daresay my ambition will seem to you a pretty poor one. I wanted to keep a shop for the gentry. I was born in a village called Brengton; that's a very small place and it hasn't got any character of its own; hardly an existence of its own. It depends on the little town next it (he gave the name, but as the people are easily recognizable it cannot be given here), and that is very small too. I never realized how small till I left it. For us—I was one of eight children—it was the centre of the universe. Father was a farm labourer, by the way. Well, this town is one of the oldest boroughs in England and among the smallest, too, I think. It's very proud of its antiquity and it's very snobbish. It's got no industries of its own, and it's not even a market town now. It's populated by rich families and their dependents, who keep up carefully the eighteenth-century customs and stop all new building. Or any pulling down of insanitary old cottages. Of course, there are grades inside the rich; the town was really run when I was a boy by three families: old Mrs. Graves with her descendants, Lord and Lady Reedham, and Colonel Wolsey-Woollis. That really was his name; he was very vexed by the advertisements of Wolseley underwear and you had to remember that his name was pronounced Woolsey-wolls, or there was trouble. To me these people were demigods. I didn't think anything could be a more desirable life then to supply them with what they needed, bowing and scraping like Mr. Wilkins the chemist— he called himself Chymist—in the High Street. I couldn't get a job with him because I wasn't properly educated—I can't spell even now—but when I left school I was taken on as an errand boy by Mr. Black of Black and Scrawns, the grocers. And even seeing the way they were treated by their customers didn't teach me anything. I was a proper little lackey; I didn't want to do anything but wait on my betters. The war didn't teach me anything about that either. I didn't see much service, you know; nothing to teach me anything about life. I went into it a kid, and I came out a kid. The one thing I did learn in it was, of all things, how to mend shoes. I was a snob already; they made me a snob in the other sense. Snob's what we call a cobbler down there at home you know. I don't remember now, why it was I got put in the snob's shop in the army. There must have been some reason. Or maybe not. You know the army. Anyway, I had learnt a trade.

(The darkness of the sky had been lightening as he spoke; the moon, still invisible, must have been rising above the horizon. The disputed flashes had been occurring more frequently; now there came an unmistakable irregular hum. Barumba, barumba, barumba; it is not exactly that, but it is a sound that once heard is not again mistaken. The bombers were on their way. Soon there began the distant crump, crump of guns. Bright, large sparks occurred among the stars and vanished; they were bursting shells. The thud of guns seemed to bear no relation to them, which was a sign that the firing was still a long way away. But both men, following instructions, withdrew under the overhanging archway of the main door. It was a protection at least against shell splinters.

Fremont pressed him; and Ransom went on, some slight embarrassment now in his tone.)

The end of the war, too, I got a gratuity. Not very much, as *you* know. Also I was stronger and healthier than I'd ever been before, or was after. And I married a girl, too, and she had fifty pounds. I don't mean I married for money; Betty and I always got on all right, and we had ideas of what we were going to do. (Ransom skirted round the word "love" and refused it.) But it seemed all right to start a cobbler shop. We had the luck to find empty a small house in the High Street, very old I expect. It was as narrow as ever you saw; I can remember every bit of it now. It just had a front room with a window, which was my workshop, and a back room which was a small dark kitchen—really nothing more than a scullery. Upstairs there was just one room, with a sloping ceiling, right under the roof. The stairs went from it down into the kitchen. The doings, the earth closet, was out in the yard, and that was all there was. The house was squeezed right in between two big shops; it had a narrow, pointed roof; you'd think they really were pinching it in. It was dirty enough, and only one tap of water was laid on. But we made it lovely. I suppose all newly married kids do something of the same, but I tell you after all these years I don't like to think of the wallpaper we put on, and some of the other work we did, especially what she did. It brings it back to me too much. She stained every board in the floor herself; and right up to the end she polished them every day. They were getting a real dark brown by then.

We couldn't afford to get much stock in, but that didn't matter. My job was shoe-mending, and the money went on the tools and leather. We just had a few shoes in the window, more for show than anything else; if anyone wanted to buy shoes I'd try and persuade them to let me make them. I don't suppose I was very good, but I wasn't bad. I was better with men's than women's, naturally.

The gentry started off being very kind. I was a returned hero, you see. And I knew how to behave. Colonel Wolsey-Woollis used to come in and talk and talk, and it was the most stupid rubbish, most times: but I never said a word but "Yes, sir," and "Quite so, sir," or maybe "Well, really." There was a certain amount of political discussion went on in the British Legion Club, but I kept off it. There were always a few who said that the gentry were the curse of the town, but it all amounted to very little and I knew which side my bread was buttered. My chief cross was Mrs. Graves; she interfered so. She drove about the town still—she was well past seventy—in a horse and carriage, and she liked everything to be as it had been when she was young. It was quite a sensation when she ordered and actually drove about in a thing called an electric brougham. I've never seen one since. It was very quiet and very high up. But it didn't work or something, and she went back to the horses. Well, she looked to everything herself; including the shoe-mending for the Hall, and there was a great deal of it. She wouldn't actually bring the shoes herself, but she would drive down with any complaints or remarks. I was expected to know instantly what she referred to. If she said: "The stillroom maid's shoes were not satisfactory," I must know at once which pair she meant out of a sackful, and be able to suggest rubber heels, or a blakey, or whatever she would like.

Of course, I always came out of the shop and stood by the carriage door to receive her orders. Once, I remember, she sent me back to call Betty out; and when Betty came she demanded to know in a loud voice in the open street why we hadn't had any children.

Still, as I say, I knew my place, and after a year and a bit we really were doing not too badly at all. The town was so small that I had very little competition. Old Mr. Mansdell was getting very old, and he couldn't cope with any more work. The only other place was Fieldman's shop—Fieldman the multiple people. They had bought up an old firm and opened a branch which offered to do repairs. But actually it mostly sold new shoes and didn't trouble me. Not then. Afterwards it did; and then when they had busted me, their head office declared the turnover wasn't sufficient and closed the whole shop down. What a laugh.

It was the depression, they said; but it wasn't the depression did me in; not directly, anyway. People want their boots cobbled anyhow; I should think my trade was the least affected by a depression that you could mention. It was prosperity did me down. I got an idea of expansion and I'd have been better advised to leave it alone.

I remember one morning the man coming into my shop. He had a small bright saloon car—and that wasn't usual about 1924; most cars were still tourers then, you know. He gave me his card; it said *Jarndis and Touran, Ltd.,* with an address in the City of London. In the corner, "Mr. A. Touran, Travelling Manager and Director." He was pretty tall, had a good manner, and I think a slight foreign accent, but the thing that struck me most was that he was dressed up to the nines. Blue suit with a crease you could shave with; everything just right so that I automatically classed him with the Colonel and the rest of the real gentry.

I at least ought to have known better, especially when it turned out that he wanted to sell me something. But I didn't. He said he was managing director of a new company, and he had decided to supervise personally the sales in the provinces, as it was far too important a branch of work to be left to subordinates. Once he had laid down the main lines and got the business going, he would, of course, hand over the running to branch managers. I believed him; I even admired his common sense. Well, the result was that after a second visit and a correspondence I bought an electric shoemakers' machine. There are such things, and they're perfectly good. A great deal of the sewing, nailing, and cutting out that shoemakers do has no business to be done by hand at all, and a machine's actually better. I'd just taken the plunge of installing electric light and a telephone—one of those old-fashioned things like a black pillar, with the earpiece separate; in the shop I kept it—and I decided to be right up to date and have a machine. I was going to take on an apprentice to work it, I remember.

The thing was to cost £175. The terms seemed to be all right. £75 down and the rest by easy payments; delivery in four weeks as there was such a rush on the machines that the factory could not keep pace with the demand, and orders were taken in rotation. Free servicing for a year after delivery. Of course, I didn't have £75 to my hand, especially after putting the money down for the electricity and the telephone. I had only £15. But I had been carrying on a steady business and the bank manager up the street knew all about it, naturally, and in a small town like that of course, the fact that the best people supported my shop counted for quite a bit. The bank allowed me an overdraft of £60.

Well, I paid the £75, the four weeks passed and nothing happened. I wrote and complained; and I got a letter from Mr. Touran, very apologetically written, saying that they had some breakdowns at the factory, and had got badly behind with deliveries, but that my machine should be sent to me on the Wednesday next. Nothing came. So I wrote again; and Mr. Touran answered that it had been despatched to me by road on the Thursday, and still nothing came. I was a bit suspicious, but even then I thought that everything was O.K. I was still one of the natural victims of the wide boys; I've learnt better since. But at least I went up to town to see Mr. Touran; even so, I hadn't sense enough to draw conclusions from what I saw. I was still a country boy; and it seemed to me perfectly all right that the head of a big business should have an office with only two rooms, and one typist and receptionist. And, by God, what a typist and receptionist. Make-up's common now, and I don't suppose she'd stand out like she did. She had painted nails and painted cheeks and absolutely brilliant pale gold hair, almost white; and she had a short bright blue skirt on, which showed half-way up her thighs, and as far as I could see no undergarments at all. She crossed and uncrossed her legs at me till I didn't know where to look. Her voice was horrible; I will say that for the B.B.C. and the talking films, you won't find any of the girls running around now who talk as hideously as any working-class girl did then. Still, that's not the point. I got in to see Mr. Touran and he was shocked and horrified. "Mr. Jarndis," he said, "is in sole charge of the manufacturing end. I deal with sales and service only here. But naturally I have been telephoning continuously about your machine; and I had it confirmed only to-day that it left on Thursday last, and everything was in order. I will telephone again at once. Pola," he called out, "get me the Crouch End works. Or no, put the line through to me." He began to dial. It was the first automatic telephone I'd ever seen, and he was on the first automatic exchange.

"The line's so frequently engaged now, we do so much business," he said. "I hope we get through quickly. There's just a chance that there was an error in the delivery chit. If the address was wrong, and it was delivered to some dishonest person, they might have sold the machine. I hope not. Or there may have been a theft on the road. But that ought to have been reported. Tck, tck. Number engaged. We must leave it a minute."

He dialled again in a minute. His face showed the same surprise and grief as he announced "number engaged" again; mine must have shown suspicion, because he raised his eyebrows: "Listen for yourself, Mr. Ransom," he said, and handed me the instrument. There was no doubt; it was the engaged signal all right.

He dialled several times, always with the same result, and generally I heard the signal myself. I was convinced then that he was really trying to telephone his factory. I didn't see how else he could have arranged it; it did flash through my mind that perhaps he might have arranged for someone at the other end to leave the receiver off; but as he hadn't known when I should come that didn't seem at all likely. At last I agreed to come back at half-past five when, he said, he would have the whole matter clear for me, or anyway we would be sure then to get on to the factory as the traffic was much less at the end of the day.

Of course, when I came back, he was gone, and the place was locked up. I never saw him or his tart again. The police caught him in the end, but it was too late for me. I never got my money back; and, as for the machine, there never was a machine. No factory, no firm, no anything at all. He had been going about the country with a catalogue and illustrations that he had got hold of from some American firm, I believe, and some letters which he'd written himself; and he'd sold quite a number of these non-existent machines. Mostly to small people like me. The police inspector told me how he worked the telephone; it's very simple. I've done it myself since. You just dial your own number. Nobody would ever suspect it; and there's no other way of being sure the number is engaged. It's a good trick.

I didn't find out what had happened at once; there was a week or two of doubt, and of course it would be just then that Betty told me we'd been careless and there was going to be a baby. And it was just about then too, that Mrs. Graves chose, for some reason or other, to get out of her carriage one day and walk into my shop. She was annoyed about something, I don't know what, I believe her eldest grandson had been doing something or somebody, and she wanted to be troublesome. Anyway, she poked around without finding anything and then noticed the telephone.

"Have you had the telephone installed, Ransom?" she said, in her usual manner. "That is very extravagant of you." I answered, rashly I suppose, that I found it useful for my customers. "Not for me, I think," the old bitch said. "It seems to me a piece of ostentation that hardly fits your circumstances." I did manage to refrain from telling her to mind her own business, but I suppose I asked her a little abruptly if there was anything else I could do for her. The butler came down two days later and collected the shoes, mended or unmended. He said that Madam had told him to ask if I had arranged to have the telephone taken away. Just literally that; I told you you'd be surprised. I swear I never knew of anything else at all that the old woman had against me. I know she told some of the others that I had been impertinent to her; and I lost quite a bunch of the good reliable trade on which I relied. It all went to Fieldman's new shop up the road. I asked the butler in the end if he'd tell Madam that I was arranging to give up the telephone; I did really; but he said Madam had made other arrangements and had said she did not wish to hear any more about the matter.

It all seemed to come together, you know. Betty not feeling herself, the money not coming in, and the bank after me. Because of course it was after me, quite naturally. The bank manager knew about the nobs blacklisting my shop, and about the machine not coming, and of course he got nervous about his money and demanded it back.

(The corporal of the guard came out with the two reliefs. He said: "You fellows can buzz off now, and settle down for four hours. You'll be on again from oh-four to oh-six. Get all the rest you can. Everything been quiet?" "Pretty quiet, corporal," answered Fremont. "There was a bit of noise earlier on, but I think they must have gone elsewhere. All Clear's not gone, though." "Righty-oh," said the corporal. "Go on in.")

4

Four hours later the two men took up their posts again. The scene was wholly different. The dead blackness had gone; there was a pattern of sharp white, grey, and black; as harsh and contrasted as the original of a Press photograph or a film "still." The moon, a not quite perfect round, was high up in the sky, having extinguished nearly all the stars; it had a large circle of light round it, seeming to be at several hands' lengths' distance. The silence was even greater than before; the railroad was still, and no buses were running. Only the school lavatories kept up their periodical flushing noises.

After they had duly walked the round of the building, Fremont asked Ransom how he got out of his troubles. If he didn't mind telling the story.

"No, I don't mind now," said Ransom, "though it's not all very creditable to me. I had to have money, as I told you; and I saw a way of getting it. Never mind just how; I don't mean getting it legally. Betty was scared and didn't like it.

But I always said there was no need ever to be found out if you knew how to dispose of the stuff. You know how the police make 90 per cent of the arrests they do in theft cases? Not by fingerprints or any nonsense like that. Because the people who pinch need the money or whatever it is very badly and as soon as they get it start using it. That gives them away. Have sense enough to wait, and they'll never catch you. Now, I wanted £60 for the bank and another twenty or thirty to keep going with. I had an idea where I could lay my hands on eighty or ninety quid in pound notes. But if like any fool I handed the sixty pounds back to the bank the day I got it, or soon after, I'd be rumbled right away. Even if I just kept it about the house I'd be waiting for trouble. So I had worked it out very neatly. I was going to divide it into parcels of £7 and £8. One lot I'd give to the bank, saying things were looking up and I'd got hopes of paying off the debt in bits in the next few months—as I would, in very irregular and uneven bits. One I'd keep in the till; eight pounds isn't suspicious in a till. I'd open a post office account for me, and another for Betty, in the next town, with one of each; and I'd use another to open one for the baby that was on the way. You can do that, you know. In another post office I'd buy a couple of Savings Bonds. And the rest of the money I'd use for paying out-of-town accounts, sending the notes by registered post. Who'd ever put all these separate bits together? And no one of them would be suspicious.

"I might as well say right away that I never took that money. I meant to. I quarrelled with Betty over it, and I began to drink to screw my courage up to it."

There had been some distant gunfire in the preceding minutes, and at this moment there was a fierce explosion of noise. A big flash momentarily showed up, black against itself, two jutting barrels; the violence of the noise caused both men to plunge backwards. "Blast it, they're getting near," said Fremont. "I hate that bloody gun going off. I never get used to it."

They edged nearer the shelter of the porch; and the gun repeated its explosion. Twice more it fired; and then there came a rattle on the asphalt like hailstones falling. "Shell splinters," said Ransom, as they both crouched right back against the door in the porch, well protected now against anything but a direct hit. The noise of the bombers was loud now. "Splinters like that, falling from five thousand feet; they'd cut your arm off easily," reflected Fremont. "What did you do then? I mean about the money."

"Oh, that," said Ransom, in the dark and taking all expression out of his voice. "I got very drunk one night—helplessly, on straight gin, which I wasn't used to. I was quite paralysed, though I got to bed, leaving Betty in the kitchen. You went through the kitchen, from the workroom, to get to the stairs to the bedroom; I don't know if I told you. I woke up early in the morning because of the smell of gas. I found Betty still in the kitchen. She had stuffed up the doorcracks and the window and chimney, and turned the gas on and put her head in the oven. She was dead, of course. You ever seen anybody dead of gas poisoning? You don't want to. They don't look nice. Especially the colour they go. Like painted dolls."

He stopped abruptly. Fremont said something, friendlily; but he did not hear it. He was seeing pictures that he had forgotten for a long time. He had sat for a very long time at the foot of the stairs. There wasn't any sort of doubt at all that Betty was dead. But he couldn't go through the kitchen to the front room to the telephone. The telephone was on the other side of "that." He could hardly look at it. He certainly couldn't pass it. It wasn't his wife; not that thing. Undertaker and police; what did they matter? After his first run forward when he had turned off the gas, opened the window, and touched Betty and found her cold—and seen what she looked like—after that he had not been able to move. Perhaps the fumes had helped to stupefy him; certainly it had been bright light before he moved. Even then he didn't telephone; he walked uncertainly out into the road to the policeman at the corner and said: "Stan. Come," and P.C. Stanley Wall had looked at his face and followed him. And later that day he had taken all the money in the till and gone across to the undertaker's and said, in carefully chosen words: "Will you take this and see to everything properly for me, Mr. Bains? I'm not quite up to it at the moment." Then he had left the key of the house in the door, taken a very few things in a bag and walked away. He'd never come back, or left an address, or written: when the police compelled him to attend the inquest he had walked straight from the station to the coroner's court; and straight back to the station when it was over.

Could he tell Fremont of what he had done since? Short periods of employment, always ending in the sack for drunkenness or bad work. Trouble; in the special sense of the word. In his case due to picking pockets, at which he had got pretty expert. Fortunately, he had done his time under a false name. No, he couldn't tell. He couldn't even explain why he had gone that way, or how it was satisfactory to him, as a sort of revenge on the state of things that had done what it had to him and Betty. And anyhow, what possessed him to start talking at all like this? Silly; and pretty dangerous. What did he know of Fremont, in the last analysis? Very little.

A long-drawn and horrible scream broke out; both men crouched flat on the ground at once. Another and another followed, each ending in the crash of the exploding bomb. Each explosion was nearer by a long step, as if a giant was striding towards them.

"Christ all bloody mighty, that's near," said Fremont.

The earth rose, and the air smote them; the thick stone of the porch and doorway rocked round them. The noise of the explosion this time was so loud they did not consciously hear it; rather, they felt it. The scream they did not hear at all.

Astonished to be alive, the thing they first noticed was a smell. It was of dirt and burning; age-long muck had been shaken out of every crevice of the building and fallen round them and on them. Something had been burnt; the smell was rather like exploded powder; and there was a background of another, a chemical, gassy smell. The playground was invisible in a thick fog of dust hanging in the air; but as they looked it began to settle.

"I thought you two poor sods were done for," said the corporal's voice not quite levelly, as the door opened behind them. "Why didn't you take shelter before? I thought Jerry'd got you."

"He's got the church all right," said Ransom, pointing.

The line of the church was now clear against the grey sky, and it was not the same as it had been. A portion had been clawed out of the roof just where it joined the base of the spire. The three men stared at it.

As if it had been civilly waiting to secure their attention, the spire now slowly bowed to one side and toppled over, the tip disintegrating first as it fell.

"The wardens'll want some help with *that*," said the corporal. "I'll turn out the guard."

5

Ransom worked in a cobbler's shop in one of the small streets to the north of the Bank of England. He had gone there in mid-1940, not intending to stay. However, the proprietor, who had lost his only other assistant through the call-up, persuaded him to stay by raising his wages; then, after joining the Home Guard in August, Ransom had begun once again to take an interest in his work for its own sake. He was a good craftsman when he chose; his change made an immediate difference to the business. He began to think—once again after all these years—of setting up on his own.

Johnny Peters owned the shop; he was thirty-two and healthy. Two nights after Ransom's conversation, Johnny Peters took him aside, and offered him a partnership.

"It's come," he said. "I'm called up. Well, I expected that and I don't complain. But the missus can't work the shop; she's expecting anyway. And I know you are looking out for something else. Well, I'll make you a fair offer, George. You're not likely to be called up, at your age; and you're a good workman and a good fellow. I wasn't sure, when you came, that you wanted to stick at this; but you seem to have changed, like. Anyway, I make my own judgment of people, and I'd as soon trust you. I want to make you an equal partner in this business. I put in the stock, the goodwill, the shop, the tools—all the business in fact. You put in your work. We share equal till I come back. Doris can keep the accounts and she can do all that need be done behind the counter till her time comes. It means trusting each other; that's all."

Ransom looked at him, cocking his head on one side. "I'll not do you down, Johnny," he said. He accented the *you*, slightly. "If Doris agrees, it's okeydoke with me."

Doris Peters had already agreed; and it worked pretty well. The business went on and up; and he liked Doris. He was long past the age of silliness with women (as he thought of it) even if Doris hadn't been the way she was. But she was pleasant if undistinguished to look at; not really good-looking, but kind and placid as pregnant women often are. Her company helped to civilize him; it kept him from being morose, solitary and slovenly.

On one Monday morning, that winter of 1940–41, he set off for work in the ordinary way. There had been a raid the night before—well, you hardly troubled to mention that now. You looked at the transport notices outside the Tube stations to see what was working and what wasn't; and judged from that whether the raid had been serious or not; that was all.

There had been no sign of its being grave, but when he got out at Moorgate station the atmosphere was strange. It was darker than it should be; heavy clouds were swirling low. Almost immediately his eyes and nose told him these were not clouds; they were smoke. But still he was disinterested; like any other Englishman or American he ordered his life on the assumption that "it wouldn't happen" to him. He walked up Moorgate with the speculative attention of a passer-by; a hell of a lot, he thought, must have been burnt. It was quite a business, to get through the damaged area to his shop.

On his right, the street was as usual; from the left he was warned off by firemen. He looked up to find out why. The tall office buildings seemed as usual. It was odd that two firemen should be standing, each at the top of one of those giant expanding ladders which stand all alone, not leaning against a building. They were playing their hoses, apparently on a roof. Ransom stared at them curiously, and from them to the black windows of the offices which he passed every day and knew well. Suddenly one window was not black any more; for a few seconds, as though it was playing a game, a little flicker of flame ran up the side of one window, and then vanished inside. Ransom realized that the whole of the interior of the block must be smouldering; what he saw, with its stone facade, its decorous notices and famous names, was a hollow outside.

He skirted round the fire engines—there was no other wheeled traffic but the street was full of pedestrians—and walked on less at ease.

When he had gone a little way further north he stepped into a strange world. Suddenly he could see only a few yards before him. It reminded him of the title of a novel he had seen in the shops recently. *Darkness at Noon.* "Darkness at Noon"; he repeated it to himself. Smoke eddied round him, blown by the wind, capriciously clearing and thickening. He picked his way over unnumbered coils of huge hoses, which lay like snakes across the road. Sometimes one would twitch as if it were alive; there is enormous power in one of those great hoses full of water. Water lay in great lakes in the road, filling the gutters. Firemen came out of the fog towards him and passed by, looking through him with the stony stare of men in the last stages of tiredness who must still go on working. He got anxiously out of their way, tripping over a hose and soaking one leg to the knee. As he walked on, anxiety now rising in his heart, he noticed the pack became closer. Women and girls, clearly office workers, formed the majority, but there was a sprinkling of city men. They seemed to him to be walking round and round, as if they had lost their direction. He was reminded of some caterpillars that he had once been shown at the Zoo; he had been told that they had no intelligence, only instinct, and that if once you started them walking round in a circle they would go on, patiently, and aimlessly, till they died.

He pushed his way through them to the corner nearest his street. Here people were standing in groups and there was a loud hum of talk; there was the sound of engines and at a distance men calling orders and instructions. He found a man he knew and asked him for news. What was burning? How far did the fires extend? The man didn't know; but others round were full of vague, and as it proved, wild information. Of one thing they were certain; the loss of life was very small. "Pretty well everyone was in shelters."

Could he go through? "You're not supposed to, but no one'll stop you. They're too busy."

He hesitated, and then began to pick his way cautiously down his own side-street. Now it was quiet and really dark; and on the north side, where his shop was, the buildings were obviously burning, and nobody seemed to be attending to them. The windows were all out, and from their blackness, hot silent breaths of air came out to him. He moved out into the middle of the street, afraid that the houses might collapse on to him. He had heard of such things happening.

The big glass windows of the "Green Man," the pub in which he took his lunches, were partly shattered, and the jagged edges remaining were blackened and opaque. Inside there was something burning—not flaming, a black pile of debris from which sprang occasional flames, and out of which stuck out what might be the glowing ends of smouldering beams. A few doors on was his own shop. The front seemed undamaged.

He walked cautiously towards it, facing the increasing heat. He put his key in the lock, as so often before, and very gently pushed the door inwards. Inside, as far as he could see, there was only darkness. His eyes were running with tears from the smoke, and he could not make anything out clearly. He took a step into the building.

His weight must have shaken something; there was a sound of a thud and a cascade. Right in front of his face, as if thrust there insolently, appeared a glowing mass, scorching him; it could have been part of the staircase. He did not wait to make sure; he backed out of the door instantly and stood in the street, well away.

There was nothing to be done but to go away.

Later in the day, he found that Doris was safe, and that every building in that part of the street was totally destroyed. Nothing was left of his stock, his tools, or anything.

Compensation would be paid, some time. Meanwhile, he could get a few odd pounds to go on with.

6

Months later, like so many others, he was waiting still while the government clerks tried to handle the enormous and complicated claims. He had taken a fresh job, at journeyman's wages, and in an ill-considered fit of generosity had handed to Doris Peters most of the temporary financial aid he had been given. He had thought that it would only be a week or two before he got an award to enable him to set up the joint business again. But there seemed to be no sign of the money coming.

He had reckoned up the amount that would be needed. Once again, it came out to between eighty and ninety pounds, as a minimum. Just what had wrecked his life before.

He was very badly in need of it, about the time Grayling died, and there seemed no obvious way in which he could get it.

Chapter V

Inspector Holly contemplated some, not all, of the history of George Ransom, and gnawed his fountain pen in perplexity. He was endeavouring to give up his habit of making pencil notes, and had substituted a pen for his pencil. Forgetfully he champed on its end. Suddenly the pen split, filled his mouth with ink, and pricked his lip with a spar of vulcanite.

He cursed aloud with surprise, and thereby covered his desk with a fine spray of ink, an involuntary specimen of spatterwork. He spent some five minutes in the washroom cleaning out his mouth and swearing; and then had to go into conference with the Superintendent with his mind not made up.

"I've got a certain way," he said, "and I've made up a theory, now, of how the crime may have been committed. But before I go on to that, I'd better summarize the results of my inquiries about another man who travelled home with Councillor Grayling. He was a Home Guard, a corporal named George Ransom. Captain Williams said he 'proved' at once when the name of the man who travelled up with Grayling was asked for. I suppose that means he stepped out of the ranks or something. He made no difficulty, anyway, about coming to see me.

"He's corporal in charge of gas protection; and that's something striking right away. But he gave me that information himself."

"You'd have found it out, anyhow; and he must have known you would," said the Superintendent.

"Yes, sir; that is so. However, for what it's worth, he seemed to regard the matter of no importance. He also said Grayling was an unpopular officer. Both Major Ramsay and Captain Williams of the Home Guard confirm that, and Williams added that Grayling had made a formal complaint against Ransom for insubordination and insolence, but that he, Williams, had decided to take no action about it, because of Grayling's disagreeable character. I asked him if the two men were generally on bad terms, and he hedged. But I think they were, and I'll look into it further.

"I found that Ransom could do with money, too. He was part-owner of a shoemaking or repairing business in the City called "Peters's A.1. Shoe Service," which the City police tell me was completely destroyed in the blitz. They say it belonged half to him and half to the previous owner, Peters, who's in the army now. Mrs. Peters, who used to be behind the counter—it was a very small place, I gather—complained to the police that they had still got no proper compensation, and Ransom was having to work like a common journeyman, when by rights a new shop should have been set going long ago for both of them. She gives Ransom a very good character, by the way."

"Well, there's something there," said the Superintendent. "Method: Ransom is an anti-gas expert. He would know how to use mustard gas, anyway. Could he have had access to it?"

"I don't know, sir. I'll enquire from Captain Williams."

"Do so. To go on—Motive: he disliked Grayling. He needed money. Have you got anything more? What sort of man is Ransom? How did he behave when you saw him?"

"He's rather a shifty fellow," said the Inspector. "A bit shabby looking, and, without being furtive exactly, the sort of man who likes to avoid attention. I would have said he had a police record, but nothing has been traced yet. I've put an enquiry through to Scotland Yard; there's nothing against him since he's been here. He was out of work pretty often before the war, but so were many other people.

"He's very fly. I thought it would be a good idea to get his fingerprints on the quiet, but there was nothing doing. I offered him my cigarette case: thank you, he didn't smoke. I pushed him a piece of shiny paper and asked him to write a few words down, offering him my pen. He preferred his own pen, thank you. And as he wrote, he kept the paper still not with his fingers but by resting his closed fist on it; and when he had done he didn't pick up the paper with his fingers but flipped it across to me with his nail. Obviously, he knew what I was up to, but he didn't give a sign. In the end I asked him outright if he objected to having his prints taken and he said yes, unless I proposed making a charge against him, which put me up against it for the moment."

"I see." The Superintendent thought for a minute but produced no comment; then he said: "You told me you had a theory about the administration of the gas. Let's hear it: I'll be glad of anything that makes sense."

"I'm not certain of it, by any means, sir," said the Inspector, "and at first sight it seems fantastic. But the more I consider it the less fantastic it seems.

"It turns on the fact that mustard gas isn't a gas at all, but a liquid. It's used in a fine spray. In reasonably warm weather it will vaporize fairly quickly. But this weather has been bitterly cold for a long time, so it would stay liquid.

"It can be handled safely by anybody who knows the ropes. Any respirator, civilian or service, is a complete protection against the fumes, and rubber gloves will guard against an accidental splash. Most people have got both of these things. It's also not very difficult to make, and there are fair stocks kept anyway for demonstration purposes. I think it's quite possible that either Ransom or Evetts could obtain enough to kill Grayling, whom anyone could see was not a specially beefy specimen.

"Now I suppose this. The murderer acquires some liquid poison gas. This has got to be applied to his victim's mouth and nose. If it is in a sufficiently strong concentration death will follow in a few hours; but symptoms will not appear for an hour or so. In fact, the books say that momentarily there will be signs of euphoria—that is, he'll feel better. How can it be applied to his mouth and nose? Clearly by his handkerchief. He had a cold, as anyone could see: he had had one some time, as a matter of fact."

"Did the murderer come up to him and say: 'Councillor, lend me your handkerchief; I want to put some cold mixture on it?' I don't believe that," said the Superintendent.

"No," said Holly. "I conjecture that he switched handkerchiefs. I think he carried a prepared handkerchief and in the crowd slipped it in Grayling's pocket. The Vicar said the platform was packed, and there was a rush into the carriage too. You and I know pickpockets have done far, far more difficult things than that."

"It's just possible," said the Superintendent, troubled. "I suppose Grayling sits in the carriage and sooner or later blows his nose, or coughs into his handkerchief, and then takes a straight snort of poison gas each time. But he'd notice it, wouldn't he? Doesn't it smell, or make you sneeze?"

"No it scarcely smells at all. And it's not a sneezing gas. It is a vesicant, which means it brings up blisters. But it doesn't do that at once."

"But it's brown. He'd see the colour on his handkerchief, even in that light."

"Not necessarily. It's only brown when impure. The purer, the more colourless. A good brew, or distillation, or whatever it is, wouldn't be noticeable except in daylight or under a strong lamp."

"But when he used it, it would begin to vaporize in the warm carriage, and would gas everybody else."

"If you remember, sir," said the Inspector, "the Vicar had a bad throat and a sore face; and Charlie Evetts had the symptoms of minor gas poisoning. They sat next to him. As he would only hold the strong concentration to his face for a few seconds, the vapour wouldn't travel far."

"It's very ingenious," said the Superintendent, wavering. "But a little far-fetched. And, come to think of it, there's a bad snag. How did the murderer manage to go about with a hanky full of poison gas in his pocket, waiting for a chance? A pocket is warm. It would vaporize and he'd merely gas himself."

"I suggest he might carry it in a tin. A flat case, like you used to get fifty cigarettes in. Many people have these about the house still. He could pour a certain amount of mustard gas in liquid form on a handkerchief, using rubber gloves and keeping his mask on. Then he folds the handkerchief and puts it in the tin, closes the tin tightly and seals it by running adhesive tape round the edges to make it airtight. He opens all the windows to clear out any gas there may be.

"Then he puts the tin in his overcoat pocket and goes to the station. He has gloves on still, of course. He waits until he spots Grayling, then he peels off the tape with one hand, keeping his hand inside his pocket, and loosens the lid of the tin. The minute he can press against Grayling—and there seem to have been plenty of opportunities, even for those who weren't sitting near him—he plants the handkerchief on him."

Chapter VI

"We mustn't," said the Superintendent, "forget there are other people who would bear looking into. The trouble, in fact, seems to be that there may be too many. You've dug up a great deal of stuff. The Vicar: he was Grayling's enemy and sat next him. He may have been fooling around with the gas, by his looks. Evetts—he's a chemist, he seems equally likely to have been suffering from gas poisoning, and though you haven't anything definite against him, you are suspicious of his manner. The German—well, we should get more on him soon, but Grayling may have had his knife into him. Corporal Ransom—a gas expert and short of money too. And no friend to the late lamented.

"You've got too many suspects. And I'm afraid you've got to add some more. Have you remembered the two workmen? One of them, the Vicar said, leant over his and Grayling's shoulder on the pretext of reading a notice. Quite an opportunity for planting that handkerchief, if it existed."

"Yes, sir; I had thought of that. But I've got nowhere," said Holly. "The trains about that time are always full of returning workmen. Shifts are different from what they were and certain places" (he gave the names of four biggish establishments in the East and N.E. districts; and a smaller one south of the river) "let a large number out just at the time when they will pack the trains already crowded with office workers. The Ministry of War Transport is complaining, and I believe there is to be a change next month. But these men could have come from any of those places or indeed from anywhere in London. We've made inquiries without result in all these factories. We've asked at the stations further up the line; and the police there have done all they can. There are three stations that that train stopped at: Whetnow, May-quarter, and Pulchayne. Each of them has a big dormitory population, of people who just go in to work in London and return only to sleep. A good proportion of them are new, since the war. The police are overworked too, as they've been having floods there and traffic has been all tangled up. But they tell me that even when things are normal they can't hold out any hope of getting us information unless we can give them something more to go on."

Chapter VII

*	Snuffly Girl	A Workman	*
*	A Mother	A Workman	*
*	Hugh Rolandson	The Vicar	*
*	A. Mannheim •	H. J. Grayling	×
*	Cpl. George Ransom	C. J. F. Evetts	*

1

The German refugee was the least difficult to investigate. For Inspector Atkins had already a great deal of information about him, from the end of 1939, when he had settled in Croxburn; and the Home Office had a little earlier information.

It did not have, however, the most interesting earlier information. Part of this was never disclosed to the police, for no dishonourable reason—for to be amateur and careless was not dishonourable in Britain, but rather a recommendation for responsible public employment.

Up till September, 1939—indeed, even later—the whole behaviour of the British towards the Nazis and the Fascists seemed to Continental anti-Fascists heartbreakingly amateur. But the amateurs survived, while the professionals are in concentration camps, you say? Yes; but through no fault of the amateurs. If at all, through their lack of a philosophy. Even in its last days the French Republic had so clear a conception of its own principles of fraternity that it opened its gates wide to German refugees. This generosity may possibly—the allegation is very far from proved—have helped a little to its ruin. Possibly, in that case too, the British lack of generosity may have helped them to their safety. There *may* have been fewer Nazi spies in Britain disguised as refugees. But this was not due to competence, for when the crisis came in September, 1940, it was clearly shown that the governors of Britain could not distinguish at all between a Nazi and an anti-Nazi; indeed, the fact was officially stated. It was due, as those who remember British policy from 1933 onwards will probably testify, to a mixture of ungenerosity and bad conscience in those who had control of policy. The trophies of the remarkable foreign policy pursued in the six years from 1933 to 1939 bore inscribed beneath their stuffed and melancholy heads the names Abyssinia, Albania, Austria, China, Czechoslovakia, the German Republic, and Spain; and each name indicated a fresh regiment of refugees and fresh reasons to doubt whether the policy being pursued was wholly wise and honourable. To those who directed it, the new applicants for admission were each one a silent (or not silent) criticism; and the obstacles placed so successfully to their entry were quite probably due to no more than the ordinary human reluctance to be faced personally with evidences of what one suspects to be one's own folly. There are few people so obstinate as the man who half thinks he is wrong.

That explanation may be wrong or right. One thing is certain; in the year 1938, those who attempted to rescue

Nazi victims received none of the official help they might have expected; Nazi agents and organizers in Britain received hardly any of the official repression and punishment *they* might have expected.

There *were* people who came to the rescue of German anti-Fascists, but their efforts were usually unco-ordinated. Most of them were unskilful; some of them approached their task in an adolescent sporting spirit, as if it was tennis they were playing against Von Cramm. They, too, were amateurs.

Most of these amateurs had no success and were of no importance. They were playing a romantic game which cost them some money, taught them a little, and aided nobody. They were not, in the French sense, "serious." There was one of these groups which had a singular success—singular in the exact sense of the word, for it was not repeated and was odd in itself. And this success it had from accident chiefly, and certainly not because it was more realist and less romantic than any other group of enthusiasts all under thirty. It was not.

It was made up of junior members of a London Labour Party who had become discontented with the lack of event that makes up a local party's history, and had attempted to team up as a sort of amateur anti-Fascist espionage organization. Those who constituted the "ring" were five. The effective leader was an unattached young man of twenty-five named David Ellerton; he had money, good looks, ingenuity, ignorance, and that sort of unruffled courage which comes of always having had one's own way. He was not a fool, though he was often foolish. The one woman in the group was a pretty young monkey named Diana Evans, fair-haired, with eyes slightly too close together. She earned a living by typing, comfortably enough since she lived with her parents. She had a half-tomboy, half-sexy relation with David. He had not yet seduced her, though he intended to if he could. His observation or his conceit did not suggest the probability of a prolonged resistance. The third member, A. W. Preston, had a little more knowledge of the world than they; he was a plumber aged twenty-seven, and a member of his union. David called him Boss, or The Boss, to indicate that he was a union racketeer, which he was not. But he at least knew his way about East and South London more than they did; and it was not inconceivable that he should get a refugee, for example, smuggled off or on to a ship. He sometimes brought with him a young dock labourer named Herron, and naturally called Smoked or Smoky. He joined the group largely because he liked to drink at David's expense; he had done fourteen days once for a fight with a policeman and was regarded by the others as impressively tough. The last of the five was a quiet clerk in a big printing firm, named Harold Birch. He came from Wolverhampton in the Midlands, he had been till very recently a strict pacifist, he had rather a weak and pale though pleasant face, and he it was who brought them their only real find.

In June, 1938, he had spent some of his money on a long weekend—Friday to Tuesday—in France. It had been his holiday for the year, and he had taken his bicycle. From Boulogne he had gone eventually to St. Omer, where he had spent one night. He was very soon satisfied and more with all the sights of St. Omer. In the middle of the wet and uninteresting Picard plain, this grey town is only remarkable for its numerous and giant churches. They are gloomy and ill kept up; the most impressive, St. Bertin, is a ruin. Even if the inhabitants of St. Omer were universally pious, which they are very far from being, the accommodation would be much greater than they could use. The churches have a black and vast grandeur of their own, but they are depressing, and Harold soon tired of them. One café in the wide cobbled Grande Place showed a little life. Harold sat in it and scraped up an acquaintance with a young man who supported the Popular Front. He told Harold that the whole police of St. Omer was corrupt and in alliance with Fascist reaction. But he soon tired of Harold's halting French. He excited Harold's interest by pointing out to him two drinkers, a fish-eyed tall man and a shiny little man with yellow shoes as *deux agents nazis*, and then abruptly stopped Harold's eager enquiries by walking away.

Next morning it rained as only Flanders rain can rain. The rain made a slightly hissing noise and raised tiny pillars of water on the cobbles where it fell. Harold had pattered in it round the Place and been driven back to his hotel, the "Hotel de France," which was dreary and empty. The proprietress sat behind a sort of counter in the salon; she had unconvincing golden hair and a varnished face. She looked greedy and not too good-tempered. The only other occupants of the room were four youths playing an unknown game of cards. They hardly spoke. There was nothing to read except several time-tables, the *Guide Michelin* for 1931, a directory, and a copy of *L'Illustration* of August, 1927, on which a considerable amount of beef had been spilt. In a sort of glass annexe there was a dead palm and six iron chairs, one upside down. Harold ordered a glass of the thin French beer and sat down to wait for lunch.

At about 11.30 the two *agents nazis* came in and went into the glass annexe after staring at Harold. They talked in low voices.

At 12.15, when at last he smelt cooking, Harold noticed two French policemen walking quickly across the Square—at least one was in uniform, and the other looked more like a plainclothes man than a true civilian. They walked into the hotel and straight towards the annexe, Harold saw the two "agents" jump to their feet and one, he thought, made a queer swift movement with his hand. He could not be sure, for an uproar had broken out, at the end of which the two men were escorted out of the hotel by the police, obviously under protest.

Harold did not follow the crowd. He went into the annexe as soon as they had gone, and examined it thoroughly, even digging his fingers into the dry earth round the dead palm. At last he found what he was looking for. It was an envelope containing papers, casually—that is, to all appearance casually—thrust inside a copy of the magazine *Je Sais Tout*. Harold was fairly sure that it had been pushed there in a hurry by one of the "agents."

He put it in his pocket quietly, ate his lunch, packed his rucksack and cycle bag and asked for his bill. As he waited, he saw the two men come back into the hotel with triumphant smiles. He paid his bill, and the last that he saw of them they were moving about the annexe. Searching, he thought; but he could not be sure.

He was a little nervous about his theft and did not look inside his envelope until he was safely on board the Channel boat a good mile beyond the coast.

These were its contents, eleven papers in all:

(1) A small piece of paper on which were written these figures in a slanting hand:

$$525$$
$$650$$
$$700$$
$$745$$
$$800$$
$$815$$
$$825$$
$$830$$
$$835$$
$$845$$

915
1015
1200
1250
1300
1310

(2) *A piece of paper the same size on which were written:*

J. Reynolds.   Ewelme Delancey Av.
O.   772 Minories.
R.R.G.   Cafe am Z.
Q.P.   Av. V.H. 7. Str.
L.A.   R. de Riv. 81.
Hot. de Fr.   Gde Place St.-O.

The last entry was in pencil. Then there was a bundle of letters which had no dates, but appeared to be in an order. At the top of the first was written in chalk, "C7: R." They were in German.

(3) Dear Sir,

I am *very grateful* to you for the arrangements for the delivery of the goods, of which I have been informed verbally to-day. I confirm that twenty-five per cent of the value of these goods shall be handed to you in return for your assiduity in fixing this up. I shall pay fifteen per cent of this sum to your agent Herr Gross in evidence of good faith on Monday, and the rest will be paid upon delivery of the goods and at the place of delivery. I confirm that the weight of the goods will be in all 140,000 grammes.

Believe me when I say that my expressions of thanks are not merely formal.

Yours very truly,
Marta Goltz.

(4) Dear Herr Opell,

I have handed 15 per cent to-day to your agent and am awaiting despatch of the goods. The instructions on your invoice handed to me by your agent will be followed exactly.

Yours very truly,
M. Goltz.

A tick was put against the above letter. The next ran:

(5) Dear Herr Opell,

I am very much disturbed at the non-arrival of the merchandise. It should have been notified to me two days ago.

The weight was 140,000 grammes and all specifications were exactly fulfilled. Please send advices *at once*.

Yours truly,
Marta Goltz.

(6) Dear Herr Opell,

I cannot understand why you send me no word. It is not possible that anything could have happened. I beseech you to communicate with me. If there is any hitch it may be possible to make further financial arrangements. But I beg of you to send me some further information. I have recently been to see Herr Gr. several times, but he is not in his office. I do entreat you to send me word.

Yours truly,
M. Goltz.

On the back of this was:

(7) Copied and sent to D.   June 20.
Action: June 22.

Typed, with a different hand in the signature:

(8) June 10th.   Berlin Office.   Memorandum.
Re Goltz goods.
Entrusted delivery to J. R.   Departure June 11.
Point: Kehl. June 12. 14.45. Please notify receiver
directly yourself. 140,000 gr.

R. R. G.

In still a different hand:

(9) Re Goltz. Received as per schedule. See *VB*
13/6/38 3, 2. Will deliver Paris 15/6/38 140,000 gr.

J. R.

A second sheet in the same hand:

(10) I much regret that I was prevented by interference
this side which I had not expected from reporting at
Paris. I shall give further details when we meet.
Only possible arrive St. O. June 25.

J. R.

An illegible pencil mark was on the last slip.

Apart from these, and crumpled as if it had been thrust into
the envelope afterwards, was a torn half sheet of the *Völkische
Beobachter*, page 3, the top half showing the date June 13th.
A cross had been marked with a blue pencil against one news
item in column 2, as follows:

(11) A fresh arrest was made yesterday at Kehl by the
admirable customs staff, which has during the past
five years been entirely renewed and imbued by the
spirit of National Socialism.
A man giving the name of Goltz was observed
attempting to cross the river on a ferry boat disguised

as an official. He had over 2,000 RM. in currency upon his person which he was endeavouring to smuggle into France. His manner was abject when he was discovered and he offered a bribe to the S.S. man who questioned him. A few good German blows from the fist of the insulted Aryan taught him proper behaviour.

He was brought within an hour before the Extraordinary Tribunal, and the double offence of smuggling currency and endeavouring to corrupt a member of the Reich forces justified a sentence of death. The proceedings were in camera, but it is understood that the criminal's name is not really Goltz and that under the degenerate Weimar regime he was a well-known banker. He is, of course, a Jew.

Sentence will be carried out to-morrow. The prisoner has not as yet confessed the names of his accomplices, but it is believed he will be induced to do so.

Harold puzzled over them for some time, but the transaction, whatever it was, was something outside the usual business of a printing office, and he could make nothing of it. As a hypothesis, he assumed that someone called Goltz who tried to smuggle out German money had been caught and the correspondence concerned that and was in a sort of code. He tried to work out the code, but couldn't do so. He noticed a reference to what looked like a rendezvous at St. Omer, but decided to turn the whole packet over to David and his colleagues for them to pick at.

2

A full session—apart from Herron the docker—was held to examine the papers, more thrilling as they were than any crossword puzzle; and approached, unfortunately, in rather the same spirit. Indeed, the clues, if such they were, were so grabbed from hand to hand by the excited investigators that Diana Evans called them in and made copies for each sleuth. After a while silence and a rough division of labour was secured.

David Ellerton took for his first subject the list of figures:

525
650
700
745
800
815
825
830
835
845
915
1015
1200
1250
1300
1310

He added them up first. 14560 was the total he got. He considered whether this might not have some relation to the 140,000 grammes continually mentioned in the correspondence. Add a nought and the sum was very similar. Suppose each group represented a packet, in tens? It didn't seem very probable. Still, it was a possibility.

He then noticed two points about the list: there was no figure of two digits, and none of five. None below 100, nor more than, a thousand-and-something. Also, every figure ended in 0 or 5. This suggested that sums of money might be concerned. $5.25, for example, might be the first. But that would only make the total sum 145 dollars and 60 cents, about £30. Or 5 francs 25 centimes would give 145 francs and 60 centimes, which was less than a pound. Neither seemed satisfactory. Nor did this idea explain why the figures went continually upwards in value. That must be so for some reason, and if he could only find the reason, he believed he would be in a fair way to interpret the whole thing. A series of figures, going upwards, by fives. He tried to find a rhythm in the spacing, but there seemed none. He irritably wished he had had a scientific education. Probably it would shout its secret aloud to a scientist. No doubt there was some graph. Or something called a geometrical or arithmetical progression.

His annoyance was not decreased by the fact that Preston was obviously making rapid progress with the second slip of paper:

> J. Reynolds.   Ewelme Delancey Av.
> O.   772 Minories.
> R.R.G.   Cafe am Z.
> Q.P.   Av. V.H. 7. Str.
> L.A.   R. de Riv. 81.
> Hot. de Fr.   Gde Place St.-O.

"This is a list of addresses," he said.

"My dear Holmes!" sneered David.

"—and some of them are fairly easy to interpret. The last, added in pencil, is where you stayed, Harold, and where they had a date to meet the 'J.R.' of the letters. You see he says in his note, 'St. O. June 25.' The other addresses I should think are the addresses of persons regularly concerned in this business, whatever it is. Possibly 'J.R.' is J. Reynolds, of Delancey Avenue. Since the next address, Minories, is a

London address, then I think Delancey Avenue is in London too. We could look, anyway."

"It might be New York. There's a street there with a name something like that," said David, anxious to keep his end up.

"It *might* be anywhere," said Preston coldly, and went on: "O. may be this Herr Opell: or may not; 772 the Minories should not be hard to find. As for the others, I can give you two and the third beats me. 'Q.P. Av. V.H. 7' is Avenue Victor Hugo number seven. There is an Avenue Victor Hugo in every French town—that was easy. And 'Str.' is almost sure to be Strasbourg: at least I don't know of any other French town important enough to be known by its initials alone."

"It may be quite a small one, which happens to be known to them all because they work there or something," offered Diana.

"It may be. We'll never find it, if so. Then 'L.A. Rue de Riv. 81' has no town mentioned, and therefore is Paris. Obviously Rue de Rivoli number 81," said Preston proudly.

"And 'R.R.G. Cafe am Z'?" asked Diana.

"Don't know."

"I do," said David, at last able to intervene. "The Cafe am Zoo is a huge café in Berlin. As famous as the Café Royal here. Look at letter 8. It is clear that R.R.G. is Herr Gross who is despatching something which Marta Goltz hasn't received. I suppose he uses the café as his office. Sounds a bit fishy."

Diana looked at document 8.

"June 10th.   Berlin Office.   Memorandum.
Re Goltz goods
Entrusted delivery to J. R.   Departure June 11.
Point: Kehl. June 12. 14.45. Please notify receiver directly yourself. 140,000 gr.
R. R. G."

"Yes," she said. "He delivered the goods to J.R. in whose hands they vanished—or something—and J.R. crossed to St. Omer to explain things away. It could be that. Kehl is opposite Strasbourg, on the Rhine. I suppose 'Q.P.' was to be there to receive it."

She hesitated, feeling there was something more if only she could grasp it.

"How would this do?" she went on slowly. "The explanation is in this cutting from the German paper. According to how you translate it, David, it means that somebody called Goltz was trying to get out with some money. That means: there weren't any goods; there was a person, Mr. Goltz. And the reason he never got through was that someone was double-crossing and tipped the Nazis off."

"I believe you're right. You've got it. You *are* a clever girl." David tipped her face up and kissed her.

"Oh, shut up being silly," she replied with a Fifth Form gaucheness, and turned scarlet.

Harold, who had been an admiring watcher till then, broke in with a comment of his own.

"I think there's a greater complication. I don't believe that the two men whom I saw were anti-Nazis. I don't think they were trying to get Mr. Goltz out. They were crooks and thugs if ever I saw one. Besides, the man told me they were Nazis."

"That's not much to go on," said Preston. "An impression of people's faces and café gossip. But if they were Nazis, they may possibly have picked up this whole pile of correspondence in rounding up people when they seized Goltz. That may have given them the chance to break up a ring. It seems pretty beastly. But I don't know what we can do. It's all over now."

"It's more beastly than that," persisted Harold, with mild obstinacy. "Look at document 9. J.R. *did* receive the goods. And what did he do with them? He says—'See V.B. 13/6/38.'

Well, you can see *Völkische Beobachter*, 13/6/38 can't you? He handed the goods over to the loyal customs service, who killed Mr. Goltz. The only trouble was about the 140,000 grammes which he ought to have delivered in Paris. And I bet that was really a bribe or something."

There was a silence while the company considered that.

"Nothing else fits in," declared Preston at last. "It means that the owners of these papers pretended to export a Jew from Germany and at the same time notified the Nazis. They presumably split the fee with the Nazis."

"That's nasty," said Diana, and shuddered.

"It's Nazi," corrected Preston, but did not get a laugh.

There was another long pause. Then Harold said: "It isn't really true there's nothing we can do. We can go and look, at least."

"Look?"

"I mean, we've got two addresses in London. We could go and see if there's anything to be seen. I might recognize if either of the two people I saw in St. Omer were around. Though even then…" His voice trailed away.

"I know where to ask about refugees," said Preston. "I could go to the Central Office in Bloomsbury and find out about people named Goltz. There's about half a dozen other places, too, which know about these things."

There was a certain amount more talk, and it was agreed that Preston should make all the enquiries he could about refugees named Goltz who had been expected and had not arrived. Diana Evans should go to 772 Minories and list the offices there, Harold Birch should find out from the directories at his employers' office, whether there was a Delancey Avenue in London, and if so, visit it in the hope of recognizing one of his St. Omer narks. David Ellerton was to receive and co-ordinate—more briefly, to do nothing.

3

Thursday night found them slightly advanced.

"Boss" Preston had been told by three refugee organizations that they knew nothing of any Goltz who would fit the conditions of the case. But at one, a dark Jewish girl clerk had hinted that she knew of certain things which were done "on the side" and she was taking time to consider whether she would confide in him. It was agreed (the meeting was formal to-night) that he should show her copies of the documents in an endeavour to persuade her.

Harold Birch had found that there was one Delancey Avenue in London, in the far south-east. You could reach it by going down the Old Kent Road, turning east at New Cross and going up the Brockley Road. Off that were a number of suburban roads, apparently rather respectable, called such names as Allenby Road, Plomer Road, Haig Road, and Foch Road. Among them were four curiously named—Delancey Avenue, Zenger Avenue, Phillipse Avenue, and Hamilton Avenue. He had not had time to visit them. It was agreed that he should go there as soon as he could and see if there was a house named "Ewelme" and watch out for either of his St. Omer acquaintances.

David and Diana had been to 772 Minories. There were several suites of offices there. One was called "The London and Hamburg Direct Importation Company." It had five names painted up in one corner on the opaque glass door. One was H. W. Opell. Diana had gone in and enquired for a Mr. Alfred Greenberg. She had been told there was no such person there, but had secured a general idea of the layout of the office.

Harold offered to go himself next day, Friday, either at lunchtime or immediately after work in the evening, down to Delancey Avenue, to look it over and watch for any suspicious characters. This was unanimously agreed; he may

or may not have thought it odd that no offer of action was
made by any of the others.

4

The fact, which he did not suspect, was that the others were
intending to act without his knowledge. He suffered from
two handicaps in their view. Firstly, he had to work. He had
to be at his desk from nine to six; and he could not afford
to be irregular. He was not available for stunts during the
day, and he disliked very much going to bed later than ten.
Secondly, he was too scrupulous and too little adventurous.
He had modified his pacifism to the extent of declaring that
a time might come when Nazism would have to be opposed
by force. But apart from that he was the most strictly law-
abiding young man south of the river, and turbulence, even
the mild turbulence of organizing reprisals against Mosley
thugs, was the last thing he liked. Therefore, when he rang
up David at lunch-time next day, he disturbed a cabal of
which he did not know. David never worked, Herron was
a casual labourer and could be very casual at need, Diana
took the liberties at work that pretty young women often
do, and Preston's services were only intermittently needed,
like those of so many workers in 1938. They were working
out a project of which they did not really want Harold to
know. Fortunately, he was not suspicious.

"Is that David Ellerton?"

"Yes."

"Harold here. Look, I've had some luck. I'm talking from
a call box near you-know-where, but I'll have to get back to
the office quickly because it's a long way. Shall I come round
after work this evening and tell you?"

"No, I've got something on. Got to go out. I tell you
what, Harold. I'll come round at two-thirty to your place
on Saturday—to-morrow, that is—and we'll have a proper

talk. Maybe I'll have some news too. Can't you tell me just briefly now, though, what's happened?"

"Well, just I've been out to Delancey Avenue and there *is* a house called 'Ewelme,' and I'm almost certain I saw a man go into it who was the taller of the two men I saw at St. Omer—the one with eyes rather like a cod. I think, if you're out to-night, I'll go back there this evening and stroll around till it's dusk and keep a watch on the place. I'd like to settle things in my own mind, anyway. Sorry, I must buzz off now. Cheer-oh."

"So long, see you to-morrow."

David put on the receiver and turned to his fellow conspirators. "Children," he said, "Harold has beaten us to it. He went down east and he found 'Ewelme,' Delancey Avenue, and he thinks he saw a fish-eyed Nazi go in. He's going to check up to-night. And that means *we* must really get on with our job."

"Our job" was nothing less reckless than a burglary. The four of them, each encouraging the other, had come to the point of deciding to break into the office of Mr. "H. W. Opell" that night, at the very time, as nearly as might be, that the various offices were closed for the night. According to Diana's observation, there were approximately twenty minutes between the time when the offices closed and the cleaners came round to clear up for the morning. In that time it might be possible to go rapidly through the files and find—what? They did not know; but they were rashly gambling on the traffic carried on there being so iniquitous that even if they were caught Mr. "Opell" would be only too glad to hush things up. Or rather, that was Preston's calculation: Herron did not think a burglary serious, and anyway, young Ellerton was well to do and would see him right; David saw no reason (as the young and rich do not) why he should not do just as he pleased; and Diana followed him faithfully for her own reasons.

5

The Providence that looks after fools, and the carelessness that comes over even Nazis when they have been left untroubled too long, saved the group from the disaster which they deserved. The three men burgled the Opell office soon after six o'clock—the lock resisted Herron a very short time—and made a rather haphazard search which left the most obvious traces if anyone had been in a position to make use of them. But it was fairly clear that the occupants of the offices were not likely to be able to. The evidence was too clear. There were a large number of files which corresponded closely to the bundle of papers which Harold had stolen in St. Omer. It might have been actually a stray from one of them. The differences consisted chiefly in the amount of the "weights" given, and the names of the victims. Four of these—Rosen, A., Vogeling, K. and D., and Leibnitz, H.—corresponded to the names of refugees of whom Preston had already heard in his inquiries. In each case the victim had been expected over this side, had left Berlin or whatever might be his home town and had been neatly collected at the frontier. The dates, so far as Preston remembered them, corresponded too.

It was a considerably sobered group which climbed into the car Diana drove, and one which rather glumly refused to give details to her until they reached David's flat. Even then, it seemed that there was nothing much to be done; Rosen, A., Vogeling, K, and D., and so on were the only gravestones. Except perhaps in one case, which was in the equivalent of a pending file. Mannheim, Albrecht, scientist. A half-Jew, a physicist, and a man of some importance.

"The record," said Preston, "showed that he has just paid the advance instalment of 15 per cent to the man called

R.R.G. at the Cafe am Zoo. He is probably arranging for his train journey now. And the German police are already waiting for him. There's nothing you can do. It's all in the bag." He spoke rather ill-temperedly, and directly to Diana, as if it was some fault of hers.

"We could tell the police," she said, uncertainly. "We could explain about the burglary. I expect they wouldn't make a great fuss, when they knew what we found out."

"Then what?" said Preston. "If they believed us at all, they'd check up, and in due course something would happen. Some day. But that wouldn't save Mannheim. Nothing will save him, bar warning him. And we have no way of doing that."

"We could *go* and tell him," said David, for whom this was already a superb game of cowboys and Indians.

"How, go?"

"There's nothing difficult about going to Berlin. I can afford it, and I've got a passport. I could just go and call on him, show him what we have found and warn him. It'd probably save his life."

"It would more probably end his life altogether. There's no doubt that he's being watched, and your visit will be recorded. Inside twenty-four hours of your call he'll be in a concentration camp if he's even alive," said Preston. "Put it out of your mind. There's nothing that Jews or Liberals in Germany like less than visits from well-meaning foreigners."

"I could bring him back with me."

"How?"

"With a forged passport. If I travel by air, looking very rich, I can almost certainly conceal it about me. They don't search the rich closely—not yet, anyway. And forged passports can be got; can't they, Boss?" He looked at Preston ingratiatingly.

"It's been done," said Preston, "but not cheaply, and not just at any time to order. I think it'd be crazy. Very dangerous to you as well as to him. I don't think you'd come back. Wash it out, David."

"It'd be better to turn all this over to the police and hope to have the burgling excused," said Diana. "You mustn't be silly."

David rather reluctantly agreed. Anyway, they would wait until Harold reported next day, if he had tracked down his St. Omer people.

6

Harold never reported.

When David went round to his lodgings at Penfold Road, Croydon next Saturday afternoon, he found the front door open, which was unlike the careful habits of Mrs. Edge, the landlady. And when he went upstairs to Harold's room, there was Mrs. Edge herself sitting in tears at the table, and a uniformed constable standing beside her in a condition of great embarrassment.

He stared at the group. "Where is Harold Birch?" he said. "I was to meet him here."

The policeman turned to him with obvious relief.

"Did you know Mr. Birch, sir?" he asked.

"Did I? I *do* know Mr. Birch. What do you mean?" asked David anxiously.

"Would you be willing to come along and identify a body which we have reason to fear may be Mr. Birch's?" asked the policeman. "We found this address on the deceased, but this lady doesn't feel quite up to the job. A most trying business, sir, and if you do know Mr. Birch, perhaps you would spare her the trial."

The room quivered suddenly in David's sight, and his throat turned very dry. To his great astonishment he found he could not speak. He had to walk up and down the room twice before his voice came back. Then he spoke creditably firmly. "Yes, officer. I'll certainly do that."

He did not move, however. He stood staring at the room which had been Harold's, as if the many evidences of his friend in it were some guarantee that he was still alive. Those books, that letter on the desk—obviously they were confidently waiting for their owner's return. He was motionless until the policeman said a second time: "Shall we go along now, sir?"

They walked down the road together.

"We'll take a police car: that is, the sergeant will take you in one, sir," said the policeman. "It's quite a step: beyond New Cross."

"New Cross," repeated David.

He said nothing more until a silent sergeant took him into a mortuary off the Brockley Road. David did not need to look more than a few seconds. Harold's face had always been white and still: it was curiously unchanged in death. The crushed-in back of his head had been mercifully camouflaged by whoever laid him out.

He walked out rather quickly and said: "Yes, that is my friend Harold Birch, who lives at the Penfold Road address where you picked me up. He works at Messrs. Evenings, the big printers. His people live in Wolverhampton, but I don't know their address. He's not married."

His face was working unhappily. "He's taken it bad," thought the sergeant.

"Would you tell me, please," said David, "how Harold was killed and where you found him?"

"It was a bit queer," said the sergeant. "I don't know how Mr. Birch came to be there, but there were few other places in the district where he could have remained unnoticed so long. The doctor says he must have died some time last night, but he wasn't found till after dawn.

"Most of the district is well-lit, but there's one place where the lamps are poor. There's an open space called Eastfields, used as a playground, and with a hedge round it. Part of it doesn't have a pavement outside at all. There's just the hedge, and a bit of a ditch, as it was when it was all country here.

"So far as we can see, Mr. Birch must have been walking in the road and been struck by a car and rolled with the impact or been thrown, so that he fell lengthwise into the ditch. The hedge is a bit overhanging and the body wasn't really noticeable until full daylight. There's practically nowhere else it could have happened like that.

"Of course we take a serious view of this, sir," went on the sergeant, talking to give David time to get back his composure. "These hit-and-run drivers are very dangerous, and they're a growing menace. There were skid-marks on the tarmac in the road, and if we find out what car did it, there'll be serious trouble for the driver."

But David was not silent from physical nausea. He was wondering what his duty was. He thought that this might well be no hit-and-run driver, but a deliberate murder.

He thought of the room he had just seen. There was an unfinished dutiful letter from Harold to his mother: no more would ever be written of it. There were clothes—a few books—a few photographs. Someone would pack these up and address them to Wolverhampton, and thereafter there would be no trace of Harold Birch in Penfold Road. His desk would remain unattended for a day or two at Messrs. Evenings, and then someone would sit down at it, rearrange his papers and finish whatever he had left undone. Immediately the trace of him would be gone. And he would be as utterly vanished as if he had been a stone dropped into a pond. The ripples would cease and with them he would disappear. Presumably there was a house in Wolverhampton where he would be remembered and missed. But apart from that he would be quickly forgotten.

He made up his mind that someone at least should not forget. He would hand over to the police the packet that Harold brought back from St. Omer, and tell the whole of that story.

He would not, yet, tell the story of his own burglary.

"I think," he said at last, "I can help you to find out a little more than that. My friend told me on the telephone yesterday that he was watching a man of bad character in this area, whom he believed to be living at an address in Delancey Avenue, a house called 'Ewelme.' I think it may just be possible that this is not wholly an accident."

"That's a very grave statement, sir. I think you'd better tell me more."

David took out of his pocket the originals of the material Harold had brought back from St. Omer. "I will, gladly," he said. "But you see most of the material is in German."

"Oh. I think you'd better speak to the Inspector. Excuse me a minute."

The Sergeant was away some five minutes, and then fetched him into a square, whitewashed room where an Inspector was sitting at a desk. David went up to the desk, laid on it the originals, and this time a copy of his own translation.

"Before you read these," he said, "I think I should explain their meaning.

"Harold Birch, as everyone will tell you, was a man of very high principles indeed. He was deeply opposed to the abominable things that are being done in Germany, and if he could impede the persecution that goes on there, he was going to do so. This summer he took a short holiday at a place in France called St. Omer. While he was there, two Nazi agents were arrested in his hotel, and he got possession of an envelope of papers which they had left behind. That is that packet you've got there. The agents were released before he left, but he kept the papers to study because he thought that they were evidence of some criminal activity.

"I think he was righter than he knew. Anyway, in his opinion, those letters didn't deal with trading affairs at all, really; but with an attempt to smuggle refugees out of Germany—or anyway, with a refugee named Goltz. If you look at them carefully, Inspector, you'll see that one signed J.R. dealing with the affair says, 'See V.B. 13/6/38,' and there is the *Völkische Beobachter*, V.B., of 13/6/38. And it tells you that Mr. Goltz was given away to the police. Harold, who knows the Nazi habits pretty well, discussed these documents with me, and decided that what he had stumbled on was a ring which pretended to give the persecuted people in Germany a chance to escape, and, in fact, sold them to the police. And he thought that this J.R. might be the J. Reynolds, 'Ewelme,' Delancey Avenue, whose address is on the other slip of paper.

"Yesterday after midday, he rang me up to say he had found out that there was such an address and he had seen one of the Nazis he met in St. Omer going into it. A tall man with fishy eyes. He told me he was going back last evening to do a bit more watching. And now you find him dead, his body hid in the only place for miles around where it wouldn't be seen. Do you ask me to believe *that's* an accident?"

The Inspector made no immediate answer, but studied the papers for a considerable time. At last he spoke.

"I don't say you're right, and I don't say you're wrong. But I will say that I want to speak with this Mr. Reynolds. If you choose to come along, since you have a description of him, I would be pleased to have you with me."

7

Nobody answered the door of "Ewelme." The house was silent and apparently unoccupied. The lady in the house next door said she thought they'd moved. Early in the morning a car had come for them and gone off with a lot of luggage on it. Them? Why, "them" was the foreign gentleman, tall, with fishy eyes, and his wife, at least supposed to be his wife, about forty-fiveish, plump, always well dressed, but with a veil and an old-fashioned hat. That morning she'd been dressed in a dark green coat and skirt, with a brown overcoat over it, and walking shoes and brown stockings, and a toque like Queen Mary's, but still the same veil and brown gloves; but the informant hadn't had time to have a proper look at her. They'd not been in the house more than a month, anyway.

The police had been all round the house: nevertheless the Inspector said: "Vansittart"—such was the improbable name of one of the constables—"I think if you went round the back you might find a window open."

"Yes, sir. I'll see, sir," said the constable after a glance at David.

A few seconds later he opened the front door.

"I found a window open, sir," he said without a trace of a smile.

"Very good," said the Inspector. "Go round now to the station at Crawshalton Road, and tell them I'm here, and what for. If there's an Inspector in charge, get him to come round here; if not, bring a sergeant. Tell him to bring along all the information about these tenants he can, and if he knows who the house agents are to bring the keys too."

He marched into the front room, an ordinary suburban parlour, and stood with his arms folded, in a Napoleonic attitude. "We'll have to tear this apart," he said.

For a time David watched, marvelling at the meticulous care with which the police went over every square inch. But before long he got weary. The house had obviously been taken furnished, and the temporary inhabitants seemed to have left no trace. Except, indeed, finger-prints: the men with insufflators seemed to be the only satisfied persons. In the end he was glad to go back to his office, with the promise that the Inspector would see him in the morning.

"The name is Johnston," said the Inspector with imperial condescension.

Next morning, when David called to see him he was still friendly, though magnificent.

"It was fortunate that you gave us that information," he said approvingly. "We've got some fine sets of prints. There's quite a mixed bunch, but two lots keep recurring. It's reasonable to suppose that they belong to the man and his wife. Crooks will do one job in gloves, but fortunately nobody's going to spend a whole month in a house with his gloves on. If this man's come from abroad, it'll help a great deal. They have no nonsense about getting finger-prints there. We are communicating with the police of Rome, Paris and Berlin—though, if your friend's idea was correct, we won't get much help from there. However, that's a matter of high politics and the less said about it the better."

"Did you find anything else in the house?" asked David.

"Not much worth mentioning." The Inspector licked his thumb preparatory to turning over his papers, and then angrily wiped it on his trousers. Do what he could, he kept on doing that trick which betrayed the fact he had spent years as a common P.C. He went on with an even more severe expression.

"The house had been taken furnished from a Mrs. Aitken, now in Egypt. Letting had been effectuated by Messrs. Horlicks and Cox, to a gentleman corresponding to your description. He paid in advance, giving the name of J. Reynolds, and said that he had to be a month or two in London on business. He wrote from the Royal Star Hotel, Leeds. Enquiry at this hotel shows that a person giving this name stayed there a few days. He entered himself in the book as: 'J. Reynolds, Finchley Road, N.W.' Do you know how many houses there are in the Finchley Road?" asked the Inspector abruptly.

"Er—no: I'm afraid not," said David with a start.

"The ultimate number on the left-hand side going north," said the Inspector contentedly, "is twelve hundred and one. We wouldn't get much out of that, even if the address wasn't certain to be a fake. An address like that looks perfectly honest and fair in an hotel book, unless you know. The other address to use is 'Romford Road, E.' That's just as long, and looks just as exact to a provincial. Well, we've got practically nothing out of the neighbours and tradesmen. The man was a foreigner: he called himself Reynolds and had a slight accent. His wife—well, you know how it is." Mr. Johnston sighed. "Thanks to you, we've got some description of the man. But we couldn't pick out the woman if she walked across the street in front of us. Plumpish! Middle age! Middle height! Undistinguished face! Probably brown hair! Wore a veil! What can you make of that? She went out very little, paid her bills regularly, and left nothing owing. No noticeable accent. Colour of eyes unknown. Generally wore gloves: spoke very little."

He sucked his lips in.

"That's all from the house. But there is something more. From the body." The Inspector turned over his notes again. "Medical evidence shows that death probably took place between one and six o'clock in the morning. Evidence from the policeman on the beat now indicates that the body was probably placed there after three o'clock. As the night was cold, it seems likely, according to the doctors, that deceased was killed shortly before being deposited, or actually *in situ*. H'm.

"The murderers had not removed anything from the body so far as can be seen. The contents of the deceased's pockets included money, fountain pen, glasses, handkerchief, packet of cigarettes, Ingersoll watch, a comb, and a pocket book with diary, containing his name and address."

"That's odd, Inspector," said David. "It suggests that they were disturbed. Surely they'd have tried to make it look like robbery, or tried to conceal his identity."

"I don't think so. I think it was quite intentional. They probably knew that we were bound to find out about them quickly. I expect they thought Mr. Birch had been to the police, as he should have done. They couldn't hope not to have the body recognized. Now, if they'd taken his things, what would they have done with them? They'd have had to deposit them somewhere, or destroy them, and that might mean leaving another clue somewhere else. So they decided that the things were best left on the body. No doubt they'd been through his pockets first and decided that there was nothing of importance.

"Were you," added the Inspector casually, "doing any of this counter-espionage yourself?"

David stayed silent and looked highly embarrassed. The Inspector went on: "If you were thinking of following this up, I would suggest you don't. If you won't take the advice as discourteous, I would ask you to leave the matter altogether to us. You've been very helpful, and I may have to call on you again. We shan't forget you, and we will let you know how things progress. But when we've taken a case over, especially a case which may be murder, there really isn't any room for the amateur, if you'll pardon the word. What could you do? You can't follow up these Goltz clues as we can. You haven't the right to ask the questions that we have. Take my advice, Mr. Ellerton, and leave it to us."

David hesitated. The Inspector rose and held out his hand. "You think it over," he said.

He did think it over. But his thoughts were not wholly those the Inspector probably hoped. They resulted in a decision not, indeed, to continue chasing after "J. Reynolds" and his fellows, but to go himself to Berlin to warn and perhaps abduct the threatened Herr Mannheim. He would travel, as he had often done before, as a rich tourist seeking dissipation in Berlin.

The rashness and romanticism of his project had shocked even his youthful colleagues. But they had been unable to stop him. Money had always cushioned him against reality. The young and rich Englishman, in 1938, still could believe that he could always do whatever he wished. It was not so much that David believed that he could buy his way out of any trouble; it was rather that wealth, without his knowledge, had in the past regularly passed over to others the troubles which any follies of his own provoked. He did not know how much his own courage was ignorance, or how little Nazis cared about the habits or intentions of rich Englishmen.

In any case, as he pointed out, not one of them could stop him going; he could and would do what he pleased. In the end, Preston even aided him to the extent of securing, by means which he did not disclose, a well-forged passport for Mannheim in the name of "Albert Manton," and even saw him off at Croydon airport.

8

David sat in a small, exactly square room, papered with book shelves, and patiently began his argument all over again. He had been talking for nearly an hour already to the owner of the flat. Albrecht Mannheim was a short, dark, squat man, with thick brown hair, and a big nose. He had full prominent brown eyes which may have derived from Jewish blood. He kept throwing his head back and brushing his hand through his hair, with what might have been a studied gesture. David had the idea that he must have been—might still be—very attractive to women. He spoke very quickly, in slangy Berlin German, and David could not always follow him.

David was wondering if he would have to go back to London without him. He had not been searched at the airport, though his luggage had been, and the faked passport was in his possession still. He had put up at the Bristol, an opulent hotel rather less ostentatious than the Adlon, though near to it. When he had left it, he had taken some precautions against being followed. He had started in directly the opposite direction. He had walked up and down the paths in the damp, dark-wooded Tiergarten until he was fairly sure no one was following him. He had examined all the shiny white statues in the Sieges Allee and received some comfort from the fact that they were still as ugly and still in the same place. Perhaps Germany did not change after all.

Then he had turned left, sauntered through the Zoological Gardens and came out at the Augusta Viktoria Platz, with its curious and ugly church on an island in the centre. Here it was he had seen the words CAFE AM ZOO, and had not been able to resist going in for a coffee. So this was where Herr Opell's agents had their headquarters! It was still the same big open café with dark red seats, and a large orchestra. It seemed rather empty, and Nazi signs were plastered about. Otherwise it was just as it had been five years ago when David first knew it. A wave of almost Teuton sentimentality arose up in him. He had been so young—there had been a girl—the band had played "Ich hab' es einmal gefragt." Camilla had been older than he was, and she had really been very kind. She had managed to leave him gently, and with no memory but that of an idyll. And in the hotel three doors down the Kurfurstendamm…He pinched his mouth wryly, and wondered if he dared ask the band to play "Ich hab' es einmal gefragt" again. They had danced again to it on their return to England as "I Asked Her One Little Time." At the Metropole in Brighton, of all places. Better not ask the band to play it: it was probably a non-Aryan tune, he decided; all the best tunes were. He gulped part of his coffee: it was a disgusting bean-coffee, an *ersatz*. He got up, suddenly brought back to the present day, paid his bill, and went out.

He took a few paces down the Kurfurstendamm. It had once been the Glittering Haunt of Jewish Vice, according to the Nazis. They had removed its glitter all right. It was decayed, dull, half derelict. He stood still long enough to make sure no one had followed him out of the café (had it been quite wise to go there out of all the Berlin cafés?) Then he crossed the broad road, walked in front of the café which had years ago been Kempinski's largest, and slowly worked his way back eastwards, to a narrow street not far from the Friedrichstrasse railway station, where Herr Mannheim had his tiny flat.

And ever since then he had been arguing with a man who obstinately refused to believe him. As if he were afraid to believe him. As if his whole world would vanish if he did. Mannheim kept saying "No!" and pushing something away with a thrust of his hand. He had a remarkable control of his emotions. For surely, David considered, he must either think that an agent provocateur was seated in front of him, or suspect that the whole of his escape scheme was a fraud. In either case, a disagreeable thought, yet he merely said: "I thank you. I find difficulty in agreeing with you."

David had yet to realize how thoroughly the non-Nazi German had learnt to keep a poker face. Mannheim, behind his mask, was deeply agitated: his mind was filled by one leaping terror after another.

David told again, with gently insistent detail, the cases that they had found in Herr Opell's files; and what had happened to the men who had paid their money. Suddenly Mannheim said to him:

"Stop. I want to think."

He turned his back on David and stared out of the window, a black, sturdy shape against the twilit sky. His room was high up over Berlin and he could see the whole flat expanse of the city. Near in the foreground was the Brandenburger Tor, unaltered and a memory of old Germany: to its left the shapes of the unfinished Nazi buildings which were making of the Unter den Linden a wholly new street. Above his head the stars were one by one coming out; below, as if in answer, pinpoints of light appeared in the city and multiplied.

After what seemed a long time, but cannot have been much more than five minutes, he turned to David and said in an unmoved voice:

"Berlin was where I was born. I belong to no other place, and to no other persons. I had nothing else to say good-bye to. I have said it; and now I am ready."

He sat down at the table, with a businesslike air.

"You will have plans," he said, "which you will tell me. When do you propose to go?"

"Now," said David. "As soon as we can. If we are unprepared it doesn't matter. They are the more likely to be unprepared too."

"It is true. Then to-night. Also," said Herr Mannheim, suddenly switching his language, "since heretofore I am to be an Englishman, I will speak English."

"Hereafter."

"Hereafter. I thank you. I explain that it is very convenient for me to go, since I have already made what arrangements I can, to go in a few days time. I have what money I can get, though whether I can it take—can take it—with me I do not know. I have entirely new clothes. My books I must leave behind, but I have sold them already to a dealer who will the unsuitable ones denounce to the authorities when he shall have removed the valuable ones. His money I have received as to three-quarters: for the last quarter I will send a letter, that he should send it by post to a place called Stentsch. This will be useful for confusion, as the place is on the Polish border; also the address that I shall give is that of a Hitler-youth organizer, which I have from the *Lokalanzeiger* copied. Yes. I will therefore only take what I can put in my ordinary brief case."

Herr Mannheim seemed almost pleased. Here, David thought, was a man of character and decision: there was little need to organize *him*. But the author had continued:

"I will write a letter to the man in the Cafe am Zoo, who to me is called Herr Gross, saying that to-day when I tried to take money from the bank, I was cross-questioned and refused. So I will say I am too frightened to come to meet him to-morrow and have gone to stay with a friend in the Wannsee region, which often I have before done—done before. So in three days will I return, I shall say, if he will also enquire so that I may be sure nothing is suspected. Also, I will leave for the concierge a note saying that I am going to the Wannsee and will be back in three days. So may we have three days of grace.

"Now you will say what I shall do. Shall I be disguised? Shall we take an aeroplane?"

"No." David had already thought this out. "It is too dangerous. Too few people cross by aeroplane, even now. Each one can be specially scrutinized. I crossed to-day, and I was fairly conspicuous. They would notice me if I tried to come back again so soon. They would also be very likely to remember that no one like you had been seen arriving at the Tempelhof aerodrome. No good: we must go by train. Perfectly openly, and by the train that is most frequented.

"I've looked it up. It's the one that leaves Berlin Friedrichstrasse, just by here, at 10.55."

He took a travel folder out of his pocket and handed it to Mannheim. Mannheim read it to himself half aloud, his expression changing slightly as he did so.

Berlin	22.55	
Hanover arr.	2.13	
„ dep.	2.30	
Osnabruck	4.10	
Bentheim	5.46	
Oldenzaal	6.48	(Dutch time)
Flushing dep.	13.50	
London	21.30	

"Bentheim is the frontier station," said David, unnecessarily.

"Yes," said Mannheim. "If ever I pass it. It will be a new life then, I suppose. I wonder what do those words mean. They do not say anything to me now." He pushed away the thought with his hand, using the same gesture as he had before. "By then, anyhow, I will know if I was wise to trust you. And if you are what you say that you are. I am sorry. It is rude, that I say this. But men like me, our minds are very tired, and often we say things that once we would only have thought."

"That's all right," said David.

"And shall I be disguised?" asked Mannheim.

"A little, I think. Your clothes will have to do. But you must wear my overcoat—I have another at the hotel. You must wear glasses—not tinted glasses, for everyone suspects them, but plain horn-rimmed glasses, which I will give you. Also, since you do not usually wear a hat, you shall wear one. And you must cut off most of your hair. I had better do that for you. It will be a nuisance getting rid of the hair, but that cannot be helped. Hair left about tells its own story."

"I will tell you what I shall do with the hair," said Mannheim, with a slightly childish smile. "I have a big envelope, also postage stamps, which I shall now not need. We shall collect all the hair which it would indeed be too suspicious to leave, and shall put it into the envelope, which I shall stamp and leave upon the table. It shall be addressed to the Assistant Burg—Assistant Mayor of Stentsch. The concierge's wife will find it and will post it. She is a bad woman, but she does these things for me when I am away because I give her tips, and also I think she reports them. Each morning, I did not say this, she comes to clean, you see. Then she will afterwards remember that she posted to Stentsch a large thick envelope with some strange thing inside, perhaps notes, perhaps explosive. This will also make pleasing confusion. Also will that official in Stentsch, whom I do not know, be much confused when he shall receive an envelope full of human hair and not any words therewith. Perhaps also will he and the Youth Leader be confused when the Gestapo shall demand explanations."

"Good man," said David. "But before I cut your hair, is there nothing that you must do? Aren't you doing something this evening? Are you going somewhere, where your absence would be noted?"

"No. I am much alone nowadays."

"Have you anyone to whom you must say good-bye? It would be better not; if you can avoid it."

"My daughter died last year. My stepson is a Nazi. My second wife has had her marriage dissolved under the Nuremberg laws. I have no one else."

"Oh."

David thought a moment.

"Then this is what we will do," he said. "I will cut your hair now, and leave you the glasses, my coat and my hat. You will write your letters and make your arrangements, while I go back to my hotel. I shall leave my large bag in the hotel, and before I go out I shall ask the hotel porter for the names of night clubs and make it very clear I am going out on a blind."

"A—?"

"Going to make a thick night of it. Get drunk and finish up with a pretty lady. I shall ask him about the girls too. No one is going to be surprised if I don't turn up till very late, or indeed if I don't get back to-night at all. It'll take them their time if they start asking all the tarts in Berlin about me when they do find I've vanished. During the evening I'll buy both tickets to London, showing the two passports, and I'll meet you fifteen minutes before the train.

"Not in the station—that would be too obvious. But in the ornamental garden between it and the river. Near to the bridge. There are a lot of people about and it is a fine night. We shall simply appear to be strolling about. Then we shall walk to the station, a little separated, and meet again inside. With any luck, we shall find a party of Americans or English, the noisier the better, and pass the barrier with them.

"Have something to eat, if you can. It'll be better not to go to the restaurant car. The fewer people who see us, the better."

9

They were lucky, on the whole, to have a carriage to themselves. In some ways, two men alone in a whole carriage were more noticeable; but on the other hand, if strange passengers had got in they might well have begun, or tried to begin, a conversation. Anything might happen then. Mannheim's English was not too good, and he could easily be tripped up.

They sat in silence, each too preoccupied with his thoughts to speak.

The carriage was a box full of brilliant light, some sort of a refuge and defence against the world beyond. Outside the night was dark, black like plush, and dotted with a thousand shiny points of yellow. Continually sudden vistas of bright light appeared, as the train passed over and above the streets of Berlin. For a moment they could see long paths of well-lit road, filled with busy, soundless people on their own errands, or almost empty with brilliant lights pouring down on unused pavements, with only a motor or two in the road running along unheard to their own destinations. Empty or full, David thought, neither he nor Mannheim would ever see those streets again.

The train began to cross the bridge over the Spree: the sound of its wheels changed, and the river appeared below, black and shiny like a giant slug. The train was running very slowly through Berlin, as if it was reluctant to leave the city. The line curved right in to the west end of the city, and the train ran slower and slower until it drew to a standstill at the Zoological Gardens station. David had to remind himself it was not unusual to stop there: his nerves were beginning to trouble him already. He risked looking out of the window: the station seemed nearly empty. A few yards away there must be the Cafe am Zoo. Curious that the train should stop, for a final good-bye, so near to that ill-omened place. He shook his head, twitching it suddenly as a horse does to get rid of an irritating fly. The train reluctantly moved forward again.

Before long it was running steadily, fast, and smoothly, out on the great plain of Prussia. Now there were no lights outside, except the strip of orange which the carriages themselves threw out on the ground beside the track. They would run on like this for hours. Literally for hours: for it would be nearly four hours to their first stop, Hanover.

David took out a thick blue time-table and confirmed the times. He closed it and dropped it on the seat beside him.

On the cover were the words REJSERUTER OG HOTEL-LISTE. Mannheim looked at them with a dull curiosity. "What language is that?" he said.

"Danish."

"Danish? Why Danish?"

David shrugged his shoulders. "I happened to find it in the Hotel Bristol's reading-room. They've got them in all languages," he said. "I thought I'd take it. If anyone happens to be inquisitive, it will darken counsel a little. Someone might be looking for two English travellers; someone who we don't want to find them."

Mannheim said nothing, and they settled down for another enormous wait.

Once they waved aside a steward who offered them drinks or food.

Once a ticket collector came in, inspected their tickets, saluted and left them.

Nothing else happened.

Neither spoke again until David said: "It's two o'clock. We should be in Hanover in a quarter of an hour."

"Um"

"2.13. Train leaves again at 2.30."

Mannheim yawned suddenly and then looked very ashamed.

Rather late—2.30—the train slowed down, passed the big board HANNOVER, and drew up into a vast, brightly-lit station.

David rose and stared out of the window without opening it. He rejected the idea of walking on to the platform, but walked out into the corridor and aimlessly moved about there for a few minutes. Mannheim remained sitting, but when David sat down again, he too rose up and looked through the window. He did not put his head out but leaned the side of it against the pane, in the corner, so as to see as far up the platform as he could while remaining in the carriage. After a minute he drew himself up.

Men do not really turn white when they are afraid: they more often turn yellow or green. Mannheim turned green. But he spoke in a steady voice.

"I am afraid that this is all," he said. "They are searching the train. I have seen get in two men in police uniform and one who is Gestapo. It is not to be mistaken. And there is nothing to do."

David jumped up.

"They mayn't be looking for you," he said, inadequately.

"If they are not, still will they find me. The one who is Gestapo I know, and he knows me. Several of my friends he has taken and not long ago he said to me that I was to watch myself. It is the end. I am sorry: I thank you for your effort. Unless perhaps," he added wryly, "this was not unexpected to you?"

David answered in a firm voice: "We have one chance; only one, but if we are both steady, it will be all right. Before I took this train I looked up other ones. There is an express which stops in this station in a few minutes. It draws in at that transverse platform which you may have seen as you came in. It goes at right angles to this train—down into South Germany—Frankfurt. When we get there we'll see what we do next: for the moment we can't bother.

"Now: this is what you must do. Now, at once, walk out of this carriage into the refreshment room. Go to the counter: order a brandy, drink it quickly. Go out by the other door, if possible while the girl is serving someone else. If the train is not in—but I think I hear it coming—sit down on a seat on the platform where there are others, not alone. When it comes in, and people begin to get out, walk to the entrance of one of the carriages where there are plenty of people. Walk along to a third-class compartment where there is someone with luggage. Sit down, don't look for me. I'll come along after the train starts."

Mannheim nodded and reached for his bag.

"No: take no luggage," said David. "You're just someone leaving the carriage to get a drink."

Mannheim walked across to the refreshment room. Thank God, David thought, he looked inconspicuous. A pity the platform was so empty. Very few civilians, but plenty of porters and two men rolling trolleys along and offering drink.

He swiftly opened his bag and distributed all that he could of its contents about the pockets of his suit and large overcoat. The spare suit must stay behind, but pyjamas, travelling slippers, shaving tackle, a spare shirt, socks, and handkerchiefs all had room found for them. They made him bulge, but he opened his coat and let it hang loose. His additional size was no longer noticeable to a casual observer, and that was the best he could hope for.

He put his case back on the rack, and left the Danish guide obviously on the seat. Mannheim's portfolio he tucked under his arm. Then he walked out on to the platform.

Everything depended on his manner and confidence now. He must not attract attention, and he must not do anything for which an obvious explanation would not appear at once to the chance observer.

He had his plan ready. He walked briskly towards the inner side of the platform—away from the train—turned along past the lighted stationmaster's office and refreshment room windows, and entered the gentlemen's lavatory. "It is forbidden to use the train lavatories while stopping at a station": that instruction is known by heart by every German, and David's trek was self-explained.

There was no attendant, fortunately, in the lavatory when he entered. It was a silent, empty hall, white-tiled and brilliantly lit. He let himself into one of the compartments and sat on the seat. He found he was sweating so much that he must stink.

He waited ten minutes, which he thought were the worst ten minutes of his life.

No one came into the lavatory. Yet they must have finished exploring the train. They might be satisfied that he and Mannheim were not on board it. They might not be looking for them at all, and might have found whoever it was they wanted. They might be dissatisfied and someone might think of looking in the lavatories. It was time to go.

He walked out, firmly on to the other platform.

Thank God, there was the long dark-green train, blowing steam out from between its wheels, filled with people, and with the white boards on its side, saying in Gothic lettering:

Altona—Hamburg—Hannover—Kassel—Frankfurt a/M.

The platform was fuller of people than the other; busy, ordinary German people. David again did not walk to the train direct. He walked towards the ticket office, examined a notice, turned about, and mounted the train. Unless anyone had been closely watching him, he had not come from the lavatory on to the train; he had come out of the ticket office.

He sat down in a corner seat of a third-class carriage with three other people in it. He did not dare to look through the train for Mannheim.

It was 2.40 by his watch. The London train should have left ten minutes ago, but it was still standing there. He could see the lights of it by looking through the ticket office windows. Something must be wrong. Would this train be allowed to start? 2.45 was its time. Five minutes to go.

Five…blasted…minutes.

David fixed his eyes on the station clock and watched it. It scarcely seemed to move. He felt his skin taut all over his face, and then wondered if his expression was giving his anxiety away. Certainly he had been breathing much too fast.

He relaxed and lay back in his corner, looking at the rest of the passengers under half-shut eyes. They seemed to have noticed nothing. The old gentleman opposite him was still asleep. The middle-aged lady in black in the far corner was knitting still. The youngish man who was reading a paper-backed novel in yellow with a red title was still reading his novel.

Four minutes to go.

David decided to clear his mind of every thought and anxiety. Let it be emptied, and rest. That was the only way to stop the jitters. Hear no evil, see no evil, speak no evil. Like the three monkeys. Hear nothing, see nothing, speak nothing, *think* nothing. Not so easy, for as you swept thoughts out, scraps of them would slip past your broom back again. Like Mrs. Partington sweeping back the sea. Still, if you were persistent you *could* empty your mind, and then, people said, you got into communication with the Beyond. Whatever that was.

That had actually consumed two minutes. Two whole bloody minutes. Only two more to go.

David wondered what he should do if Mannheim was not on the train. That would mean that Mannheim had been arrested. There wouldn't be any other explanation. And there was nothing that he, David, could do, but go on to Frankfurt, take a train to France there, and be damn grateful if he didn't get it in the neck himself.

He half rose to start searching the train *now*. But that would only attract attention, and what good would it do?

Suddenly the porters began to shout to passengers to take their seats. Last minute good-byes began.

This train was going to go! This train was not going to be held up and searched! David nearly laughed aloud.

A few seconds later the carriages jerked and the train began to move. 2.45 exactly. As it moved slowly away, David looked back at the station. The London train still stood there, all lit up and motionless. The Gestapo was still looking for something it had not found.

David waited until the train was well out of the station and running in the open country before he began to walk down the corridor looking for Mannheim.

10

He moved cautiously along the corridor. The train swayed, and bumped him from side to side. Each German he met he seemed to cannon into; he who was above all anxious not to be noticed. And still he had not found Mannheim.

Tired. So tired. A monstrous yawn seized him. Worried though he was, he could not help wishing he could sleep. Just at that moment, when his attention had wandered, he collided with a short man dressed in his own yellow overcoat.

"Mann—" he said, and then cut himself short.

Mannheim pushed by him with unseeing eyes. "Excuse me," he said in German. "Is this the way to the restaurant car?"

"I believe so," said David.

"Many thanks." Mannheim rolled on like a teetotum bouncing from side to side of the corridor. David pressed back against the window, to allow passage to the man following Mannheim. He was taller, sallow and had a soft hat pulled over his face. He had a bony nose, and nothing in his manner or appearance gave any indication whether he was some kind of policeman or not.

After a few minutes of hesitation, David decided that Mannheim's words had been a hint. He followed him along to the restaurant car.

It was in semi-darkness. One or two tables alone were illuminated, and only one waiter was in attendance. At one table sat Mannheim, eating a plate of mixed sausage and drinking lager.

There was no sign of the tall man with the bony nose.

David looked round for a minute and then sat down at Mannheim's table.

He ordered a Munich Export-bier. Nothing to eat.

Neither spoke for several minutes. Then Mannheim finished his beer, rose up, bowed to David, and said in an undertone: "I will see you on the platform at Frankfurt."

"Bitte," said David. "Nine o'clock."

He finished his beer slowly, went back to his carriage and composed himself to rest. Anxiety, he thought, would prevent him sleeping; but it did not wholly. He had dozed off, with his mouth open, and was snoring most disagreeably, when a sharp jerk occurred and the train stopped.

He woke up in acute terror, sweat pouring down his face. He cursed himself under his breath when he saw that they had only stopped at a station. *Kreiensen.* "Kreiensen? Never heard of the place," he said to himself with a sense of personal injury.

But the same thing happened to him at each station. Sweat poured off him and his eyes bulged out with fear.

Gottingen.

Eichenberg.

Kassel.

At Kassel there was a wait of ten minutes and the train did not pull out till nearly six. Then, to his surprise, he fell deeply asleep and did not wake until the train was nearing Frankfurt. It was broad daylight by now. There was a steady rain, and a ticket collector was gently shaking him by the shoulder. David looked round the carriage. All the fellow passengers who had been in the compartment at Hanover had gone. The middle-aged lady had got out at

Gottingen; the others must have left during his sleep. That was a convenience.

"I got on at Hamburg," he told the collector. "I was late and am without a ticket. I must pay you."

"So," said the collector, holding the conversation in suspense for a moment while he considered. David looked respectable: moreover, the mere fact that he asked to pay from Hamburg was in his favour. A swindler would have pretended to have got on at a nearby station.

He took out a large yellow paper pad and made out the ticket. A short while later, David was standing on the platform at Frankfurt and watching Mannheim go out through the main exit. He followed him at a safe distance, saw him cross the square and join the queue for a tram. He joined the same queue; got on the same tram; and sat several seats away from Mannheim as it rattled through the crowded streets.

His heart was singing with relief and he grinned with delight as he watched the people pushing to and fro. Once again they were two ants in an antheap. Let the Gestapo hunt for them: they were safe for the minute. Bless all these busy, nameless Germans.

They picked on a crowded café and talked over coffee.

"Where did you tell the collector you had come from?" asked David.

"Gottingen."

"I said Hamburg. So when they check the tickets they will find two persons, one from Gottingen and a foreign speaking one from Hamburg. That will not be suspicious. Not for the moment. How good it is to drink coffee, and not to have to be frightened."

"We have only gone a little way," said Mannheim, more chillily. "Where can we go now?"

"Saarbrücken. Only four hours by train; and very near the French frontier. After that we must walk across the border. Somehow. We'll work that out when we come to it. But for the moment we can just take a peaceful train, like two peaceful citizens, from one German town to another. There are plenty of good trains. One goes at eleven. It gets in at twenty-past three.

"Meanwhile, let's eat."

11

Next morning two tourists left the *Zwei Schüssel* inn at Saar-brücken, both with rucksacks on their backs and with stout walking-sticks in their hands. Both were dark, but one, who spoke little, was tall and thin, and the other was older, shorter and stouter. They talked in German, clearly and in distinct voices, well in the hearing of the inn staff. It was made quite clear to everyone that they were on a walking tour and were going south-west, along the banks of the Saar. The taller man spoke chiefly in monosyllables, but the shorter was loquacious and had a north German accent.

A remarkable thing about them, perhaps, was that when they left the hotel they did exactly what they said they were going to do. They walked south-west, and they took the road that followed the course of the river. This was David's idea. If they were not being followed, he argued, there was no harm in telling the truth. If they were, their pursuers were sure to be aware that they were dodging and double-crossing on their own tracks. Consequently, if they left a heavily-marked trail pointing in one direction (and that the direction of France) their hunters would be certain it was false. That place would turn out to be the safest of all places to go to.

Mannheim had not been convinced, but he had said: "It is very well. I trust you. I have no other plan, even if I do not." He had, however, stipulated that they should talk German and appear to be German. The latter at least they did: nothing could have been more Germanic than their appearance as they walked along in the mild sunlight (the rain had passed with the previous day), the elder one at regular intervals pointing out the beauties of the countryside and receiving suitable expressions of admiration in return.

The road had but little traffic on it, but not until they had walked five miles did David decide that he could pass out of his assumed character.

"I think," he said, still speaking in German, "that we could almost decide we have not been followed. It would be funny if all this journey of ours was a complete mistake. I wonder whether we might not have gone straight on to Holland in the first place. After all, it is most probable that they do not even yet know you have escaped from Berlin."

"It would be more than funny," said Mannheim dourly. "It would be miraculous." He looked round as if expecting a policeman. But the road remained empty.

It should have reassured them both. But Mannheim's words had destroyed David's ease of mind. The road was so long, so straight, and so easy to be seen along all its length. Nothing could save them, David reflected, if a car searching for them were to appear even four or five miles away. They could be seen for miles. He felt as though an invisible watcher might be behind them all the time. Against his will he kept turning his head to look. Nothing, always nothing. And yet…A scrap of verse, half-remembered, kept running in his head:

> "As one that walks a weary road—"

What was it? "And having once turned round—"? And then it went on—

> "And turns no more his head
> Because he knows a frightful fiend
> Doth close behind him tread."

He found the strain too much. "Mannheim," he said. "We must get off this road. It's too obvious. Look at this map. If we take the next turning on the right; it's an old country road, winding and probably not much used. Certainly you can't see for miles along it. And it's in the direction of Forbach. We'll be on our way to the French frontier. Let's take it."

Mannheim nodded his head. They took the turning. It was a roughish road, with trees on each side. David felt unreasoningly as if the fiend had fallen at least several steps behind.

A short while after they had left the main road a powerful black car drove slowly along it, in the direction which they had been going. They saw it from a corner of their road, which had begun to climb. They stood still, behind a hedge, and watched it. They could not tell whether it was in fact looking for them. But it increased their disquiet. "I think," said Mannheim, "we had better separate there, where the lane divides. We are near the frontier, and one man can get across more easily than two. I will meet you at the Buffet de la Gare, Metz, in three days or four days. Or if not there, I will ask at Harry's Bar in Paris, and will leave a message. And if not there, and if I can get to London, I will present myself at your flat. Good-bye, my very kind and very generous friend." He spoke the last words in English, removed his hat, and gripped David's hand in a firm grasp.

12

Yet they never met.

Three days later, a very dishevelled German, still square and with a rather imperious manner, but exhausted, dirty and hungry, presented himself at the refugees' relief centre in Metz. He demanded to see the chief of the Bureau, startled him by offering an apparently valid British passport, and startled him still more by recounting briefly the story of

David's mission. After a little hesitation, the chief accepted his story, and went with him to the prefecture of police. How much he told the police is uncertain, but it secured for Mannheim the issue of a *permis de séjour*, which enabled him to live in France—with the exception of Paris, the north-eastern departments and the frontier departments.

He obeyed this order unprotestingly, until May, 1939, when he gained permission to cross to London. He settled in Croxburn and quietly and carefully observed all the regulations, and in due course was given employment in the chemical research side of a large munitions factory. He was arrested with others in the panicky round-up of 1940, but was released early. He lived a solitary life, renting the top half of a small furnished house. Nobody paid him much attention until Councillor Grayling suddenly denounced him to the police. Two days before the death, a Home Office man had called on him and made a few preliminary enquiries.

The same day as that on which the two had parted—indeed, only four hours later—David had been arrested in a German village. The charge was attempting to cross the frontier illegally and possessing seditious papers. If there were further charges connected with Mannheim, they were not published; but the sentence was five years in a fortress. There was immediate intervention by the British authorities; the German government reduced the sentence to one year, but would do no more.

In June, 1939, David was ceremoniously brought back to Saarbrücken, released, and put across the frontier. He took a train to Metz, and then another to Dijon. Here he fulfilled one of the projects which had occupied him for twelve months in a Nazi jail. He put up at the Hotel des Trois Faisans, and ordered the best dinner that he could conceive. He found that his memory tricked him. He could not construct as good a dinner as once he did. Still, he had eighteen different kinds of hors d'œuvre, with two glasses of manzanilla sherry; a sole cooked with mushrooms and red wine (*red* wine—there is such a way of cooking it, but this is not the place, nor is it now the time, to discuss it) with a 1924 Bâtard Montrachet; a roast pheasant with a Clos de Vougeot 1929; pancakes with Grand Marnier, flaming; coffee and Armagnac.

His stomach tricked him too. You cannot eat like that after twelve months in prison. He was wretchedly ill in the night, and spent the morning in bed. Only by 12 o'clock was he well enough to ask for a railroad time-table; and then he could not study it.

After some black coffee, he dressed, and examined what had been left in his wallet by the Germans. Nothing had been taken: not even his cryptic notes of the cases he cited to Mannheim. There was even the list of figures, the first and most puzzling of the Goltz documents, which he had failed to solve and had still been carrying around. He laid it down with a sigh and a smile: it reminded him of a much younger and, he assured himself, much more foolish man.

Then he turned to the railroad time-table again.

Dijon—Laroche-Migennes—Paris (P.L.M.), he read.

That was the line. He painfully ran his finger along the columns, and then suddenly a little mystery became clear. There was something familiar about this line:

Laroche-Migennes: 5.25 6.50 7.00 7.45 8.00 8.15 8.25 8.30 8.35 8.45 9.15 10.15 12.00 12.50 13.00 13.10. He checked it up. Yes. The figures were the same as on his slip of paper. Someone had jotted down the times of trains at Laroche-Migennes. That was all. Hours of subtlety had been wasted on trying to decipher it. All it meant was, a man had wanted to catch a train.

David laughed aloud, and wondered if Mannheim got through, and what Preston and Diana were doing. That stirred memories and hopes. He decided to go to Paris that night, and, after a little reasonable enjoyment, on to London.

Less or more expeditiously, that was what he did. He made no effort at all to find Mannheim when he got to London, and had only a perfunctory contact with Preston; Diana he sought out with more zeal. Prison has a marked effect on a human being, but they are in error who claim that it has a purifying effect. It had given David a more exact knowledge of his wishes with regard to the fair-haired young woman, and a stronger impetus towards securing them. It had dulled and coarsened his technique: her first evening at his flat was partly spent in resisting rape. He also talked a little crudely about a month in France.

She escaped from him and sat on the floor, her chin on her knees.

"France," she said. "Paris."

"Paris in August?" he said, too quickly assuming consent, and already trying to amend her choice.

"Yes, Paris in August," she said, looking at him queerly. "You don't have to offer me France, you know. I'll…" she hesitated, and turned pink. "I'll do what you want. Not *now,* instantly: keep off. But I will, and you don't have to pay me. But if you want to give me France as a present too…" She looked much less a woman of the world as her sentence trailed away.

For that portion of life which remained for him, David's most vivid memory was of the next three weeks; his most acute single picture that of a short-haired golden head on a pillow, a white shoulder, and an arm folded beneath the head.

September, 1939, called them back to London: David was one of the earliest casualties of the R.A.F.

"I'm not ashamed he had what he wanted," said Diana, violently and unprovoked, to her mother.

"Not ashamed!" exclaimed that pale lady. "You're openly delighted."

"Yes. I *am* delighted," said her daughter, and added: "It's funny. We never even hunted up that German, and it really was all because of his rescuing him that I did anything."

"I don't know what you mean," said her mother.

Chapter VIII

*	Eileen Doreen Grant •	A Workman	*
*	Gladys Grant •	A Workman	*
*	Hugh Rolandson	The Vicar	*
*	A. Mannheim	H. J. Grayling	×
*	Cpl. George Ransom	C. J. F. Evetts	*

"I've got reports now on most of the people in the Grayling case," said Inspector Holly. "They don't take us much further. The strongest motive seems to be that German's. If we actually knew who he was, I feel I'd be almost certain. If we knew what Grayling was going on when he denounced him, that would probably answer the question. But I can't find out if Grayling had any reasons, and Inspector Atkins tells me the Home Office are rather worried too. He left no papers except bills and such things, his widow says.

"Grayling was right about Mannheim having, or anyhow using, a bicycle; and there is a radio set in the house to which he used to listen. That's forbidden, and Mannheim has been arrested. He'll be fined. That's all there is about that. The serious thing is, of course, Grayling's charge that this person isn't Mannheim at all, but a Nazi spy impersonating him. Nobody seems to be able to check on that at all. Mannheim, of course, denies it fiercely. Grayling was quite capable of imagining the story out of spite, at that."

"Surely," said the Superintendent, "they can find out a thing like that. Somebody must have vouched for the German when he came here."

"Yes," said Holly. "An R.A.F. boy who's dead now, and a French official who lived in Metz and hasn't come out of France. It seems, too, that there's no German refugee here whom they trust who knew the real Mannheim in Germany at all well."

"He's a skilled chemist, though, whoever he is, isn't he?"

"Exactly so, sir."

"If Grayling had evidence which would prove him to be a Nazi spy, he'd have been shot, I suppose. Certainly the best motive up to date for murder. If a Nazi needs a motive for murder. Knowledge, motive, opportunity."

"Yes, I know, sir," replied Holly. "But as yet we've no direct evidence. Still, he's under lock and key, and *he* at least won't get away.

"I've been enquiring about the other passengers in the carriage, just to complete the list. There was, you remember, a middle-aged lady who had a small girl with her, who had a cold. They sat in the corner farthest away from Mr. Grayling. Well, we found them fairly easily. They live in Whetnow. The lady is a Mrs. Gladys Grant, wife of a small builder, Grant Brothers Ltd. The child is her daughter, Eileen Doreen. The daughter goes to a High School in London, very superior the mother told me, called The Lady Marguerite's School; and that day the Principal had rung up to say that Eileen did not look well, so Mrs. Grant had gone down to town to fetch her home, and true enough she developed flu; but you'll be glad to know she's better now. Mrs. Grant says she never heard of Mr. Grayling, and didn't notice him at all, having other things to think of. And Eileen says she was much too ill to notice anything at all; she just nestled close to Mummy all the way.

"The Grants are a very respectable family, the local men say; and I don't see any reason to question the story."

"It's a relief to find somebody of whom one needn't be suspicious," remarked the Superintendent.

Chapter IX

*	Eileen Doreen Grant	A Workman	*
*	Gladys Grant	A Workman	*
*	Hugh Rolandson •	The Vicar	*
*	A. Mannheim	H. J. Grayling	×
*	Cpl. George Ransom	C. J. F. Evetts	*

"Hugh," she said, sleepily, "you'd better go." She must have forgotten she had already told him once to go, and he was standing outside the bed looking down at her. She flung one arm out of the bed and it fell along the counterpane, drawing down the bedclothes and exposing one white breast, small and unspoilt; if it was not quite such a firm round as it once had been, Hugh Rolandson was not the man to know it. She turned her head towards him, but did not open her eyes. She let herself sink into the pillow, profile outlined against the white, and in a few seconds was deep in the sleep of satisfied exhaustion.

Hugh wrapped the thin silk dressing-gown round his chilling body and watched his lover. *I shall never know another moment like this in all my life*, he thought. *I cannot ever have a sharper happiness or a greater pleasure. I am going to fix every detail in my mind so that for years afterwards the memory shall be as clean and clear as this minute is.*

The common consensus of opinion is often right and convention may be a good guide even in unconventionality. Could any place but Paris have provided so perfect a romance?

There are no good words to explain, to those who do not know it, the keenness of the emotion he was feeling. It is a special thing. He was young; he was romantic; eight hours earlier he had been a virgin. It was six o'clock in the morning, in Paris in the year 1939, in spring, in an hotel on the banks of the Seine. His mistress was a few years older than he, experienced, and undeniably lovely. There was such a concentration of delight that he could scarcely contain it. He had the serenity of full satisfaction and at the same time a consciousness that he was only at the start of the most exciting and pleasurable period of his life. He had had all—much more than all—he had ever hoped for, and yet knew it was only the beginning.

Long bars of pale reddish light from the rising sun flooded into the bedroom from the tall french window. He saw every detail of the room, in the thin light, with the sharp-edged clarity of early morning. He imprinted on his mind the disorder of the narrow room. There were some lilies of the valley, which he had bought the evening before, drooping a little in a glass placed in front of the mirror. There was a pile of feminine clothes, half on and half off a chair, with small silk garments at the top. Even an unfinished quarter tumbler of brandy on a small table was important to him; he fixed its position in his mind. Underneath the heavy scent of the flowers was a sharp smell of alcohol. He walked to the long window and looked out. The street was empty in the weak sun; he stood for several minutes and watched the river run smooth and silent beyond the parapet, looking through the range of tall, slender, closely set trees, already bursting into leaf. This was Paris; here Renata had been his lover.

He turned round to look at her again. Brown, short hair on the pillow, finely traced features, eyes closed but with shadows beneath them; arm, shoulder, breast. Still, but breathing gently and quietly. He felt a sudden rush of feeling that he could not analyse, a constriction as if he was going to cry.

He waited for the crisis to pass, and when it had, deliberately remembered the night, passing from the clear light to the warm darkness. With no passion left, he recalled carefully every detail; and the blood rushed to his face again. Earlier in the evening, touched by his devotion and remembering her own past, she had said to him: "You make me feel secondhand." He had not understood her; he was not capable, at the moment, of comprehending anything that seemed to suggest a criticism of her. It had only underlined his own feeling of yokellish clumsiness and inexpertness, and the greatness of her condescension. He stood at the door a minute before he slipped away to his room, and again recorded to himself that he did not deserve what he had received.

Neither later that day, nor afterwards, did Renata show if her emotions were equally stirred. She was as graceful as a cat, and she was as secretive. She gave him plenty of evidences of affection, but no signs that she had been shaken off her balance. Yet she had taken a very great risk. Her husband, the Councillor, was jealous and morose; and to go to Paris for a long week-end of adultery was at the least rash. The alibi she had constructed for herself might easily collapse. Once before she had taken a much less risk; and before her marriage she had made one experiment. This was more serious.

But if she was worried she did not show it.

It was a Saturday morning on which Hugh had watched the sun rise. They spent the day at Versailles because it was the cheapest way they went by the State railway. The carriage was packed and Renata—he was beginning to learn to call her Renée—sat on a folding seat at the end of the carriage, near to the unclosed and uncloseable door. The railway runs through narrow, bush or tree-covered cuttings. Hugh silently watched her sitting there, motionless and calm, the green leaves racing past her head. When they came near the station, she rose, smoothed her dress, and called him by lifting her eyebrows. He came as swiftly and adoringly as a dog.

As there has not been, for two hundred years, any town to equal Paris for what the journalists call a week-end of love, so there has never been a park for lovers to equal Versailles. There are no fountains to equal that astonishing battery when it plays; no trees like the monster quincunxes that Louis planted; no ornamental gardens like Marie Antoinette's playground. The long vista of squared waters seen from the Palace has been imitated from Leningrad to Washington; but this is the original.

They walked away from the Palace, down the great steps and past the first of the great rectangles of water. They turned off among the huge trees, among the partly overgrown and wholly overshadowed gravel walks and perennial green hedges, dark and a little damp after the brilliant warmth of the sunlight. Soon they came to a dusty, white side-road, with a waiting line of horsecabs in the sun and shabby cabmen, a kiosk, and large notice-boards containing *Regulations for Hippomobile Vehicles*. They stood in the sun; and laughed at the notice; and refused solicitations to ride in a hippomobile vehicle.

After a minute or two they turned and went to the Petit Trianon. Renata stopped on one of the bridges in the Queen's play-village and looked at the thickly struggling mass of fish in the stream. "Those are carp," said Hugh, remembering the guide book. "They're very old. They saw the Revolution. Marie Antoinette stocked the stream. Or perhaps they're only the descendants," he corrected uneasily.

"I know," said Renata, and held on to the stone parapet silently for a second or two. "I never walk about here—I've been here before—without feeling unreal," she went on. "I don't mean feeling that *it's* unreal, but that I'm somehow out of place; or rather out of time, I suppose I mean. Did you ever hear about the two English spinsters?"

Hugh indicated ignorance.

"I forget exactly what the story was intended to prove. Something about reincarnation, or perhaps it was Dunne's time theory. Anyway, I read about it once. There were two middle-aged English spinsters before the war—about 1906, I think it was—walking in the Trianon, just about where we are, I suppose, when they noticed that it all seemed very empty. I think the first thing definitely queer that they saw was a man in what they thought was fancy dress, outside one of those wooden imitation peasant huts, walking up and down waiting for something or somebody. He was in a very bad temper and dressed like the eighteenth century. I forget whether he saw them or not; but the next person did see them; he was a woodman or park attendant in uniform and he seems to have been very surprised. And one of the old ladies described exactly what his uniform was, and it was something like the uniform of the attendants about 1788, but not quite right. So, because it wasn't quite right, it was taken as proof that the old girls' story was made up; but apparently later investigation into the records kept here showed that the Court was always fiddling round with the uniform and for quite a short period of one year just exactly those changes had been made. Well, when they got out of here into the main gardens the two Englishwomen began to hear some thin and pretty music and one of them was able to reproduce it afterwards more or less. Also they saw a great crowd of people in the distance, all in eighteenth-century dress. I forget how it ended or what exactly the proofs were; but I believe the evidence seemed to suggest that they had actually found themselves somehow in the middle of a *fête champêtre* given by Marie Antoinette on some particular day for which that music had been composed, and while those changes in the uniform had been enforced."

"Do you believe that?" said Hugh.

"Of course not," she answered. "There is some explanation—some sane explanation, I mean. But while you were reading it it was very convincing. I only mentioned it because I feel like those two old women. All this doesn't belong to *us*, or to the rest of the tourists wandering round here. I wouldn't in the least be surprised to find the trees suddenly smaller and younger, the peasant houses inhabited by courtiers, and the fish only a few, small, new, carp. It's we who aren't real; this belongs to other people; and it isn't dead yet, like a museum is."

"I don't mind being a ghost, in a place like this," said Hugh, smiling and looking up, to where the branches of the elms interlocked and formed a green ceiling through which bright blue shone in squares and diamonds and broken shapes.

"'Your ghost will walk, you lover of trees,'" she answered, a half-embarrassed quotation, to cover her lapse from reason.

"I love other things than trees," he said, looking down at her with an affection that was almost fatuous.

They walked back to the main gardens, found a warm place on the edge of the trees, not too far from the artificial lakes, and lay down. They watched the sun make patterns on the grass, through the leaves of the trees, and flash irregularly in the water as it was troubled by the fountains. Both were tired; dark rings were under Renata's eyes.

"Don't let's be ashamed," quoted Hugh suddenly, "'if the knowing know, We rose from rapture but an hour ago,'" and then blushed scarlet and nearly apologized. She held his hand firmly for a moment; her fingers were thin, long and strong. "You ought," she said contritely, "to get to know more about the facts of life. I'm really rather a bitch, but I suppose it's no use telling you that."

It was no use. He did not even trouble to say so. She chose, for her own reasons no doubt, to say such things about herself; but they had no meaning, and he did not regard them. All that mattered for him was how to keep the unexampled privileges he had secured, how to retain the graciousness of this marvellous, self-contained and experienced lover, how to hide his incompetence and rusticity. To this he devoted himself steadily until they caught the early morning Boulogne–Folkestone train on Tuesday. He recollected anxiously all that he had ever known, or been told, about Paris restaurants and cafés. That night he took her down to Montparnasse, and they had aperitifs on the terrace of a café called the Closerie des Lilas, looking at an iron statue of Marshal Ney on a horse, half-hidden among young yellow-green leaves. They drank a mixture called mandarin-citron, a bitter highly alcoholic brown liquid, with a dash of syrup, soda, and ice. It was exhilarating and (though they did not find this out till later) slightly purgative. They went on to a small restaurant called for unknown reasons the Negro of Toulouse, and ate what was no more than an ordinarily good Parisian dinner; that is, it was greatly superior to anything that could be got without prevision and thought in London or New York. A dignified man in black, with a flowing cerise tie and large belly, stopped in front of the restaurant, took a violin out of a shabby case, tucked it underneath his partly-shaved chin and began to play and sing "I kiss your little hand, Madame." The French was "*Ce n'est que votre main, madame.*" He noticed the English couple, bowed, and began to sing and play a more ambitious number, unknown to Hugh and obscure in tune, which seemed to be called "*Ce ne fut qu'un moment de folie.*" Hugh was enraptured and sent him twenty francs: Renata said nothing, but watched her lover. Her expression might have been anguish, guilt, maternal anxiety, plain love, or even for a moment humility; it passed almost at once.

Lovers' nights are all the same, and yet never the same. He felt, in the quieter delights of Saturday, as if he had been shown, in order that he might know everything, what love would be like with Renée (the name was coming easier now, though he still sometimes pronounced it Renie) after years of married life. An absence of hysteria, a quiet confidence of affection. He did not hope for married life with her; he knew it was impossible, and why, anyhow, should he expect it? (If he could have expected it, would he have felt the same way about her? He would have had to have been much older to ask, let alone answer, such a question.) Only, he wished for a fleeting minute that he could have stayed all night with her. Surely, in a small Paris hotel, there was no one to ask questions. But she had said what she wanted, and he had to do as he was told. Perhaps she just preferred to have her bed to herself. He looked for a longer time, that dawn, out of the window. He craned his neck and could see the statue of Ste. Genevieve, patron saint of Paris. It is (or was; it may not still stand) a white torso rising from one of the pillars of a bridge across the Seine. It looks eternally, watchfully, and ultimately in vain, to the East. He wondered about it for an idle minute. It was probably, he thought, symbolic.

Watching for the German invader. He disliked the thought and forgot it.

That Sunday, wiser than he was, she demanded exercise and made him take her to Fontainebleau. They walked the whole day in the forest, among the great trees, and had lunch in a small inn on the western edge of it. The road outside was white and sunny; inside it was dark and almost too cool. The room was furnished with wooden tables on a few of which were blue and white check cloths. On the walls were an advertisement of Rossi vermouth (an orange), the faded text of the LOI SUR L'IVRESSE, the words DUBO DUBON DUBONNET and an elaborate announcement of a society called *La Chablisienne*, which had been formed to combat the pernicious habit of *le cocktèle*, so destructive to population, and had therefore arranged that a glass of genuine Chablis could be purchased for 3 fr. 50, which was an *œuvre de remoralisation,* and in this work of remoralizing they joined.

The meal was simple and very cheap. The hors d'œuvre contained most of the things that they expected, and in addition a dish of what looked like sliced rubber and gristle in oil and vinegar but which turned out to be very tasty, masticable (though only just), but ultimately enigmatic. There was next a great deal of veal in a dark orange-coloured sauce, fruit which was no more than reasonably good, and the cheese which is called Pont l'evêque, in excellent condition. The wine was a light red burgundy named Juliénas, which does not travel well but is very rarely bad (as it is also very rarely extremely good; it was in this case neither). Hugh, who was still young, took with his coffee a liqueur called Parfait Amour, and wished he had not. Renata asked for brandy—*fine maison*—and to her distress realized she had humiliated him once more by showing a greater knowledge of the world. She did all that she could by holding his hand under the table and smiling at him.

That was their Sunday. At night, their lovemaking was little more than the equivalent of the brief kiss of two tired but affectionate people; he did not stay with her and was, to his surprise, glad to lie in his bed and sleep uninterruptedly, peacefully, and very late into the morning.

They spent what was left of the morning wandering Paris like tourists. There was a flower market by the riverside, not far from the Prefecture of Police; she prevented him with difficulty from loading her with new bouquets of lilies of the valley. They walked around the tiny Ile St. Louis, and were surprised to see how much it still resembled a small French village set down in the middle of the city. They went north of the river and spent a lot of time and some appreciable amount of money in a shop called Le Bon Rire Gaulois, on small practical jokes, including a toilet roll which released a black snake, a sort of whistle which could be placed beneath a cushion and would make an indecorous noise when anyone sat down on it, and a cruet which was composed of tiny models of necessary domestic china articles. In the afternoon they went to the pictures, to see a French film that Hugh did not understand.

That night, Monday night, was their last night. They said good-bye ardently; at one point Renata told Hugh to look away (which he obediently did) for she found she was quietly weeping for no reason that she knew. They separated next midday at Victoria, hurriedly and without a word. Fear and calculation had returned to them as soon as they passed the Customs at Folkestone.

◇◇◇

It is almost certain that Renata Grayling's chief anxiety, as she sat in the train for Croxburn on that morning of 1939, was not for her husband's possible clairvoyance, but for her own balance. Ever since she had begun to think about herself connectedly at all, her chief object had been to secure her own poise. She must be in control of herself and, so, in control of what happened around her. She could not order the world, that she knew; but she could make sure that the world did not overcome her. Her chief characteristic—she had decided it as early as fourteen years old—should be a calm superiority to outward circumstances, an elegant nonchalance, a self-adequacy which would not be upset by anything outside herself. Dignity was not the word: it was rather the sure self-possession of a woman of the world which was (she decided) the only reliable protection except money.

Age is more important in women's lives than in men. Here, then, are the dates. Renata Grayling, *née* Torrens, was born in 1904. She was fifteen in 1919, the first year of peace. She was twenty when she married Grayling. She was thirty-five when she went to Paris with Hugh Rolandson, probably as beautiful as she ever would be (which was, at the least, exceedingly good-looking), full of vigour and ambition, but not with the future before her. She was thirty-eight when her husband died. Nearly forty.

All through her life, she had concentrated her attention, successfully, on controlling herself, on being (as she phrased it to herself) in the driving seat of herself. Only in Paris had it seemed, for a minute, as if the car would run away with the driver; and that would be terrifying. For all her life had enforced on her the moral that "They"—the outside world—would oppress her if they could, if she let anyone but herself for one minute gain any control.

Her father, Clarence Kirkpatrick Torrens, had been Senior Classical Master at a reputable boys' school on the South Coast which was already in 1904 at the beginning of slow decline. Parents even then were wondering whether

they were really wise to send their boys to be flogged by
Mr. Torrens and taught Latin and Greek and very little else;
in the years in which Renata grew up, more and more of
them decided they were not. Mr. Torrens had never been
a jovial man: the slow decay of his prospects and the death
of his wife in 1909 made him finally into a morose one.
His six children were named Alexander, Desiderius, and
Augustine (the boys) and Alethea, Sophronia and Renata
(the girls). It might have been conjectured from their names
that he was a classical scholar, and a second deduction could
have been that he was High Church. In fact, he had not
taken his religion seriously until shortly before the birth of
Renata: he then became consciously an Anglican (he had
been nominally one all his life) and proceeded slowly but
steadily towards Roman Catholicism. Shortly after his wife's
death he became convinced that he ought to have been a
priest, and celibate. He found in this belief a consolation
for his worldly ill-success; but at the same time the sight of
his children became an offence to him. They were present
reminders that he was not a priest, that even if his convic-
tions did, as they intermittently threatened to, carry him
into the Roman Church, it would have to be at the cost of
repudiating his whole past life, or of remaining a layman.

He treated his family, as he believed, with exact justice.
He did not reflect on any need they might have for the
affection their mother would have shown them, or on his
possible duty to replace her. He showed them the way to
the love of God, which was greater than any mortal love, by
means of morning and evening prayers; he disciplined them
for untruthfulness, uncleanliness, or noise. For the rest, he
treated them exactly as he did his pupils, without favouritism
of any kind. That, incidentally, included punishing them not
infrequently in the somewhat indecent manner common in
boys' schools of the last generation. He made, in pursuance

of his principle of fairness, no difference between the sexes. There is nothing like intermittent beating on the bare posteriors in adolescence to encourage in after life an almost morbid determination to keep one's life wholly private, and to forbid others even the most indirect control or the most innocent and emotional rights.

Renata was not worse treated than her brothers and sisters, but she was ill-served by her age. She was thirteen and fourteen in the last two years of the first world war: that is to say, like most English children, she suffered from a slight lack of sugar and meat and a grave lack of fats in 1917, intensified in 1918. This left a marked effect on her physique—she was pallid, leggy, spotty, and underweight. She wanted to be called "Diane," because of a picture entitled *Diane de Poitiers* in her father's encyclopaedia, but the family did not encourage romantic dreaming. Her brothers called her Skinny and told her the only place she had any fat was on her bottom. They could be excused: she was not pretty. Her brown hair was sparse and done in two plaits, she was gauche and ill-mannered.

Her emancipation was by no act of her own. The very day after her decision already mentioned to cultivate poise and self-adequacy, her father spanked her quite smartly with the study door wide open. The younger children laughed, with the treachery of their kind, and tears and humiliation were all her lot. It was an event which was repeated more than once, even after her fifteenth birthday: twenty years later she had not quite forgotten the sensation. One July evening in 1919, her father, finding some fault with her and Desiderius, her seventeen-year-old brother, strapped her moderately severely—enough to reduce her to tears—and then turned to her brother.

Desiderius, watching his sister's ignoble struggles, had made up his mind. He seized his father's right hand and twisted it sharply, so that the strap fell out.

"How dare you?" thundered the schoolmaster.

Desiderius' answer was to twist his father's arm in the way he had learnt at school. He discovered his muscles were better than the older man's: he nearly twisted his father to his knees.

"If you ever try to touch me again, I'll *break* your arm," he said.

The two glared at each other. After a minute the father walked away.

"And leave the kid alone too," called Desiderius after him, with lordly generosity.

◇◇◇

There can have been fewer young women of eighteen more unfit to take care of themselves than Renata Torrens in 1920. Her father never attempted to reassert himself after his defeat by Desiderius, even though his son left the house three months later. He withdrew himself, allowing her the minimum of pocket money, offering neither enmity nor affection, nor, for days on end, even conversation. He would not, if he could avoid it, speak to her or to any of his children. He expected of her, as his financial circumstances declined, more domestic duties, which she fulfilled fairly adequately. She was not well clothed, but gained considerable skill in making a good show from poor materials. She still regarded herself humbly as an ugly girl, the automatic derision of her family preventing her knowing that she was developing a brown-haired, pale, slightly elfin beauty. She read all the modern books that she could get from the local library, indiscriminately but eagerly. She was not qualified for any work—not even as a shop girl or a typist—and her acquaintances in the High School she had just left were silly. It was an especial misfortune that not one of her friends' mothers took an interest in the lonely girl.

She was in consequence, as Brandon Lee told his friends, a pushover. He seduced her, with an ease that astonished himself, on a July afternoon. She had been flattered and surprised at the short but enthusiastic court paid to her by one who was incontestably the beau of the town. He had been a pupil at her father's school, and even there had been adored by his juniors of both sexes (including herself), and by at least one indiscreet senior, wife of one of the staff. That he should have picked her out from among the girls of their acquaintance, even for a week, astonished her. She walked proudly with him along the esplanade, dressed in a blue coat and skirt, which she had herself made over into a well-fitting garment, hands thrust clenched into its pockets, swinging along with a free long stride, a wild surmise forming in her mind. Perhaps she was not the ugly duckling she had been; perhaps others than the great Brandon could see beauty in her. When, after scarcely a week, he claimed, and with smooth efficiency took, complete intimacy, she made no resistance. She was not, yet, sufficiently proud to do so; and in any case she wanted to lose her ignorance. He reassured her against possible consequences and called her "my sweet Ipsithilla." Not till she consulted her father's Catullus at home did she discover that Ipsithilla was a cheap harlot, and that all she had immediately received from Brandon was an insult in Latin and some physical discomfort.

But she had ultimately been given something else. Brandon wanted to continue to hang round her: she gave him his *congé* with serene assurance. His attentions, and her mirror, had assured her of one thing. She was no longer an ugly gawk, a skinny Lizzie, a duck's-bottom or any of the things that the nursery had called her. She knew now she was a pretty young woman—perhaps more than pretty—she could cut others out, she could charm men, and (she considered) she had experienced all life had to give and found it worthless. Immune from temptation, new in poise and assurance; she would marry for money and remove herself from her father's home as soon as she could.

Her fulfilment of that programme had not been as successful as she wished. Two years after Brandon Lee's exploit she became engaged to, and shortly after married, Councillor Henry Grayling of Croxburn, who was staying for a fortnight's holiday at the Grand. He was over forty and already established in his habits, which consisted of regular attendance at the office and the Council, with the sole relaxation of bridge with fellow councillors. He wanted a wife who would increase his position in the community, entertain his friends as he wished, and give him children. He picked on Renata because she was very attractive, because she encouraged him openly, and because she had no money and would be in his power. He did not get what he wanted: she would not have children, and was bored with his friends. He was not even able to control her financially to anything like the extent he had expected.

She, on her side, wanted a rich husband who would make few demands and would provide her with a comfortable home and the base for a full life. She found she had married a man who was moderately well off only—his salary was not high and his peculations limited—and very parsimonious. His friends were dreary, middle-aged and dull; he disapproved of the books she read, and of the conversations she tried to carry on. He was as narrow and tyrannous as her father; though he did not try to beat her he had other physical rights over her which he exercised according to a punctually kept time-table. She was convinced (being twenty years old, healthy, and a woman) that she had cast from herself all illusions of the flesh and of romance: she was greatly surprised at the annoyance caused her by the continued proximity of this grey, sour husband, smelling perpetually of stale tobacco.

Her second escapade, which she remembered in humiliation in Paris, was undertaken wholly in revenge on her husband. She found in Cellini's memoirs a phrase about one of his models whom he rather disliked: "I lay with her to vex her and her family." Appreciating it, she lay with Richard Grannison (a cheerful, rather greedy reddish-faced man who had entertained her expensively) in order to vex her husband. She never told him of her evening's occupation; her revenge was private. To her mild surprise, she rather enjoyed the experience, though not sufficiently keenly to wish to repeat it. She found Grannison a very kind and quite unsentimental man: she learnt in one afternoon that a cynical attitude to affairs of the heart was quite compatible with gentleness and (as she thought) a fundamentally civilized behaviour. He talked to her afterwards with the ease of a practised man about town, assuming at the first an equal degree of sophistication in her. "Why, you're blushing," he said after a minute. "Let me see. Do you blush all over, or only your face?" She burned even redder and held down the clothes. "You…" she began to say and stopped. What she really meant was the equivalent of "You are a one!" or "You do say such things!" observations she had abandoned about the age of fifteen; and she felt humiliated that she had advanced no further. She said something, inevitably incoherent, about "broad daylight."

He sat upright, and bent over her, his eyes bright with the zeal of the propagandist. "Darling," he said, "you mustn't be Victorian. You have got to consider these things practically. Afternoons are the time for seduction. Anatole France proved it long ago."

He stood up to deliver his discourse. He picked up his dressing-gown, which was silk, purple with large yellow sunflowers on it, put it on and strode up and down in it. He looked Neronic, and the subject of his oration would have suited the early Roman empire.

"Consider the whole question in the light of reason," he adjured her. "The conventional night out. What does it mean? Why, creeping home about five in the morning, very tired and uncomfortable, with none of the buses or trains running, and probably no taxi available. One is unshaven and probably has an unpleasant mouth. If you are a man who runs the usual ménage, you are terrified of making a noise as you come in and facing questions afterwards. You are exhausted and irritable the rest of the day; and what, I ask you, are your last recollections of the girl friend? You saw her in the light of early morning: she was probably half asleep, with her mouth open, and she might be snoring."

He stroked her hair with his hand and reflected that there was no point in adding that her make-up might be disturbed. Two small dashes of lipstick were all that Renata needed in those days.

"And then think of the afternoon" (he resumed). "You get up—you have a cocktail (I am going to order one in a minute). Your last intimate recollection of your friend is of her in complete command of herself, in what the eighteenth-century poets called a sweet disorder. As lovely as you look this moment, my dear. You part about four or five o'clock—bland, cheerful, unchallengeable. Nobody knows that you have been occupied otherwise than innocently. You remember each other as we, I hope, will remember each other. I hope you will think of me as clean and well-shaved, and as cheerful after a large dry Martini. That is what I am going to order, and I have remembered that you like a Clover Club. And I shall certainly remember you as beautiful as you are now, and as chic as you were when you came—and as you will be when you take my arm downstairs. I shall say 'Good afternoon, Mrs. Grayling! It has been a pleasure meeting you,' and that understatement will end a perfect afternoon."

He sent her flowers for two years running on the anniversary and thereafter forgot.

It was much more her continued association with her husband than her one escapade with Grannison which had made her feel grubby and secondhand in face of Hugh's adoration. It made her, too, a little frightened—not that Hugh would "find out" in any vulgar sense, for she had told him her history and been listened to without comprehension, but that some time the excitement would pass and he would see in her a not-so-young, cheapened suburban councillor's wife. Was she deceiving him? No. Was it her duty to prevent him deceiving himself? No. Could she prevent him, if it had been her duty? No. The sequence of question and answer should have been satisfactory and was not.

◇◇◇

The partner in her bad bargain did not know quite how bad his bargain was, but he too was discontented enough. He was the more consciously, and the more quickly, discontented, because he had from the beginning regarded the marriage as a transaction—as an important step in a career which had consisted in a steady, if slow, acquisition. He had acquired money, a limited amount, but satisfactory according to his standards; power, limited in area but satisfactory in its area; possessions and position of the kind to which he aspired. He had made no serious error before, and if anyone had been worsted in his life it had not been he. This was his first failure.

He had been an only child, late-born, of hardworking and poor parents. He had been sickly in his youth, a spotty, timid boy in knee-breeches attending a private school which taught him indifferently and had pretensions to snobbery. His education had consumed nearly all his parents' money. What remained had been just enough to send him to a London commercial college where he was taught "business method," of which the only valuable part was accountancy. He had taken a junior clerkship at Barrow and Furness's before 1914. His career was interrupted only a short while by the war. He "attested" early in 1916 to avoid conscription, was passed B 1 by an indolent doctor, and broke down in two months. He was invalided out, was taken on again at the bottom of the ladder by his firm, and had never left them since. His progress had been maddeningly slow, not because he was inefficient (he was noticeably neither efficient nor inefficient), but because in 1919 the management reinstated such of their old employees as returned from the war. They demoted him to make room for them; he bitterly resented this as an injustice, but dared nor protest. He restarted climbing the ladder. One year was like another year; promotion was very slow, salary increases small but regular. He lived with his parents till they died; then he moved to one of the innumerable houses built in the London suburbs which he purchased, as did a thousand neighbours, on a mortgage through a building society. He employed a middle-aged cousin as a housekeeper. It was partly to get rid of her that he married.

It is not in his emotional but in his financial history that the mainspring of his life could be found. Henry Grayling was honest in private and in business, but publicly dishonest—a system of morals more common than is often realized. He would have regarded it as crazy to attempt to swindle his employers, and as bad policy to cheat his friends, but he had no hesitation in robbing the public. He recognized, indeed, that he had better be careful, just as a man who rides in a train farther than his ticket entitles him to go realizes he had better be careful. But he had no more sense of guilt than the thousands of London tram, tube, and bus passengers who override their stage each year. He regarded himself quite honestly as a man with a high standard of morals.

He did not enter local politics originally with any corrupt intention, but merely as part of his plan for social advancement. He had joined the Conservative Club (from which the local "Ratepayers' Association" was run), while his parents were still living. When Croxburn was first constituted as Urban District and allowed a Council, he was a candidate at that first almost uncontested election; by the time it achieved the rank of Borough he was so well established that it was unthinkable that he should lose his seat. At most elections he was unopposed; all he had to do was to issue a brief election address, printed locally on shiny paper with a smudgy half-tone of himself (in an oval frame, and taken by a local photographer), assuring the citizens of Croxburn of his continued devotion to their interests.

Quite possibly he would have been contented with the increase in importance that his new status gave him, if he had not been elected to the Finance and General Purposes Committee, on the grounds that as the cashier of a big firm he would be highly qualified. He watched the proceedings of his colleagues silently for some time: he suspected irregularities and even partially exposed one. Nothing came to the ears of the public on that occasion, nor to those of the District Auditor, but it was understood by fellow councillors that Mr. Grayling's broad hint was the cause of the resignation of the Deputy Mayor on grounds of ill-health. Taxed with it one evening by an Alderman—P. H. Robbins, a stationer, not very influential—Grayling declined to reply except in general terms. "I don't," he said, "claim that for a man to make a reasonable profit out of his knowledge is a serious crime. I have moved about the world; I am a practical man.

But what I say is this: municipal finance nowadays is very closely overlooked. If a councillor or official is found out doing what he shouldn't, it shakes public confidence as well as ruining him. And he *is* very likely to be found out. As to whether I've had any reasons to suspect anything recently, and whether I've acted on these suspicions—that I ought not to say. All I will say is that, if anything like that occurred, it would be to everyone's advantage if the person who had been so ill-advised decided of his own will to retire from the scene."

Alderman Robbins looked at the Councillor admiringly over the edge of his cup of cocoa and repeated these profound aphorisms during the next week to all who would listen. Grayling's reputation went up among all municipal politicians of sense; a week later he accepted membership of the small committee which controlled the Croxburn Municipal Gasworks.

He had had his eye on this committee for some time. It consisted of five: the Town Clerk, the General Manager, who was the Town Clerk's brother-in-law, Councillor J. G. King (whom Grayling replaced), Alderman Robbins who was insignificant, and Councillor Peter Fairley who was interested in a local tileworks and was believed to have a finger in several other enterprises.

By opening his eyes and shutting his mouth he noticed reasons to believe that peculation could, and probably did, occur, though direct monkeying with the funds was impossible: the District Auditor made it far too dangerous.

He spent an enormous amount of time trying to find out what was going on, and how he could get in on it. It was for a while the problem of his life, on which he spent more thought and energy than on anything that had come his way—certainly more than on his marriage. He lived with the question—slept with it, ate with it, worked with it.

Ultimately he decided there were probably four methods of corruption, and began to make notes on them in a private shorthand. But he was a careful man; it was just possible that some day someone might find his notes and decipher them. He recast them, therefore, heading them "Matters for investigation," and writing out at length preliminary reflections upon the duty of every councillor to prevent corruption and to check on every possible loophole through which it might creep.

The first method which occurred to him as probable was the undercharging of favoured customers. He suspected that somehow the Town Clerk and his friends got their gas for something like a third of the fixed price. But how it was done he could not imagine. It irritated him to the extreme. It would be too risky to tamper with the Accounts Department. There would be someone who would notice. The statement would not agree with the meter record; and that could not be explained away. He wrote: "*How? How?*" in the margin; he was indignant at not being able to see what must be under his nose.

Still, this was small stuff and risky. A second method seemed, at first sight anyway, to be more hopeful. He noticed, as everyone who has had anything to do with public contracts has been noticing for a good many years, that the competitive character of tenders was pretty bogus. All the large tenders for equipment, coal, and so forth, corresponded almost exactly when they were received in the Council offices. A few shillings difference, indeed, only separated them. In one case the firms in the ring had not even troubled to make that gesture, and the tenders were identical to the last 8s. 6d. Yet one firm had to be preferred to another in the end. How was that firm chosen? The answer did not seem doubtful to Grayling. Bribes. Not a large bribe; perhaps only £20 passed across in a public house. All that the obliging official had to do was to remark to the Committee that all the prices were much the same and so what really mattered was that So-and-So's service was much better, by past experience. Or perhaps the same amount would be more wisely spent scattered among the councillors. Grayling noted this as a possible source of funds; but he also noted (as obscurely as he could) that it couldn't be good for long. For, in his opinion, it would soon occur to the contractors that their agents were undoing by these bribes the chief benefit which they had anticipated from forming a ring. They were reintroducing a kind of competition even as if was only a competition in corruption. Before long, Grayling considered, the firms would go into a fresh huddle and allot the market scientifically. Then, the firm to which Croxburn business was allotted would always enter a tender appreciably below that of other firms. The Committee would have nothing to debate. The Council would find its choice in effect made for it. And there would be no more handouts.

Grayling did not note down that he was witnessing a fundamental change in economics and the structure of society. He was not inclined for reflexions upon the structure and implications of the late stage of finance-capitalism. All he saw was a system of graft beginning to wither away before he had had a real opportunity to exploit it.

He noted with more respect a third way of preying on the public funds (the phrase comes from his own notes). This was unnecessary expenditure of a kind which was sure to be for the benefit of one of the gang. He noticed that the amount of re-tiling that the Gasworks had required in the past three years had amounted to almost complete re-equipment. Mr. Fairley had, of course, withdrawn from the Committee when the contracts were discussed. He had indeed only just resumed his seat on it. But his presence had not been necessary. Once it had been decided to re-tile, the thing was in the bag. There was no other firm near which had the equipment and material or employed local labour. Mr. Fairley could show the most complete indifference to the debates; as indeed he did. There were several other, smaller contracts, mainly with builders, which Grayling suspected. But, alas, he owned no firm which could work a similar racket. He had to console himself by marking this practice "Dangerous."

Finally, he viewed with cold contempt the stuffing of the payrolls which went on. The clerical staff of the Gasworks was much too large, and very incompetent. The reason was, fairly clearly, the considerable number of otherwise unemployable female relatives of local politicians who were on the staff. Grayling had no relatives to park on the Gasworks, and he was annoyed. The telephone was answered by halfwits, and he disliked having an institution with which he was connected publicly shamed. He felt what might, with gross flattery, be called an embryonic stirring of civic consciousness.

He had by now a brief Rogue's Manual of local government, but found only one opening for himself. He decided that the only thing he could do was to push in to the contracts racket while it was still profitable. It needn't be dangerous. He could just wait until there seemed to be something going through and then obstruct in Committee. Then the others would have to move. They would have to offer him something. They should take the risks; not he.

He waited some considerable time; the whole project was of a risky kind that made him uneasy. Indeed, when he did move, it had to be after all on a guess. The biggest single contract which came to the Committee was, naturally, for coal. Five years earlier this contract had been changed over, on the pretext of a very small saving, from a firm which had supplied the Council from the beginning to a relatively new coal merchant. Grayling knew of no evidence that there was anything wrong. He merely assumed from the character of his colleagues that there had been some dirty work. He therefore decided to say as little as possible, consistent with playing his hand at all. When the contract came up for a renewal, which all the rest of the Committee assumed to be automatic, he muttered over it, and then suddenly said aloud that he thought the question ought to be gone into thoroughly. He felt that the needs of the ratepayers required the figure to be examined by an independent authority, and perhaps some other tenders ought to be solicited. He suggested that the engineers be asked to report in detail on the quality of the fuel delivered; at that point the General Manager's expression showed him he had found the weak point. He then looked at his watch, exclaimed at the time, begged his colleagues not to make any rash decision and left the committee-room at high speed.

Two days before the next committee meeting an envelope arrived through the post, addressed to *H. J. Grayling, Esq.*, and containing thirty-five one pound notes and nothing else. At the committee meeting when the subject came up, Grayling said nothing at all, and the contract was unanimously passed for acceptance by the full Council. At the Council meeting he said nothing also.

A few nights later the Town Clerk took coffee and an evening's bridge at his house. As he helped him on with his coat, Grayling said to him smoothly and in a low voice: "About that coal business. I hope your brother-in-law, the General Manager, is careful." The Town Clerk blustered a little, said he didn't know what Grayling meant, and then, as the Councillor remained coolly silent, was rash enough to say: "Well, you're in it now as much as the rest of us."

"I don't know what you mean," said Grayling.

"Why, you got thirty-five pounds, didn't you?" asked the Clerk.

"I don't understand you," repeated the Councillor and stared him down.

When the Committee sponsored a great "forward move" by which subscribers got gas cookers provided by the Corporation at a nominal rental in return for signing a special "all-in" contract, Grayling got the biggest "cut" of his career. He also allowed himself to go as near as he ever did to indicating a request. "Well," he said, as the meeting rose, "I hope my gas will cost me less now." The General Manager was wreathed in smiles. "I expect it will," he said.

Two days later two of the Corporation engineers called at his house. "I understand the Councillor's complaining about his meter," said the elder one to Renata.

She showed no surprise; indeed, she felt none, for her husband rarely told her anything. She took them down to the cellar, where they disconnected the old meter and attached another which they had brought with them. It recorded consistently 40 per cent of the amount that the old one had. Thereafter Grayling knew how the second habitual swindle was worked.

Grayling reckoned that he saved £14 a year on that, and an average of £60 or £70 was delivered in pound notes. He never took anything else but pound notes. Once he received a cheque, signed personally by one of the directors of the firm which supplied the gas cookers. He rang them up, and said to him: "This is Grayling speaking. That was a very foolish thing that you have done. You know what I mean," and rang off. He received the sum in notes next day. But he did not return the cheque, nor did he destroy it. It was evidence.

He knew his position was far from absolutely secure. But he frequently reviewed it to himself and decided that there was no evidence against him, while he himself had evidence against his colleagues.

The gas meter? He had never asked for it to be changed, nor had it ever occurred to him to question his bills.

The coal contract? He had suspected it, and the minutes would show that he had queried it. He had inspected the accounts (yes; he had made a point of going down to the office and looking at them, but had found nothing, as he knew he would), and they were in order, so he had not pursued the matter.

The cheque? Precisely; an evidence of his incorruptibility. He would tell a fine story of his having rung up the director of the company, upbraided him, and reduced him to humbleness. "I told him that I believed he meant no harm; that I knew such things did occur in circles in which I did not care to move; but that he must understand that Croxburn Councillors had nothing to do with such behaviour. I warned him I would keep the cheque by me, unused, and if ever I heard the least thing against his company—if the least breath of suspicion occurred—I would throw it down on the table in the Council Chamber and he could explain it if he could."

All that was necessary for him to do was to be sure to move first. If it ever looked as if the game was up, he must leap in with revelations. The episode of the Deputy Mayor would be in his favour and he would be almost sure to gain rather than lose in reputation.

He was, indeed, in a position to put the squeeze on the General Manager, and through him on the Town Clerk. He did not, in fact, do so; he merely allowed himself the pleasure of occasional equivocal remarks at the end of the evenings of bridge which so bored his wife. His sole disquiet came from the Vicar; the man had made two disagreeable speeches on the Council and he wondered whether perhaps the Council staff had not been chattering.

◇◇◇

Marital disharmony began in the first week of the Graylings' life together. The Councillor had had good reasons to expect that everything would be as he wished it. He had the strong position. Renata was a stranger; he would supervise all her friendships. One by one she would be introduced to his friends and their wives—all considerably older than her and unquestionably good influences. She would learn which acquaintances deserved dinner invitations, and which (such as the Vicar, for example) should be kept at a short distance and invited only to tea. When the first of the two children on whom he had decided was on the way, she could have some daily assistance in the house; till then domestic duties would keep her busy during the day. If she had time to spare and needed entertainment she could join the Ladies' Bridge Circle: she did not, it was true, play bridge, but she could learn. For the first month he would inspect all the household bills and check over each item. By that time sufficient data would be accumulated to fix a figure of a proper weekly expenditure: this he would thenceforward pay over to his wife without further question. Should she need any extra money, she would explain why, and he would either give or withhold it.

This was his idea: it was broken in seven days. The first of his "bridge evenings" was attended by the Town Clerk, and his wife, Mr. and Mrs. Alderman Robbins, and the next-door neighbour and his wife. Renata refused to play bridge. She even declined to be instructed, saying flatly she was not interested; so there was only one four. She talked about literature, of all things, to the enforced sitters-out; she chose for the subject of her discourse James Joyce's *Ulysses.* She had not read it, though she managed to sound as if she had: neither had her chief antagonist, Mrs. Robbins. Mrs.

Robbins had acquired the general idea that the book was an obscene work, the equivalent of *Suzy, Petite Dactylo* (if she had known of that work); and in any case she disliked being instructed by a wife so noticeably younger and prettier than herself. The ensuing argument was sufficiently loud and ill-tempered to disturb Grayling at the card table and make him lose half a crown. Later in the evening he had his first quarrel with Renata. He told her it was important that he should not quarrel with the Robbinses, and that she was never to mention "that filthy book" again. She told him he was an ignoramus, that his friends were fools, and that she would do as she pleased. If they had been brought up differently he would have beaten her, or she would have thrown the ornaments at him: as it was, they merely nursed their anger.

As a consequence, she refused to submit the second week's bills to him. She merely said what the total was and declined to discuss the details. He paid; but the next week would not pay. She said nothing, but opened accounts at the chief tradesmen's shops: they were glad enough to do so, as it made them sure of her custom. At the end of a month she handed the tradesmen's books to him; the weekly entries were merely, "To Goods." He asked for the individual bills; she refused to show them.

"Then I won't pay," he said.

"As you please," she answered. "*I* can't pay them. I shall give the shops your city address and tell them to present the bills to you there."

He jumped up in anger and alarm. "You're not to do that—I forbid it!" he shouted.

She made no answer; and that evening he gave her the money to pay the books. She didn't show him the books again: she merely told him each week of the total (which varied very little), and he supplied the money. She asked him for a pound a week for herself, in addition. He refused, and she replied: "You ought to have sense enough to realize I shall only take it."

There was another long wrangle, at the end of which he allowed her 12s. 6d.

As for having children, she saw to it that that did not happen; but she complained of continual minor illnesses which fed him with false hopes. The illnesses were almost wholly, but not quite wholly, imaginary; her diseases were really only slight anæmia and great discontent. She completely charmed, however, old Dr. Hopkins: he assured the Councillor with absolute sincerity that it was imperative that she should have help in the house. Grayling himself, however, chose the maid: he picked on Mrs. Buttlin, whom he had met in connection with his church work. She regarded him as "the master" and her employer; she distrusted her mistress, and suspected her morals long before there was any justification. When, in 1941, she stood in front of the Vicar and said: "A whore. That's what I said," she satisfied a longing of some years' growth. The full round word gave her as much pleasure as a ripe orange.

The second week of her marriage, Renata, flushed and perverse because of the time of the month, chose to pick a quarrel with her neighbour's wife. She told her that religion was nonsense and that she, Renata, would never go near the Church. "My husband," she added, "is a churchwarden, but that is a matter of business."

She cried, for once, a little when Grayling reproached her afterwards, but she would not withdraw. It was for only a minute, too, that his reproaches were effective. He almost immediately changed over to the terms in which he really thought. He told her to cease trying her superior airs on him and his friends, as she was cheap, and ought to be grateful to him for picking her out of an intolerable existence. She froze at once; but he did not perceive it, for he saw nothing offensive in what he said. It was a mere statement of fact. All his life at the office the firm had, openly or by implication, made a similar statement of fact to him. He had never resented it.

He had little hesitation in forbidding her friends the house. He came home one afternoon to find Mrs. Callaghan, wife of a man who had once run as a Labour candidate for the Council. He behaved so icily that she soon rose to go, and he saw her to the door. As he opened it, he said, in an equable voice:

"Please do not come here again."

"What did you say?" Mrs. Callaghan asked incredulously.

"Please do not come here again," he repeated. "I think your opinions are likely to have a bad influence on my wife. You would not be welcome."

She flushed and answered: "I shall do whatever Mrs. Grayling wishes."

He did not seem affected. "If necessary," he remarked, "I shall write to your husband."

He went back into the house. "I have told that woman not to come back," he informed Renata. "She is a bad influence, and you are not to drink in this house."

There was a pathetic and deplorable half-bottle of Australian wine which Mrs. Callaghan had brought and out of which they had each had a glass. He poured the contents down the sink and put the bottle aside for the dustman.

◇◇◇

A border warfare of this kind must in the end close in a compromise (or a slaughter). Before 1939, Mr. and Mrs. Grayling had achieved the compromise: a method of living satisfactory to neither; agreed, if not agreeable. He paid her weekly a fixed amount for household expenses. Since prices, on the whole, fell from 1931 onwards, this was convenient

to her; she could, and did, annex the margin for herself.
He did not question her accounts, nor expect from her
affection or anything but a civil friendliness. She, on her
side, ran his house, provided food for him, and at not too
frequent intervals entertained his friends. She was aloof in
her conversation and attitude, but avoided shocking the
guests; he, in return, made no effort to discover whether
she invited Mrs. Callaghan or other undesirables while he
was at the office. They disliked each other decorously: the
ménage might have gone on for years on the same basis, as
many others have done.

Externally, both of them seemed to have learned calm:
whether it was feigned, in order not to give the other an
advantage, or real, they both seemed satisfied with a life of
limited courtesy and limited hostility. Underneath there was
a strain: it perhaps was as well that this strain was relaxed
shortly before the outbreak of war.

The Munich Agreement in 1938 was supposed to bring
"peace in our time"; but even the Chamberlain Government
doubted that. What it immediately brought was the institution of a national Air Raid Precautions Service, and this
was not an unmixed evil for the Grayling family. It enabled
Mrs. Grayling to enrol for A.R.P. work; it ended an idleness
which was eating out her heart without her knowledge. Her
husband's authority had, despite her resistance, limited her
acquaintance. When she enrolled she was suddenly thrown
into the company of men and women whom he would never
have wished her to meet. Croxburn was a snobbish suburb,
and the enrolment of the A.R.P. staff was a compulsory
churning up of social strata which would have preferred to
remain separate. Theoretically, Renata Grayling approved
this, though for no better reason than that it annoyed her
husband. She had, in fact, some difficulty in adjusting herself
to the sardonic and robust conversation of the ex-charladies

and workmen's wives whom she met, but she made the effort, and was rewarded by the verdict that she was "superior" but "not uppish."

Perhaps equally important in making life easier for her was the uniform that she received. Dark blue trousers and dark blue tunic, not unlike an army officer's tunic, were hard on some of her plumper colleagues, but for the slim and not too young were a gift from heaven, so long as they remembered not to wear shoes with high heels. Renata knew, as she walked about confidently and with a strictly limited make-up, that she looked at once delightful and efficient. Trim, slender, charming: those were the adjectives which she cynically decided a Woman's Page Editor could honestly apply to her. They were the adjectives which a colleague had already used. Hugh Rolandson, twenty-nine years old and unmarried, had joined the A.R.P. because the club foot with which he had been born prevented him taking more active work. He had not been in the service a fortnight before he knew he was in love with Mrs. Grayling.

He was a young man—born in 1910—innocent and ardent, not rich, with a handsome fair face, and singularly bright blue eyes. She was older than he was, unhappy, and sorely in need of affection. She made some effort at resistance. She reminded herself that he was the sole support of his mother, that he was wholly dependent upon a not-well-paid job in the gift of a narrow-minded employer, that baby-snatching was ignoble. But she had been used to taking responsibility on herself. She did so once again, and in the spring of 1939 went with him to Paris for a long week-end, Friday to Tuesday, by the Folkestone-Boulogne route, on specially cheap tickets provided by the Southern Railway.

◇◇◇

It was not very surprising to anyone but himself that Hugh Rolandson fell so helplessly in love. He was twenty-nine when he first saw Renata, but he was young for his age. And he was in addition unusually inexperienced. His only relative was his mother, to whom he was devoted. He lived with her in the small house in Croxburn in which he had been born, and which, with a very small income, was all his father had left her. She was not precisely an invalid, but she was in indifferent health, and he had very rarely left her for as much as a night. As soon as he had left college he had gone to work for the old-established publishing house of Brown and Summers, and he still was working with them. He was underpaid, but loyal; and until he met Renata his thoughts were almost wholly concentrated on deserving his employers' approbation.

Brown & Summers Ltd. was a publishing firm of a kind that was very common fifty years ago, but is rarer now. It was a family business, run paternally and economically. After eight years' service Hugh was still only getting a basic wage of £4 a week, but he received frequently extra payments according to a carefully calculated system laid down by Sir Herbert Brown-Cotton (in those days only Mr. Herbert) in 1910, when he became senior partner. It was not an unjust scheme; its only considerable fault was that Sir Herbert failed to realize how much the value of money had decreased since 1910. Hugh was paid his original salary of £4, and to this was added a low rate of extra remuneration for anything that he wrote which was used in any of the various magazines which the house published. Editorial work, cutting, proof-reading, and corresponding with authors he was supposed to do as part of the job for which he was paid his original fee. Should anything that he wrote be regarded as worthy of book publication, for that he would be given a contract identical with the contracts offered to outside authors, which might mean quite an appreciable extra sum. He had never yet achieved that honour. Ideas that he produced for other authors to use were the firm's property.

Each man or woman who joined the staff, Hugh included, had been given a brief history of the firm to read, written by an elderly compositor now living off a pension (granted by the firm to all old employees, as part of its fixed policy). It gave a full account of Josiah Brown, founder of the firm, whose marble bust stood at the head of the main staircase of the huge offices in Holborn. It gave only a few words to Edwin Summers, who had stayed with the firm but a short while, and none of whose descendants were to be found in its employment to-day. It recorded how Mr. Gladstone had so strongly approved of Josiah's policy that he had overborne the objections of his regular publishers in order to allow the new firm the honour of publishing his *Essay* upon the advantages of religious education in schools. It told a totally apocryphal anecdote to the effect that Charles Bradlaugh, the great atheist, had been struck silent in the midst of a passionate oration by the voice of Josiah crying out "Blasphemer!" It noted how he had been disappointed of male offspring, though the Lord had blessed him with seven daughters, of whom but one married. Her husband was Mr. Aloysius Cotton, who had been educated in the Roman heresy, but shortly after meeting Miss Rebecca Brown became an Anglican, a very Low Church Evangelical. (Josiah was a Methodist.) After fifteen years' work in the firm, Mr. Cotton took the name of Brown-Cotton and became a junior partner. He succeeded to sole control of the firm on his father-in-law's death, which occurred at the age of eighty-three. On his death at seventy-two, the firm passed to his sons, Mr. Herbert, Mr. Albert and Mr. Gilbert. He left some shares, but no right to interfere, to his daughter Leonora, married to a tea-broker named Hopkins; and instructed his sons to find employment for any of her sons who desired to enter the business in due course. One, Reginald, did so; he was Hugh's immediate superior.

Mr. Herbert, made Sir Herbert in 1911 by Mr. Asquith, was the head of the firm, in title and in fact. His brothers' photographs, greatly enlarged and framed in silver, hung in the reception room. His portrait, painted in oils by an A.R.A., was in the boardroom. It was not hung; in the rebuilding of the offices in 1920, it was actually built into the fabric of the wall and could not be removed without tearing down the structure. He controlled the policy of the firm and supervised every department. Mr. Albert concerned himself almost wholly with the accounting side; he was a placid, bald man with pale blue eyes. Mr. Gilbert did not come to the office regularly. He was unmarried, with longish dark hair, and lived alone in a large house at Purley, where he gave musical evenings at which he himself played the piano. It was understood that he was artistic; he was asked his opinion upon the typography and the jackets of the new books; and no catalogue went out without his approval. He attended board meetings and supported the opinions of Sir Herbert.

Sir Herbert, tall, white-moustached, a little bent with age but still impressive, carried on the profitable policies of Josiah Brown and Aloysius Brown-Cotton. Hugh had only once had a lengthy interview with him, but that was enough. The old man was as clear in exposition as he was immovable in judgment. Nor had this judgment been wrong; throughout three long lives the same general policy had made money; and at this day it was supported consciously by three men whom their colleagues admitted to be among the most successful publishers in London. "My uncles," as Reginald Hopkins always referred to them, were a triumvirate who passed assured verdicts on every form of printed matter except daily papers, who had been until recently always right, and who still had no conception that they would not always be right. Whole areas of literature fell under their condemnation: "my uncles" warned Reginald when Hugh once rashly spoke of D. H. Lawrence, "consider that a great deal of modern fiction would have been better left unwritten."

Sir Herbert had explained to Hugh that he was never to forget that the great British reading public was deeply moral. It was not, perhaps, as consciously religious as it had been, but all the same the annual balance ("which my brother Albert will show you if you care to see it") showed that the most substantially profitable section of the firm's list was the large theological section. Some of these books, which were still on the list, had cost the firm originally no more than a couple of hundred pounds' payment to a struggling clergyman who had been deeply grateful for it; and had then sold for as many as thirty years and were still asked for. Next to them, and possibly soon to become more valuable, were the educational books, headed by the famous series of Elementary, Intermediate and Advanced Dictionaries. More aleatory (Hugh blinked at the word) in Sir Herbert's opinion, but still profitable were the series of magazines with which Sir Herbert hoped that Mr. Rolandson would henceforward specially concern himself. They ranged from *Wireless for Boys* to *True Stories of the Empire*, and from *In the Steps of Our Lord* to *Science for You*. These three main lines, Sir Herbert explained, were what brought in the bread and butter. Year after year, orders for them could be predicted; they had stood the test of time, and though the firm was far from unenterprising or unreceptive of new ideas, it could not fail to remember that the opinion of the British public was that in this sphere at least the old ideas were best.

"I was almost forgetting," he continued with a benevolent smile, "what is after all the department which certainly gives the most honest and simple pleasure, and, though it is far from being the largest, has in several years given the highest percentage return per book. I mean our juvenile department. My grandfather, Josiah Brown, really started it with some moral tales for children, which I'm afraid would make the modern child chuckle; but it was my father who first developed the big picture books and annuals which were unique until Mr. Blackie copied them." As he made this outrageous charge against a highly respectable rival firm, Sir Herbert did not seem angry; he spoke indulgently, as headmaster might of a promising but pretentious schoolboy. "I remember well how pleased I was when father said my suggestion to call them the Bumper Annuals was a good one, though for some reason he did not adopt it. I felt I was on the way to becoming a real publisher. Ah-ah." He sighed and resumed. "Then and then only, my dear Rolandson, we come to the biography and fiction, which alone the reviewers seem to notice and which, despite their considerable number, really play a relatively small part in assuring the prosperity of the firm. I think you know this part of our list fairly well. Now tell me, what strikes you about it particularly?"

This was an appalling question to be fired at a junior employee by the head of the firm. Hugh sought round desperately for something not too inane to say. What *was* the list like? Well, the biographies were mostly of builders of empire, established literary figures, well-known political characters (all reputable), written by honest craftsmen and rather on the dull side. None of them was a debunking or a "fictionalized" biography. The fiction list contained several good stodgy names of older novelists, safe for a first printing of five thousand each time, a big number of simple romantic woman writers, a few Wild Westerns, and some detective novels of the puzzle type. How could you sum that up politely? He played for safety: "Well, I had always regarded it as a very solid list, sir."

"Yes, that is a fair comment," Sir Herbert smiled; it seemed that the answer was all right. But to prevent any mishaps Sir Herbert took charge of the course of the conversation henceforward himself. "I wonder if you have observed what gives our list its solidity. What is the common feature which runs through all sections, and is to be found as much in the religious section, where you would expect it, as in the fiction where perhaps you might not? It is, that all our books have a moral basis—a Christian philosophy and aim, using the word Christian in the very widest sense. I do believe, and I trust you will not ridicule this" (Hugh would never have dreamed of doing such a thing) "that what is good religion is also good business. The public, despite certain flurries of fashion, does not *want* pornography and mocking. We don't publish risqué novels. We don't issue a series of biographies of King Charles's mistresses, written by hack journalists to order, like our colleagues who live a little further east. We decline politely the offers we get of American gangster stories. Sometimes my brother Gilbert tells me we go absurdly far. He was pulling my leg outrageously only yesterday because in Miss Nina Opal's new novel an oath by an Indian captain is given as D-dash-N. He asked me if I felt it safe to spell out the words 'Oh bother.' I told him—only in fun, of course—that he would be asking me to print out in full the word Mr. Bernard Shaw tried to popularize some years ago in a play called *Pygmalion.* It was a very witty play.

"Don't let me give you the idea that we are narrow-minded. I am not in the least afraid of the Captain's oath, though I don't use it myself. My education taught me to give the word its original meaning, and if I said a man was damned I would mean I thought he was on the way to eternal fire; and that seems an extremely violent term to throw about in daily conversation. We aren't narrow in politics; in fact, we only yesterday decided to approach Mr. J. R. Clynes with a proposal to write a book on Socialism; and we shall be delighted to publish it if it can be arranged. We aren't narrow in religion; if a scientific book, written in decent terms and the product of honest thought, led its author, for example, to deny the truth of revealed religion, neither my brothers nor I would consider that alone a reason for declining it. I admit I might have a certain private prejudice against it; but I would not allow that to influence me. I hope not, anyway. We are not narrow even in matters of sex; we long ago dropped the ban on the mention of divorce except for reprobation, on which my father insisted.

"But we believe this. Every publisher has an individual responsibility to see that his books are fit for all to read. No firm can limit the circulation of its books. You may label a book 'for adults only,' or 'for doctors only.' That is quite meaningless. Even if all booksellers were scrupulous, there are innumerable libraries which cannot supervise withdrawals and many of which don't try to. So we try to keep off our lists anything that encourages a love of blood and slaughter. These sickening stories of gangster massacres—just consider what effect they are likely to have on a boy of fifteen, for example, sent out to earn his living—say, in London as a van boy. Or on an older man of twenty-five or so, unemployed and with a grievance against society which is by no means wholly unfounded. Tacking on a happy ending is no good; he reads the story and learns to admire the Big Shot. And he ends up in Thames Police Court, convicted of some sordid little crime and wrecked for life. And as for these sex novels—well, there is nothing, nothing in the world, more likely to destroy the happiness and future prospects of a young man or woman than to have learnt a frivolous attitude to unchastity. Believe me, I am not quite an old fogy; I have been young; and I do know what I am talking about."

Sir Herbert spoke with great emphasis and a trace of embarrassment. Perhaps he was conscious, as he stood against the mantelpiece underneath a large framed portrait of Mr. Asquith, that he was an imposing figure of a silver-haired old man, but he was not acting. There was real earnestness in his voice; he seemed as he continued almost to be imploring Hugh to assure him that these views still seemed sound to the younger generation.

"My nephew Reginald," he said, "will be giving you great latitude in the work he will hand over to you. I do want to feel sure in my mind that you will care for these magazines as the firm would wish you to. I hope you will share these ideals and help us to carry them out. May I have that assurance from you?"

Hugh gave him the promise he wanted, and was not insincere as he did so.

◇◇◇

Hugh's club foot prevented him going to the war; "Mr. Reginald" (Hugh sometimes expected the staff to refer to him as "Master Reginald" to distinguish him from the Olympian uncles) joined the Army in 1940. More responsibility, and more frequent interviews with Sir Herbert, resulted; Hugh was now in general charge of half of the variegated periodicals which Reginald had controlled. The other half was under the control of his most immediate rival, a woman of fifty, Cornelia Shotter. He knew little about her, except that she was pious and did not dissemble her dislike for him. Each of them was of opinion that Mr. Reginald's work could have been devolved on the one alone, without the other's assistance; but Hugh was less obviously irritated by that belief than Miss Shotter.

As the size of the magazines was progressively reduced by paper rationing, Sir Herbert correspondingly reduced the amount of material provided by outside authors. Soon no more than 5 per cent., all over, was provided by writers not on the payroll of the firm. Hugh was not asked to write any more than he had been, nor were the Wireless consultant, the Home Problems consultant, the Religious adviser and the rest of the industrious gentlemen and ladies who had desks in the office and provided a named amount of satisfactory copy each month; but, because they wrote the same amount, their contributions were proportionately larger. The only material which Sir Herbert felt could not be satisfactorily written in the office to order was the fiction. And this was no inconsiderable expense: several magazines had either a serial or short stories; one was nothing but fiction. He considered but rejected a scheme put up by Mr. Albert for changing the contracts of those who like Hugh had shown an aptitude for fiction, and requiring them to turn in a proportion of fiction in the material that might be demanded of them. He told his brother it was an immoral proposition, and the two had as near to a quarrel as they ever did. The most that he would agree to do was to send a memorandum to each member of the staff who had shown any ability to write the sort of stories that were needed, in which he said that the firm would welcome even more eagerly than before anything that they could offer, but that as before this work would be paid for separately. Hugh, who had written two or three adequate short stories, received this note and set ardently to work to provide all the fiction he could. He needed money badly. Not only was his mother in poorer health than ever—the track of some of the raiders in the London blitzes had gone straight over Croxburn, and the A.A. racket as well as jet-tisoned bombs had wrecked her nerve—but he now had a mistress. Renata was not expensive—indeed, she vetoed whenever she could his least expenditure—but she could not invariably refuse what he brought. Flowers, chocolates and cigarettes when there were such things, cinema tickets, fares, new clothes for himself to feed his new found vanity, half shares in a very rare week-end or night away. Adultery may or may not be sinful, but is never cheap.

In November, 1941, he had a long session with Sir Herbert which for the first time offered him the hope of a considerable increase of income. It opened inauspiciously. He submitted to him an idea for a romantic serial by one of their most reliable authors, Mrs. Blodwen Griffiths.

It was an adaptation of an idea he had read somewhere— he no longer remembered where. It was to be about a thyroid deficient, a young man who was cast aside on a desert island with his girl friend; and realized that without his thyroid extract he would shortly become an imbecile. It had seemed an excellent idea. But Sir Herbert dismissed it as "morbid," and as inclining to immorality; then perceiving how cast down Rolandson was, sought for a way to comfort him. "I am very sorry to put aside so promising an idea—a brilliant suggestion which does you every credit, my boy," he said, "but I cannot see how we could make it acceptable. No, I really cannot." He paused. "You offered a suggestion the other day which I would far rather take up. I am trying to recall exactly what it was."

"Arsenical egg," said Hugh Rolandson, distinctly.

"I beg your pardon?" said Sir Herbert, frowning.

"It was an idea suggested to me by a young woman I know," Hugh explained. "It was to be a murder story in which the villain injected eggs with arsenic, using a hypodermic syringe through the shell. So he was able to have an alibi for when the victim ate an egg and was poisoned. But I asked a chemist and he tells me that the arsenic would make the white of the egg set at once, and you couldn't get away with it. I'm afraid it's no good, sir." He spoke depressedly.

Sir Herbert's kind heart was troubled. "I wish we could get something that you could write yourself," he said. "Something which would use the magnificent possibilities of modern science. You do that so well. Something on the lines of the early H. G. Wells stories. Or Jules Verne, if that name means anything to you."

It did not, but Hugh had an idea. "I have got a plot," he said, "but it seemed to me too fantastic. However, if you think we could do with something on these lines…"

"Let me hear it, please," said Sir Herbert.

"I haven't got it worked out yet," said Hugh. "But so far as I've gone, it's this. The man who writes the book writes it about a friend of his, an eccentric but brilliant scientist. The scientist is primarily an astronomer, and for that reason has become a great expert on telescopes, lenses, photography, light, and all that. He has built himself the finest telescope ever made, far better than the Mount Wilson one, and it is mounted on a peak in the South American Andes, among the wild Indian tribes of Ecuador."

"Good," said Sir Herbert.

"One day the hero gets a wire from the scientist. *Come at once*, it says. Well, we pass over his various travels and adventures, until at last he comes to the scientist, alone with his vast telescope, strange instruments and valuable stores, in the middle of tribes who use poison arrows and juju, or voodoo, or whatever it is in Ecuador. And then the scientist tells him a wonderful story.

"You know, sir, that light travels infinitely fast, but that the distances in space are so enormous that what we see in the stars is what happened hundreds of years ago. I believe that it has been worked out that the nearest star is one called Alpha Centauri, and that what we see there is what happened in the days of Julius Caesar. I'll look that up to make sure, but that is the general idea. Of course, all we can see is the chemical composition of the star, which is found out by breaking up the light into a spectrum. But that's because it's so far away and our instruments are so weak. The light travels on, undimmed and unchanged in space; and everything is there, if only we could see it.

"This scientist has been experimenting in taking enormously enlarged photographs through his giant telescope on to a special film, and then enlarging and enlarging the film and throwing the result on to a screen. For a long time he has got nothing more than fuller information about what we know already. Especially he has got an enormous map of Mars, with even small details of the canals, which turn out to be belts of quick-growing jungle, with four-legged things moving about in them. He has been able to raise the power of his instruments so much that he can make out their general shape, but that is all."

"Excellent. Go on," said Sir Herbert.

"He never lets his telescope rest, of course. All the time it is trained somewhere on the heavens, and the photographic attachments are clicking away. He looks at everything that comes through to the film, and projects it on the screen. Most times it is nothing of importance. But once or twice he finds the whole of the screen occupied by a pale grey picture which looks like an actual view of countryside, seen from above. It positively seems as if he was up in an aeroplane, looking down, sometimes clearly and sometimes between clouds, on fields and houses and people moving in them. Everything is in black and white, or rather grey and grey, like an old, bad film.

"Gradually he discovers what has happened, as he finds out how to make sure of this peculiar phenomenon being repeated. He is put on to it first by getting a continuous 'run' of these strange pallid pictures, which seem to show him the beginning of a story. Something is happening, though he loses the connection one night, and a month later when he gets the thing adjusted again he is looking at a wholly different scene. But the explanation in both cases is the same. It is this:

"Brilliant light is pouring off the earth every second. If we were in the moon, for example, we should see the earth as ten times as large and ten times as bright as the moon. Even with our naked eye we could pick out the outlines of sea and land and so forth. If we had powerful telescopes we could see much more. Well, the earth's light, pouring out like this, has simply struck against one of the dead, dark bodies which we know are circling in space, and has been reflected back to the earth. Here the scientist's instruments have infinitely enlarged it. And now he is looking straight on to what happened a hundred years ago. He sees men and women long dead moving and acting, though he cannot hear them and cannot move his position. It is not a picture he sees, but them themselves. After a vast journey through space their images have returned home.

"That's the basic idea, sir. I haven't yet worked out *what* it is he sees—it may be something of great historic importance, or it may be something which has direct bearing on the hero's life—a will, for example—or just a plain story of passion. Perhaps there could be more than one story. But the end, of course, will be that superstition destroys the scientist. The Indians are set on to him by their sorcerers, who declare he is bringing evil magic down to the earth; and they storm the house and kill him. They wreck the delicate instruments and the hero only just escapes with his life. Months later he makes his way down to a coast town, starving, racked with fever, continually mouthing and repeating a story no one will believe."

Sir Herbert fixed him with earnest blue eyes. "Amazing, my dear boy. Amazing. Absolutely first rate. It has everything we could wish—adventure, terror, marvels, and a good moral. No morbidity, no sex business. Nothing against it at all. It is wholly admirable." He rose and paced up and down the room. "You think you can work out this idea, Rolandson? Can you get down to it right away?"

"If you think you can use it, sir, certainly," said Hugh.

"Use it? Certainly we can use it. You may consider that settled." Sir Herbert thought a moment, and went on. "If you can make a full length feature of this story, of seventy thousand words or more, we will take it on the usual terms for *Home and Beauty's* serial. We will also, if it proves satisfactory, and I am sure it will, take it for book publication, either in the spring or the autumn of next year. We shall pay you two hundred pounds advance for this, and fifty pounds above that if our American colleagues use it, as I expect they will. There will be a commencing royalty of 10 per cent., rising to 15 per cent. after the sale of three thousand copies. You know our usual contract form."

Two hundred pounds, and more. Hugh was so delighted he was hardly able to convey his assent.

◇◇◇

One end of a telephone conversation, late December, 1941

"May I speak to Mr. Rolandson?"

. . . . .

"Mrs Grayling speaking."

. . . . .

"Mr. Rolandson?"

. . . . .

"Hugh. Can you meet me at lunch? I'm coming up to town. It's something rather important."

. . . . .

"Oh. I see. If it's Sir Herbert you can't, of course. But I must talk to you: and you can't come here this evening. Are you alone in the room?"

. . . . .

"I won't risk your telephone girl listening in. Can you go outside your office, *now*, and ring me up here? I've got to talk while Alice is out, and she may be back any moment."

. . . . .

"I'll be waiting."

An interval of under three minutes, and then a telephone ringing:

. . . . .

"My dear, Henry has found out."

. . . . .

"I wish it had been. I wish it could be that before I'm too old. But it isn't. He just found out. It is going to be very disagreeable, as disagreeable as Henry can make it, and he is an expert at that. Apparently Mrs. Buttlin had been watching us for a long time, and we must have been careless. You've only been here twice, after all. From what Henry says she took her evidence to the Vicar, and either she got no change from him or she was told to go to Henry. And Henry had a magnificent scene prepared for me yesterday. I tried denying it, but it was obviously useless."

. . . . .

"Oh, *News of the World* stuff. Rumpled beds, and envelopes taken out of the wastepaper basket, and torn up letters. That was my fault. I began a letter *Darling Hugh* and tore it up, but not small enough. And apparently on the day you were here when I gave her the afternoon off she was suspicious and waited to see who came. We didn't draw the blinds, did we?"

. . . . .

"That's the sort of thing she said, anyway. You must just imagine the rest. The thing which made it worst was the cruet. I had no explanation of it."

. . . . .

"Yes, yes; the cruet we bought in Paris, in the joke shop. Made up of poes. I put it in a drawer, hidden away, and he found it. You can imagine his moralizings about it. He and Mrs. Buttlin must have fairly enjoyed themselves. Anyway that, he said, warned him of my depravity and started him making inquiries. I don't know if there's any truth in it, but that is going to be his story, for public consumption, anyway. It serves me right for being sentimental, and about such a thing too."

. . . . .

"Hugh dear, you must be serious and pay attention."

. . . . .

"But that is just it. He's not going to divorce me."

. . . . .

"Well, he's *not* going to. He has a better idea. He told me all about it last night. I asked him, as coolly as I could, if he thought he had evidence enough for a divorce, and he said he didn't approve of divorce on religious grounds. He only puts on that sort of pretence with me—religion, I mean—if he's very angry. He said he was going to sue you for seduction and alienation of affections. I think those were his phrases. Anyhow, there is a case which he kept quoting, which he called the Helen of Troy case. I didn't remember it, but it was in the papers. Somewhere in the provinces a man got quite a lot of money off his wife's lover. Cambridge, I think it was. And because it wasn't a divorce the papers could report it. They let themselves go, and the two people were driven out of the country by the scandal. They couldn't marry, either; because there was no divorce. That didn't matter so much as the fact that they were ruined. Henry gave me all the details. He enjoyed himself thoroughly.

"What he proposes to do is to sue you and ruin you. He said just that. He is going to have the papers served on you at the office, on the pretence of not knowing your address, but really in order to make sure you are sacked."

. . . . .

"That is just what he *will* do, my dear. Of course, he offered a way out."

. . . . .

"For me to give you up and be a good wife to him. And, my dear, I think it's got to be done. He's got the whip hand. There's nothing we can do."

. . . . .

"Of course I do. More than anything in the world. But you'll be dismissed at once, won't you, and that two hundred pounds will be gone, and all…

. . . . .

"It's not probably, you know it's certainly. And you've got to think of your mother."

. . . . .

"Hugh, you're being unjust. I don't want to. I shall find life almost impossible to live. But I don't see any way out. Henry's vanity and his sense of property have been attacked and he's quite merciless then. And he is quite sure he has you trapped. I won't have you ruin your life for me."

. . . . .

"I will: indeed I will. But I must stop now. You know why. Good-bye, my love."

◇◇◇

"Well," said the Superintendent to Inspector Holly, "did you get an earful from Mrs. Adelaide Buttlin?"

"An earful indeed," said the Inspector. "And a few extra notes from her successor, Alice Williams. It's remarkable what minds respectable women have. She sounded just like the old *News of the World*, before they stopped printing the divorce reports. She even mentioned 'a suspicious condition of the sheets.'"

"What did it all amount to?"

"Briefly, that Rolandson and Mrs. Grayling had been having a hot affair for some time, and there is no doubt they'd been going the limit. Mrs. Buttlin is as malicious as any witness I've ever heard, but if a divorce case had come on I think her evidence would have settled it. As far as I can judge it, she suspected what was up long ago, but did nothing about it till after Mrs. Grayling sacked her. Then she turned nasty; but she first went to the Vicar. I don't know what he said, but I gather she got no satisfaction. After that she went to Grayling, and then there was a real uproar. There have

been scenes in that house, first-class scenes, for the last fortnight or so. Alice Williams heard enough to give the whole
story away. Mrs. Grayling didn't raise her voice much, but
Grayling did. He shouted. He wasn't going to divorce her,
apparently. He was going to sue young Rolandson for dam-
ages and ruin him. Rolandson works for an old-fashioned
publisher in Holborn, and it probably *would* ruin him. Also,
as it was not to be a divorce case, all the evidence could be
printed in full in the papers. Grayling said he would brand
them so that they would be run out of town. He was certainly
all out to make himself unpleasant."

"What do the guilty pair say?"

"They won't talk. I am fairly sure that they've got together
on this. Their answers are so damn similar. Mrs. Grayling
repeats over and over again the story of the evening when
the Councillor died, and apart from that regrets she cannot
agree to discuss her relations with her husband with me.
When I remind her she can be asked on oath at the inquest
or perhaps even at a trial, she says that she will answer what
questions she must answer when she must and not before.
I tried to suggest to her how much easier it would be if she
would only speak freely—how the police could be discreet,
and so often things need not come out in court. My most
fatherly manner. I might as well have talked to a lamp-post."

"Rolandson?"

"I think he'll make a fool of himself in court. She will
freeze the coroner, I've no doubt. But he's all nerves. However, at the moment, he, too, has 'nothing to say,' but just
repeats the story of his train journey with Grayling. It's just
the same as all the other stories of that journey."

"There's motive there, all right," said the Superintendent.
"Have you anything more against them?"

"Knowledge," said Holly. "They're both in the A.R.P.
service. They've done the complete course of gas—

decontamination and all. There's a supply kept as you know there, for the gas chamber and other purposes. The A.R.P. people say it couldn't be tapped, but their precautions are childish. They go on the principle—reasonable enough, normally—that people are too frightened of the beastly stuff to want to touch it. A label saying: GAS, KEEP OFF, and a Woolworth padlock. That's all."

"Your trouble," said the Super., "isn't that you don't know who did the job. It's that you've proved too many did it. Almost everyone had both opportunity and motive. Just count them up."

"In a sense anybody is suspect," protested the Inspector. "There's too much opportunity. The only firm facts we have are that death was caused by mustard gas and that the gas can't have been administered much before the time when Grayling's train started home. It could have been administered, theoretically anyway, before he got on to the platform at all. There was a lot of jostling, you remember. Supposing that the mustard gas was administered by someone slipping a soaked handkerchief into his pocket—and that's a big supposition—then that could have happened any time after his leaving the office. Even before, I suppose, though that's not very likely. It might have been planted on him by any of the people who crowded into the carriage with him. I am supposing he sniffed it up in the train. But it might have been administered by someone setting on him on the way home and clapping it on his face like a chloroform pad. Nobody was seen lying in wait for him, but that doesn't mean much. I'd think, though, that Grayling would have raised the devil's own racket if anyone tried that on him; and there aren't any reports of any disturbance that night."

"Did you ever find anything more about those alleged workingmen who leant over his shoulder to read the notices during the journey?" asked the Super.

"No. No luck at all." The Inspector sighed. "I'll count them up, as you said, sir. There's the beginning of a case against everyone who saw or might have seen him, right up to the time he fell in his own front door dying. Apart from the workmen, there's the Vicar; he's the least likely. But the condition of his face suggested that he might have had something to do with poison gas recently. Still, it might have been nothing but a cold and the revival of a barbers' rash that he had before. He disliked Grayling, we know. On the other hand, all the evidence that we have is to the effect that he had something on Grayling and had reason to look forward to putting him out of public life. I wouldn't dismiss him; but I don't think he's a good suspect. But as for the rest—!

"First Corporal Ransom. He's a gas expert, with access to the stuff. He's quarrelled with Grayling, who had his knife into him and is his superior officer. He was close to Grayling on that journey, he may possibly have a criminal record, and he quite certainly needs £120. Ordinarily, you'd say all the signposts pointed to him. But wait a moment. Think of Mr. Rolandson. He is Mrs. Grayling's lover, bitterly jealous; and Grayling has threatened him not only with losing the girl-friend but with getting him sacked and branded all over the country. He knows all about gas too; and it's pretty sure he could get hold of some. He sits in the same carriage with Grayling that night; and plumb opposite to him. A very curious choice. *His* neck may get a crick in it yet. Then there's a third. This German, whom Grayling was trying to get taken up by the Home Office people and dealt with as they do deal with Nazi spies. He was close up against him. And whoever he is, fake or genuine, he knows all about chemistry. He doesn't need to have access to that stuff; he can make it. If it comes to that, so could Evetts, the young man who was sitting next to Grayling and whose bag fell on his head so that he could have planted a handkerchief as easy as kiss-me. He is a qualified chemist; and his appearance, more than the Vicar's, was like that of somebody who'd been mucking with the gas recently. Though that, too, may just have been a cold. Also, his behaviour to me was more suspicious than that of anyone else's at all. Not that I go much by manner, of course."

"Well, you've got six people, or six and a half, against whom there's part of a case," said the Superintendent. "There it is. What am I to do with it?"

Holly looked at him gloomily. One does not reply to superior officers with the suggestion that he wished to give. After a minute he said: "I'll have to ask everyone more questions, I suppose. I'd give anything to be able to bring them all in and beat them with rubber hoses. Never before seen what a good idea that is."

They both remained silent some minutes. After a while the Superintendent spoke again.

"About your theory of the administration of the poison gas," he said, not very hopefully. "Does it hold water? Have you gone into that with Dr. Campbell, for example?"

"Dr. Campbell is not very helpful," complained the Inspector, resignedly. "But I have consulted him, and tried to think out the mechanism of the murder for myself. It does seem to be possible, this way:

"The murderer has either to make the stuff himself, or he has to abstract it from somewhere. Supposing he makes it, he apparently needs only the sort of apparatus which is to be found in most chemical labs. By this the liquid is distilled, or whatever be the word, into a sealed container. There is no danger to him at all. The only difficult point comes when he has to soak the handkerchief with the liquid. The temperature can be low, so that the liquid will not be volatile: still, in the nature of things it will have to be exposed. What he does, therefore, is to put on rubber gloves and his civilian gas mask; and use a pair of tongs to hold the handkerchief. He lays it in the stuff and leaves it, under cover, long enough to get saturated. He has to have a flat tin immediately to hand to plunge the soaked handkerchief into. When he's done that, he closes it up at once. He puts the stopper or whatever it is in the bottle, and runs adhesive tape round the edges of the tin box; and that's that. I suppose he would need to open the window for a short while to let any fumes clear away.

"If he stole the stuff ready made, he could transfer it to the handkerchief and tin the same way, in any room that was convenient. I talked to Dr. Hewitt, at the Civil Defence Divisional Headquarters, in charge of Gas Protection, putting it up as a hypothetical case. He said it was perfectly possible.

"Then about planting the handkerchief on Grayling. I've checked this up myself. I walked with the crowd going to the station, with a flat cigarette tin bound with tape in my overcoat pocket, and a damp handkerchief inside. I had rubber gloves on and kid gloves over them. It took me 25 seconds, 20 seconds, and 35 seconds, in three experiments, to do the whole business. I mean by that, to strip off the tape with my right hand, inside my overcoat pocket, open the tin, take the handkerchief out of it, and hold it in my hand inside the pocket ready to slip it into someone else's pocket. I didn't go the further step and actually do so. It might have been difficult to explain to anyone that I tried it on, and anyhow I'm not good at pickpockets' tricks. But far more difficult things than that have been done, as you know. So the whole thing is *possible*, anyway.

"A direct attack on him looks like the only alternative. It's not very likely. He would have fought and yelled—he was certainly not a meek or accommodating person at the best of times—and would probably have had to be knocked out or chloroformed. There was no trace of a bruise, and no one has mentioned traces of chloroform. And anyway, when he came to he would have made the devil's own uproar. Suppose he had been attacked between Croxburn Station and his home—that's the only place it could have happened—well, I know it was a dark and lonely night; but the streets are less empty then than at most times. People are coming home from work and we have our men on their beats. I don't believe it could have passed unnoticed."

"Are those the only alternatives?" asked the Superintendent.

"Practically the only ones, sir," said the Inspector. "The doctor talked about the possibility of a gas bomb dropping practically on to him. I inquired into that, and both the Air Ministry and the wardens' service said it was impossible. I think that is a dead end. I'm forced back to assuming my first theory is right. And then, as you said, I have six and a half good suspects."

"Any hope of tracing the means used?" asked the Superintendent.

"Very little. The handkerchief should have been in Grayling's overcoat pocket, unless he dropped it. But Mrs. Grayling sent the overcoat a couple of days later to the cleaners. He had vomited over it. I asked the cleaners if they had noticed anything about the coat—that is, if it had produced any symptoms of mustard gas poisoning. They said half their girls had running noses and wretched colds, anyway. As for a handkerchief, they had no record of one. But they volunteered the remark that since the war they had lost most of their competent staff and that records of such things were no longer properly kept. I got the impression that things found in pockets were more likely to be pinched than not.

"The murderer could quite easily dispose of his own traces. The tin would go into a salvage dump, the tape be dropped in a gutter. If he had worn an overcoat, the gas would vanish from it after wearing it once out in the rain; if he had a mackintosh it would never have soaked into it at all. If there was anything left in the bottle—supposing he stole it in a bottle—he need only pour it into a gutter or on a bit of waste land on a rainy night and it would be washed away. In a few hours, I'm told, there'd be no traces. And we've had plenty of rainy nights."

He rose heavily. "I'll just go on asking questions," he said, depressedly.

Chapter X

1

"They were both young, in dungarees, and fair-haired: one taller than the other," said Inspector Holly into the telephone. "I'm afraid we have no other description…No, just that they travelled up by that train…They needn't necessarily have been travelling home, of course; they might have been sent out on a job…I hardly expected anything…Of course, if you do find out anything, tell us at once…What, still? It's dry enough here."

He had been talking to the police of Mayquarter. They, like those of Pulchayne and Whetnow, had found no trace of the two workmen who had travelled down with Grayling. They did not expect to have any, either, unless the Inspector could give them more details to go on. And without wishing to be unhelpful, they had to remark that they were still kept busy by the effects of recent floods.

The report on the results of a thorough examination of the railway carriage lay before him. Several buttons, two pencils, part of an old newspaper, and a hairpin had been discovered. There was no trace of any chemical or any other unexplained feature. Thrust down behind the seat was the following letter, without date or address:

Dear Joe,

   If you did it, shut your silly mouth. If you didn't,
least said soonest mended too. The doe had eleven. With
love from

                                                              Rosie.

None of these, however enigmatic, seemed to be concerned with his immediate problem.

The Inspector reviewed in his mind his round of interviews. He had done exactly what he proposed to do: he had visited every one of his suspects and questioned them again. Some he had even bullied. He had got peculiar results: he was not certain that they were informative as well as peculiar. The shortest and most unorthodox in every way had been the interview with Hugh Rolandson. The young man had come into the police station to see him, dressed in very light flannel trousers and a pale yellow linen coat, dragging his club foot. Fair-haired, bright-blue eyes, very obviously nervous, he sat on the edge of his chair, alarmed, and looking rather like a rabbit and liable to bolt at any minute. A pet rabbit, thought the Inspector contemptuously, and decided to use rough methods.

"I must warn you," he said, without preamble, "that you are not bound to answer the questions I propose to ask you. I merely advise you to do so."

Apparently incapable of speech, Hugh nodded.

"Is it correct that you have taken the full gas course at the A.R.P. centre?"

"Certainly."

"Do you know where the poison gas is kept?"

"I think so."

"You must *know*."

"I mean," said Hugh more spiritedly, "that I believe it is kept in a particular cupboard, but I have never tested the fact."

"Humph. You travelled up with Grayling on the night of his murder?" continued the Inspector.

"I did."

"You might as well know we are perfectly well aware of your relations with Mrs. Grayling, and the excellent reasons you had for wishing her husband out of the way. Our evidence goes to show that you would probably have lost your employment and would have found it very difficult to support your mother if he had lived."

Hugh looked sullen and made no answer.

"You left the station immediately behind Councillor Grayling?" asked the Inspector.

"I don't know. I may have done."

The Inspector rose to his feet, pointed his finger at Hugh, and spoke in a savage, fairly loud voice. "Rolandson! You followed him out into the darkness. You came up behind him. And you gripped him round the neck with that pretty little hold they taught you in the training at the Centre— the Japanese stranglehold, don't they call it? And then you clapped a pad soaked in mustard gas over his face and held it there until you knew he couldn't live. Didn't you?"

Hugh leapt from his seat, yellow with fear. "No!" he said shrilly. "I didn't. I didn't." He pulled at the door and ran out. He pulled at it so suddenly that he hit himself on the forehead, but he didn't seem to notice. "Very interesting," said the Inspector to the empty room, and made no effort to stop him.

On the whole, he thought, Rolandson had come much higher up the list of suspects as a result of the interview. Charlie Evetts, on the other hand, had dropped back several points. He had seemed almost at ease in the Inspector's room—physically and mentally a new young man. His cold? Thanking *you* for the kind enquiry, all gone long ago: never felt better. Pretty well all the office had had equally rotten colds: they'd all cleared up now. Mr. Grayling? Any information he could give, only too pleased. The Inspector was not to bother about that cautioning stuff; Charles Evetts knew all about it—taken down, altered and used in evidence against you; ha, ha, ha. But really he had nothing to hide.

The Inspector was a little dashed by this exuberance, though he noticed it cooled down a little when he asked Evetts some vague questions about his manner of life. It ended suddenly when he asked him right out if he had recently been in need of money. Evetts slowly pulled out his pipe: "Mind if I smoke, Inspector?" he asked in a very quiet voice.

"Go ahead."

"I don't know how much you know," went on the young man slowly, "but I'm going to tell you something. Two things. One is, I'm going into the army. I'm exempt, but I've volunteered." He turned full face towards Holly, expecting admiration. Holly merely nodded, but was unable—indeed, did not try—to prevent a more benevolent look appearing on his face. Charlie Evetts promptly dropped into the back rank of suspects, illogical though he knew he was.

"The other thing is this. Maybe I ought to have told you this before. You'll say so, anyway. I *have* been in need of money, as you call it. I've been being blackmailed.—No, I'll not tell you details. I once was foolish enough to pinch something I wasn't entitled to. I've paid back the value of it long ago, and no one knows about it bar one person, who was bleeding me for money. I made up my mind, a day or two ago, I'd tell him to go to hell. What's more, I've laid a little trap for him."

Evetts smiled broadly. "Don't ask me any more," he said. "I'll not tell you." He radiated contentment. How fortunate that he had remembered that he had once introduced Ann Darling to Harry, when Elmer was there as witness.

He had already drafted out in his mind the letter he was going to post to the Chairman of the Board of Directors of Barrow and Furness at the end of his embarkation leave. No, better the night before actual embarkation, so as to be sure he was really gone beyond awkward questioning when it was received. The phrases danced through his mind. "…so moved by your generosity that I see now loyalty to the firm transcends loyalty to a colleague…great struggle with myself…noticed a suspicious action by Harry Kelvin and afterwards examined the chits…promised to respect his confession of the theft of two ergot bottles, but cannot go a journey from which I may never return with deception on my conscience." Would it be wise to point towards Ann Darling's death or not? He wasn't sure; and he became aware the Inspector had said something. "Awfully sorry, old man: I wasn't paying attention. Thoughts far, far away," he said. "It doesn't matter," said the Inspector, and dismissed him.

He had not troubled to make further enquiries about the Grants, mother and daughter. Mrs. Grayling he had interviewed in her house, and had had no more success with her than he expected.

She sat upright in a hard chair, tired and looking fully her age, but all the same unquestionably a good-looking woman. Her greenish eyes looked him full in the face, and before he could start questioning her she said:

"So that there may be no misunderstanding, Mr. Holly, I must explain to you that I am not going to answer any questions concerning my relations with my husband. If I have to answer such questions in court, I shall no doubt answer them. But meanwhile I consider them impertinent, and it will serve no purpose if you ask them."

"Very well, ma'am," replied Holly, coolly, but disappointed. "In that case I can only ask you to go over with me the events of the evening that your husband died."

"On that, you may ask me what you wish," she replied equally coldly.

"What time did your husband come home?"

"I do not know exactly. After eight, I think. I remember noticing some little while before that he was half an hour late."

"Will you tell me exactly what happened then?"

"I opened the door and he fell in, on his hands and knees. I expect I said something to him in surprise, but I do not remember. I helped him in and then looked out of the door. I was puzzled, and as the hall light could not be on I did not see how bad he was. I suppose I thought somebody might have knocked him on the head. I think I even took a few steps out. But I am not quite certain. Anyway, I found nothing."

"Did he go—or did you take him—straight up to bed then?"

"No, I helped him into the kitchen. I thought he would need a glass of water; and supposing he had been attacked he might have a cut that needed bathing. I thought there was blood on his face. I could see indistinctly."

"After that you saw him in the light and discovered how bad he was?"

"No: the window in the kitchen was broken and the black-out torn down. It had only happened that day, and I was waiting for him to mend it. I couldn't turn on the light. It was quite a while before I realized how ill he was."

"How long was it before you sent for Dr. Hopkins?"

"I am not sure. It was some time."

"An hour? Two hours? Half an hour?"

"I wouldn't like to guess. The doctor would probably be able to tell you. He didn't come at once. He had to arrange for a nurse, I think."

The Inspector gave it up at that point. Further questions seemed likely to be equally aimless.

His interview with Ransom had been stormy. The corporal had come in Home Guard uniform, though there was no parade that day, and had been truculent from the beginning. "Are you the same George Ransom," asked the Inspector, "as the one who ran a shoemaker's business about 1924 in such-and-such?" (He gave the name of the small town.)

"If I am, what has that got to do with you?"

"There's no need to be quarrelsome. I know it came to an end in a very tragic way," said the Inspector, civilly enough.

"It's not likely I'd discuss it with *you*," answered Ransom.

"What did you do between then and when you began work for Peters?"

"Mind your own bloody business," answered Ransom, without heat.

"Ransom, have you got a police record?" snapped the Inspector.

At this Ransom lost his temper. He seized the arms of his chair, as if to prevent himself from leaping at the Inspector, and cursed him for several seconds. His phrases, literally taken, reflected on the Inspector's legitimacy, chastity and normality: except by inference, they contained no answer to the question. When the flood had subsided, Holly said:

"I'll be straight with you, Ransom, though you're not being straight with us. Grayling was murdered by the use of poison gas. You know all about poison gas. You had access to it. You detested Grayling. You were in a position to administer it. And you could have done with the hundred and twenty pounds he was carrying, which have completely disappeared. There's no use shouting abuse at me. You ought to have sense enough to realize that you're under suspicion. Why don't you co-operate with us?"

"Go to hell," said Ransom; got up and walked out.

Holly rang a bell. "Don't touch that chair," he said to the constable who answered. "There are fingerprints on it I want taken, and compared with Scotland Yard records."

Next day he got by telephone the news he hoped for. "Picking pockets, was it? I'm not surprised…gave the name of Gordon Richards, did he? They always keep the same initials…That's very helpful. It fits exactly." He put Ransom at the head of his list now.

Mannheim—if it was Mannheim—he spoke to in the corridors of the police court after the doctor had been fined twenty pounds. Inspector Atkins was with him, and the German started uneasily at the sight of him.

Holly told him briefly why he lay under suspicion, and—with Atkins' permission—emphasized that the most sinister charge against him was that he was not what he pretended to be. "Will you tell me frankly," he said in conclusion, "what Councillor Grayling had against you? Why did he make this charge?"

The German turned his square, dark head towards him. "I am still surprised," he said, "that the police are courteous to me here; it makes me still a little frightened. Believe me, I would tell you all I knew, if I knew anything. But what put this idea into his head I cannot guess.

"As for me, you have just heard in court that I have used a bicycle and a radio set when I should not, and it is very expensive for me. Perhaps also you heard me say that the bicycle I borrowed one night when I was too late to come home before curfew; and I was careless and did not return it. Because you have treated me well and as a free man, so I have become careless. Perhaps, too, you heard it said that the radio set was a cheap one, which could not be used for short waves. All this was foolish of me, but does not show me a Nazi. Indeed, I may say that if I was a Nazi, then would

I have been very careful not to be foolish, and to make the police enquire when I did not need to.

"But still I have for days, ever since I heard of what Mr. Grayling said, asked myself: 'How does a man prove that he is himself?' I do not have an answer. In Berlin are those who know me; they are in Berlin. The young David, who rescued me, he is dead. In Metz was held an investigation, at which the Bureau was satisfied with me. And now for long the Nazis have been in Metz.

"So do I tell you of my books, what I wrote in them, and who published them?" He bowed towards Inspector Atkins. "But as you have truly said, I could copy all that from the British Museum. I tell you where I lived, and whom I knew: that, too, I might have been told by the Nazis, if I am a spy. I did not take part in politics very much: I do not know those who are refugees here. In Germany I was not the sort of person who was photographed in picture papers. I can think of nothing else."

He waited for an answer.

"Well, don't go away from Croxburn, anyway," said Inspector Holly, awkwardly. Mannheim bowed again, and turned away. The two men watched the squat figure walk heavily off. "The factory speaks well of him," said Atkins. "We're inclined to think he's O.K. He wouldn't be about if we didn't, anyhow."

The Inspector's last interview had been with the Vicar, but he had not thought it worth while to make any pressing inquiries. He did not seriously include him in the list of suspects. The only information he got, indeed, was that the Vicar was quite recovered from his rash, which had yielded within the day to the ointment left over from the last attack. There was nothing whatever to show, indeed, that it *was* anything else but a recrudescence of that disease.

He drew a line under the record of that conversation and stared at the list in front of him. It was half-past ten: perhaps in the morning, he thought, he would get enlightenment.

He pushed the papers aside and deliberately let his thoughts wander. He began to think about the characters in the case separately, as individuals. When this case was over, how would they appear to him? When he met Ransom in the streets—if Ransom was not guilty—he would be quite a different person. Only another Home Guard, a slightly touchy, insignificant-looking, hardworking man, with nothing mysterious about him and no aura of danger and cruelty. Those two fair-haired and undiscoverable workmen, who kept troubling him—who were they and what were they? If they were nothing to do with this case, they would probably be, and remain for ever, just that—two fair-haired workmen with a liking for childish and vulgar jokes. They could not ever be of interest to him again; they were only of interest to him now because of something which, very probably, did not concern them at all and wasn't even known to them. At one minute of time, if he was successful, all but one of these people would suddenly become not significant at all to him. They would vanish, and one important figure alone would remain. The story of Councillor Grayling, for all but one of them, was an irrelevance in the pattern of their lives. The light it threw on them and the character it gave them was for all but one false and meaningless. Indeed, there was no pattern.

These people were unrelated. They were each one individual persons—who were important—"valid" would be the literary cant word—in themselves and must be looked at alone. Then, maybe, he could find which one would carry on into the next episode and which would vanish and be forgotten. They did not, in fact, did they, have any other connection than that they had travelled in a single coach on a single journey, which had a relation with the crime. If it did have.

He stopped there and looked at the figures. Rolandson; take away the pattern-making and what remained? A rabbit. And rabbits don't kill. He looked at the workmen; only this thirst for correlation could have made him continue to trouble about them. The Vicar? Well, he had never thought very seriously about him any way; he at least was certainly a man with a life of his own, which had nothing to do with this problem. It was centred round St. Mary the Virgin, that ugly and unwanted church, and made up of small rebuffs and well-meant but ill-directed attempts to reform the parish. He inclined, too, to regard the German doctor's appearance on the record as accidental. Suppose he was a spy. It was still not likely that a German spy should travel the very strange path that would lead to killing a disagreeable and unimportant town councillor. You could make yourself think so; he had done so for a moment. But it was not sensible. Ransom too—Holly had the policeman's usual respect for the importance of a "record," but the record was only of picking pockets; and he too seemed an accident.

Forethought; where could he suspect forethought? There was only one person whose connection was not accidental, whose life itself was necessarily intertwined with Grayling's life, and death, whom he could not picture as surviving unchanged after all was over. And that was the person whom he had least pressed, Mrs. Grayling.

She had seemed "out." But that was because her statements had been accepted as true, with only a limited checking up. Suppose they were all false—as they would be if she were guilty. He decided to test them—to tap them all over as one taps a wall to discover a hollow sound which may indicate a hiding-place.

She said he had come home late, and ill. Suppose that he had come home at the ordinary time, perfectly well. Would anyone have noticed? No, it was the maid's night out and the night was pitch black. Could anything have happened between then and the time when the doctor came? Well, how long was that time? He looked again at the papers. Mrs. Grayling had refused to be exact; the doctor had not noted the time, but knew that it was "after ten." The Vicar had been sent for by Mrs. Grayling for what seemed on consideration to be insufficient reasons, and it had been eleven by the time he came. It could have been Mrs. Grayling's idea that he would help to provide a sort of alibi; he certainly had helped to create the atmosphere she wanted and frame the picture of the dutiful wife doing all that she could for her stricken husband. But he was no use as a witness to time. If Grayling had arrived at the usual time, soon after seven, there were some three hours to be accounted for before the doctor had arrived. Did an innocent wife, with a telephone to her hand, leave her husband dying all that time? Or, what was perhaps a more pertinent question, could she have killed him in that time, and how?

The door of his room opened and the sergeant-in-charge came in. "Working late to-night, sir," he said. "I thought you'd like a cup of tea."

"Thank you," said the Inspector. The tea was hot, dark, sweet and made with tinned milk. Holly poured part of it into the saucer, which was not very clean, and drank it slowly and with noise. He filled up the saucer again afterwards, and, that having finished the tea, said: "Thank you. Yes, a cup of tea's a comfort. I'll be going along now."

He had hoped to continue his thoughts as he picked his way along the dark street, but within five minutes he had stepped hard against a fixed sandbin, and had realized that he had better give all his attention to his journey. He had broken the skin of his shin and blood was running down inside his clothes, forming a thick and sticky clot lengthwise in his heavy woollen underpants. In bed, the trivial wound tied clumsily up with a handkerchief, and aching, he took up his disturbed argument.

There was time enough for Mrs. Grayling to have murdered her husband by the use of mustard gas. Yes. That was sure. If she could have induced him to breathe the gas for much less than those three hours he would have died. But how on earth could she? Supposing she had drugged him somehow? There were no traces mentioned of chloroform, but that was not final; it could easily have been missed in the surprising and highly noticeable symptoms caused by poison gas—and, as a matter of fact, he reflected, these would conveniently conceal the usual symptoms of chloroform. But it was incredible that he could have meekly consented to be chloroformed. He would have fought her; and she was not noticeably a strong woman; he might have won. Certainly, there would have been some noise; and inquiries of neighbours on both sides had shown that they at least had noticed no noise. If she had come behind him and slugged him without warning, then there would have been marks of a bruise on the head or the body. There were none; as a matter of routine he had inquired about that at the very beginning.

He fidgeted in his bed and turned on the other side. The solution was slipping out of his hands. Yet he felt sure—well, fairly sure—that his eyes were at last fixed on the guilty person. And then an even more vexing objection occurred to him. Suppose somehow Mrs. Grayling knocked her husband out silently, without leaving a mark and then calmly gassed him—as she would have been quite capable of doing. What happened to the gas? The house would have reeked of it, if he had had enough to kill him. She would have had to receive

Doctor Hopkins with her gasmask on; and everyone who had been in the house would have been as sick as a dog in the morning. Yet nobody was affected at all.

It wouldn't work. The poison must have been administered in the open air. Possibly, as he had thought before, the victim might have been tricked into giving it to himself, in little packets each time he used his handkerchief in the railway carriage. But apart from that theory, which he now thought was far-fetched, it was inconceivable that it could have been administered except out of doors. By no other means could the murderer have got the stuff to clear away under some hours.

He grunted, threw out his hot-water bottle, and went to sleep.

In the morning, drinking tea and eating, to his great pleasure and surprise, a kipper, he reconsidered Mrs. Grayling's evidence; and quite suddenly a light came in his face. Hadn't she said that she took her husband into the kitchen where "the window was broken and the black-out torn down"? Why had she said that? No doubt because it was true; and because she thought he might discover it anyhow. What did it mean? Easy, go easy! He held the thought, and almost watched it. *She* broke it, and *she* tore down the black-out. She wanted a room where no one could go into—during the hours of darkness, anyway—and a room from which poison gas would clear away easily. No one could go into that room until nearly eight the next morning, or the wardens would be down on them when the light was turned on. No doubt she had put a notice on the door—probably, locked it, too. By the morning even a high concentration of gas would have escaped through the broken windows. Certainly, she told the truth when she said that she had taken her husband into the kitchen. And when he was there she had stunned him or made him powerless some way (that could be left vague for the minute) and kept him under gas for as long as she felt it necessary. Holly felt he could see her calmly doing this, wearing her gasmask and probably a pair of rubber gloves, quite coolly and efficiently in the dark. He wondered whether she stayed by her husband to make sure that he died and did not recover his senses, or whether she went out and shut the door, sitting in the front room and pretending to wait for him, while he slowly choked to death beside the kitchen table. She was a good liar, he thought respectfully; she obeyed the central principle of skilled lying, which was to tell as near the truth as you possibly can, and omit or change only the essential. She had told the police almost everything that occurred, and almost exactly. He would be prepared to swear that all minor details were correct, even where they could not be corroborated. He was pretty sure that she knew nothing about the missing money, for example.

He had spent longer than usual over his breakfast, but at the end had decided that he would that morning consult the Superintendent and ask him whether he thought there was enough evidence to take out a warrant against Mrs. Grayling. He was not yet sure of his hypothesis; he wanted support. He arrived twenty minutes late at the station, to be told that the Super had left seven minutes before. He had been called to London, to a conference of suburban police heads summoned by the Home Office. It was announced to be of considerable importance and was to be addressed by Mr. Herbert Morrison in person. It would probably last all the day, and it was quite out of the question to get a message to the Super, still less bring him away from it.

Holly reflected a few minutes, considered abandoning his plans for a day, and then decided that he must at least do something. He would not himself apply for a warrant. That was a very grave step; if he turned out to be wrong there would be a deep black mark against him. But he would do the next best thing. He would go and call on Mrs. Grayling, taking with him a shorthand writer, and he would warn her before he questioned her. He would do his very best to shake her by his manner; and he would take her through every detail of the evening. He would end by warning her not to leave Croxburn and he would have her watched—not making too much concealment about it, either. He might by these means get enough evidence to persuade the Super to-morrow to ask for a warrant.

He arrived at the Graylings' house, in uniform and with a uniformed shorthand writer, at eleven that morning. Mrs. Grayling's maid had left her, and she opened the door to them herself. She invited them in civilly; Holly marched into the sitting-room without replying a word.

"Certain facts have come to our knowledge, madam," he said, "which make it necessary for me to question you again. You are not, of course, compelled to answer these questions; I shall, naturally, however, draw my own conclusions if you refuse. The constable who is with me will take notes of your replies and I should warn you that they may be used in evidence."

Renata Grayling said nothing. She licked her lips, and looked rather white. But she was probably no paler than usual, Holly reflected. As she did not answer, he began:

"What was your husband's usual time for homecoming?" She waited perceptibly, and then said: "Ten past seven."

"You told me before that it was half-past seven."

"I do not remember doing so. I was mistaken if I did."

"I think I know why you did. Never mind that now, though. Where did you take your husband after, as you said, he fell in at the door?"

"I told you. To the kitchen."

"Why?"

"To bathe his face."

"You said, I think, that the window was broken and the black-out destroyed. When did you break that window, Mrs. Grayling, and why?"

"I did not break it."

"Who did then? The servant? She will remember, I suppose."

There was again a pause, and Mrs. Grayling said: "I suppose a boy must have thrown a stone, or something. I haven't thought about it."

"Indeed?" Holly did as good a sneer as he could manage. "Very well then. Now let me ask about times again. Do you still claim that your husband did not come in till nearly eight—taking almost an hour for a ten-minute walk?"

"I—I am not sure. I did not notice the time. It may have been earlier."

"It may have been earlier. I see. Now, when did you telephone for Dr. Hopkins?"

"I don't know."

"Would you be surprised if I told you that it was well after ten o'clock?"

Renata said nothing.

"Come, Mrs. Grayling, this will not do. You tell me that your husband is in this house, in state of collapse and in the most obvious pain and danger, and you let three hours pass before you even trouble to telephone the doctor?"

Renata seemed at last a little disturbed. "I do not think it was so long," she said at last.

"It was," said Holly. "You must see that for yourself. Mrs. Grayling, isn't there something that you wish to add to your statement? You have not been telling the truth. That we are sure of. If you are protecting someone else, you should stop doing so now. It is no good; we know too much now. Was Mr. Rolandson here?" A pause followed, but no answer. "If it is yourself you are thinking of—believe me, it is still no good. Mrs. Grayling, I beg of you. *Haven't you something to say to me?*"

The last words were spoken with all the solemnity he could manage. Renata only put her handkerchief to her mouth and shook her head.

"I must ask you not to leave Croxburn till further notice," said the Inspector as he went. He did not look back as he left but nodded to a plain clothes man standing at the corner.

2

Hugh Rolandson was a badly frightened young man. The Inspector had scared him very competently. His mistress, to whom as usual he had carried his troubles, had been silent and unwilling or unable to help him. Three days later he was still sleeping badly: he lay awake, the fear of death close to him, until five in the morning, and then fell from exhaustion into a heavy slumber. As a result he overslept and did not get up till nearly nine o'clock. He refused the hot coffee his mother querulously offered and ran for his train, thrusting into his pocket without reading it the one letter waiting for him on the hall table.

It was not until after the train had started that he drew the typewritten envelope out of his pocket and began to read the letter it contained. Then the change in his appearance was so remarkable that the woman opposite him thought that he was gravely ill. When he got in, she had seen a rather slovenly, unshaven, fair young man, with dark rings under his eyes but otherwise in no way unusual. Her attention was called by a hoarse noise coming from him, something between a rattle and a choke. His face had gone completely yellow and the whole of it glistened with sweat. His mouth had fallen open; unconsciously, he was dribbling slightly. His eyes were fixed on the paper before him: they gave the illusion of protruding. His nostrils were twitching curiously.

She expected a fit, and held her hand ready to pull the alarm cord.

The letter was from Renata Grayling. It had been their old habit to type their envelopes, for concealment's sake—a habit recently and disastrously abandoned. It said:

My darling Hugh,

I have written and rewritten this letter so often. I do not know if even now I can say exactly what I want to say, but it will have to do. I have all my life taken my own decisions and acted on my own responsibility. I am going to do so again now. I did so once too often before, when I killed Henry. For I did kill him; I am afraid that has got to come out now. It can't be hidden any more. I have thought about it very carefully. I did not realize that the Inspector could make such a case against you: I never knew till too late that you had travelled home with Henry. I would not, my dear, anyway send you to the gallows. But I don't think that I have that choice any longer. The Inspector called on me after he had talked to you and asked me a series of questions that made it quite clear, when I thought about them afterwards, that he knew what had happened and was collecting the last evidence. He took me carefully and slowly through a sort of time-table of that evening, asking me each little thing that I did, and as soon as he did that it was quite clear that nothing would be left of my story.

This is a very confused letter, but it is a confused and unhappy woman who is writing it. I suppose you will have to know what exactly I did, because of the police. Henry didn't come home late, as I said, he came home just at the usual time. I waited till he had shut the door and then knocked him senseless. You know we had been taught how to do it in the unarmed combat lessons, with a blow from the side of your hand on the side of the temple. It doesn't leave a mark. Then I pulled him into the kitchen and put a pad of chloroform on his face for a few minutes. I gave him enough to keep him under an hour or so and then burnt the pad in the kitchen boiler. Then I put on my gasmask and gloves and put another pad soaked in mustard gas on his face, with oiled silk on top of it to keep some of the gas from filling the room. But I also turned out the light, broke the kitchen window and tore down the black-out, so no one could go in and the fumes would have vanished by the morning. I left him breathing in thick poison gas for about two hours, I suppose. I didn't call Dr. Hopkins till I was quite sure, later than I pretended. I carried him upstairs just before the doctor came.

I took his hat and bag and dropped them in the road. I don't know about the money. Somebody must have stolen it. I left the bag nearer the house than that.

Darling, I don't think we could ever have been happily married: I always knew I was too old for you. It doesn't make any difference now. Either they will arrest you or they will arrest me. Either way, there is nothing more in life for me; but there may be for you.

I am posting this so that you will get it in the morning, when I will have been dead some hours. I wanted to die in what I have always thought of as our bed. But it is too difficult to seal that room and I shall have to go down to the kitchen and turn on the gas oven. I shall be lying almost exactly where Henry was. I kissed you good-bye, though you did not know it.

Forgive me and forget me.

R.

At the station at which Hugh got out there was one taxi. The driver was going to refuse to take him on the unprofitable journey out to Croxburn, alleging shortage of petrol, but after glancing at his distorted face he said nothing.

The taxi ran fairly quickly through the suburban streets. Each semi-detached villa, with its neat garden, looked exactly the same as usual. A few tradesmen were about, one or two dogs prowled in the sun, a few wives were on their way to the shops. There was nothing to mark the fact that this morning was different from all others—not until the taxi turned into the Graylings' road and Hugh saw a white van drawn up there. As he watched, a tall man standing at the Graylings' gate gave a signal, and the van started towards him. As it came near he could see the Red Cross and knew it was an ambulance.

When he got out, he recognized the tall man: Inspector Holly. He tried to speak, but found he could not say anything. The Inspector pitied him. "They are taking her to the mortuary," he said gently. "If you want to see her, they will let you see her there." He looked away as Hugh turned round stumbling, and hung on to the door of the taxi, unable to answer, to stand, or to think. He stood there waiting long after the taxi had taken Hugh away. He found he was unconsciously twisting in his hand the note that the charwoman had found that morning. It was written in a firm, fine hand, unwavering, folded in three as Mrs. Grayling's messages for the charwoman invariably were, and equally deliberately ordinary in its phrasing. *Mrs. Adams: Do not go near the kitchen: it will be full of gas and dangerous. You should call the police as soon as you have read this. You may tell them I killed my husband.* She had not left any other message.

To see more Poisoned Pen Press titles:

Visit our website: poisonedpenpress.com/
Request a digital catalog: info@poisonedpenpress.com